I0526669

Hope and Honor

by

Marilee Brothers

The Soul Seekers Series, Book 3

This is a work of fiction. Names, characters, places, and incidents are either the product of the author's imagination or are used fictitiously, and any resemblance to actual persons living or dead, business establishments, events, or locales, is entirely coincidental.

Hope and Honor

COPYRIGHT © 2018 by Marilee Brothers

All rights reserved. No part of this book may be used or reproduced in any manner whatsoever without written permission of the author or The Wild Rose Press, Inc. except in the case of brief quotations embodied in critical articles or reviews.
Contact Information: info@thewildrosepress.com

Cover Art by *Debbie Taylor*

The Wild Rose Press, Inc.
PO Box 708
Adams Basin, NY 14410-0708
Visit us at www.thewildrosepress.com

Publishing History
First Fantasy Rose Edition, 2018
Print ISBN 978-1-5092-1870-7
Digital ISBN 978-1-5092-1871-4

The Soul Seekers Series, Book 3
Published in the United States of America

He scoots his chair back and pulls me onto his lap. I lift his cap to check out his hair. It's pale blond and growing out from the spikey do.

He says, "Is it true blonds have more fun?"

"You get to decide."

He leans and whispers, "Believe me, I will."

Heat spirals through my body, settling deep into my belly. I want to grab him by the hand and drag him out to my car. Have my way with him. Until I see Mick, I don't realize how much I've missed him. But, this is not the time or place. I push away and stand. "Are you going to introduce me to your friends?"

I suspect they are fellow officers. Not that he'll tell me.

Instead, he says, "This is Mel."

He points at the men and identifies each one by first name only. Now I know for sure they're his work buddies.

I say, "See you around, guys. Enjoy your evening."

Mick looks a little panicked. "Hey, wait. I'll see you later. In Number Ten. Right?"

Now, it's my turn for payback and I love it.

"Wrong." I walk away.

"At least leave bread crumbs."

I hear a hint of desperation in his voice and return to the table. "You're Homeland Security. Remember, you have no rules. I'm sure you'll figure it out, big guy. Bye, bye."

His buddies burst into laughter as I sashay away.

Praise for Marilee Brothers

"Wow! I had such a hard time catching up...but finally got the time to read [AFFLICTION]. And boy am I glad I did! What a wonderfully written story. As the mother of a child with actual Aspergers, I was a little intrigued by that aspect. I was so happy to see it was never seen in a bad light, and this was so well-written I came out of it wishing it could be real."

~*The Naughty Librarian*

~*~

"Love a cheeky heroine...Mel is back taking on prejudice and a hate-crime mystery in [ALLEGIANCE] book two of the Soul Seekers Series! Author Marilee Brothers does what she does best—gives you relatable characters that engage you more and more with each turn of the page."

~*Dawn Miller*

Chapter One

"This is my colleague, Detective McKenzie," Candy Talbot says, tipping her head in my direction.

Talbot and I are across the table from a whiney, ferret-faced individual with greasy black hair and a sporadic twitch in his left eye. The twitch complicates my job, since it's up to me to determine whether or not he's lying. Some call me a human lie detector. I prefer the term soul seeker.

The title 'Detective McKenzie' is fake, just like the blond wig and dark-rimmed glasses I'm wearing. My real name is Honor Melanie—Mel—Sullivan. I'm not an officer of the law, but a paid consultant, hired by the 3 Peaks Police Department. Although the results of my unique skill set are not admissible in court, the detectives use my lie-detecting ability to decide whether or not to pursue charges against possible lawbreakers.

Candy shuffles papers and gives me a significant look. When I don't respond, she kicks me under the table. Oh, yeah, my turn. We're still getting out act together, Candy and me. We'll never be besties, but we make a pretty good crime-fighting team. I lean forward with a winsome smile, doing my best to look friendly and unintimidating. "I have a couple of questions, Dwayne. Is it okay if I call you Dwayne?"

His eyes narrow in suspicion. "What the hell is

this? Good cop, bad cop?"

Note to self: cut back the smile wattage. "I believe you have a girlfriend by the name of Judy Moss."

"Former girlfriend," he mumbles, left eyelid fluttering like a wounded moth.

I stare into the non-twitching eye. "She filed a complaint against you. Her right arm is in a sling. Her left eye is blackened. She says you did it."

His eyes widen and he snarls, "Bullshit, the sling is fake and she punched herself in the face. She's a human cuckoo clock."

Candy shifts in her chair. I know she's dying to lock Dwayne in a steel cage and throw away the key.

"So, Dwayne," I continue. "Why would she beat herself up and fake a broken arm?"

His lips curl into a sneer, revealing tobacco-stained teeth. "I just told you. She's got no toys in the attic." He aims his pointer finger at his temple and twirls it, the universal sign for mental disorders, also known as crazy.

Candy and I remain silent while Dwayne searches his impoverished memory banks for a plausible excuse.

Finally, he says, "I'm guessing she's pissed at me." His voice trails off. He slumps in his chair.

"Because...?"

"She threw all my shit onto the front lawn and changed the locks."

"I think it's safe to assume she's pissed at you," I say. "Did that happen after you punched her?"

He snaps to attention and glares at me. "I *told* you, I never hit her. The bitch is into revenge. She wants to punish me for a little mistake I made."

"Tell us about your little mistake."

He hangs his head and mumbles, "I slept with her old lady. She kept coming on to me and she's not bad looking. I felt sorry for her."

"So, it was a pity thing."

He stares into my eyes. "Exactly. What's a guy supposed to do?"

Candy snaps, "Keep it in your pants."

I stand. "Detective Talbot and I need to confer. We'll be right back."

We huddle together in the hall.

"He's a creep, but he didn't do it," I say.

Candy's eyes narrow. "Aw, come on, Mel. He's got guilt written all over him."

"He may be guilty of screwing his girlfriend's mother, but he did not beat up Judy Moss."

Candy likes to second-guess me. I've learned to trust my soul-reading ability and stand my ground.

"You're sure?"

I sigh. "Yes, Candy, I'm sure. Did she go to the hospital to get checked out after Dwayne supposedly beat her up?"

"She didn't say."

"Okay, bring her in and let me look into *her* soul. Sound like a plan?

Candy sulks for a moment, but finally nods in agreement.

"Okey dokey, then. Let me know when you need me. Gotta run. It's moving day for Mel."

Her eyes brighten with curiosity. "Moving out of Nick's?"

"Yep, catch ya later."

As I dash down the hall, I hear her call, "Hey, wait. I need details."

Actually, she doesn't. She's being nosey, probably wondering if I'm back with Billy the Kid, now a detective with the 3 Peaks Police Department. Speaking of whom steps out of his cubicle just in time to make full body contact with yours truly. He places his hands on my shoulders and gazes into my eyes, making no attempt to put space between us.

I take a step back, even though my body instinctively wants to curl into his, like it did before our relationship flamed out and became a pile of ashes. Well, maybe not ashes. A few smoldering embers remain, waiting for a chance to re-ignite.

"Whoa, it's Minnie Mouse in disguise. What's the hurry?"

"No more motel living for me," I state proudly. "Steve is moving in with his boyfriend and subletting his place to me." I fish the key out of my pocket to prove my point. "My car's packed. Today's the day."

The warmth of his smile reaches his eyes. "Need any help?"

I fully understand the subtext of the question. It has to do with the off-and-on-again relationship I have with my Homeland Security boyfriend, Mick Petrov. Billy is checking to see if he's in town. That's the off-and-on part. Mick is a great guy. I know he cares about me. He's an ideal boyfriend when he's around. Attentive. Loving. Generous. The problem is, he's on an upwardly mobile career path. His undercover assignments may last for weeks, during which time we have no communication. As far as Mick is concerned, huge gaps in our relationship are part of the job, and I can take it or leave it. I'm still trying to decide if this works for me.

4

I pretend to take Billy's question at face value. "I can manage. Thanks, though."

He looks disappointed. "Call if you *need* me."

Billy has a competitive nature and has thrown his hat into the ring, so to speak, in an effort to renew our relationship. Mick is well aware of Billy's intentions. Thankfully, no animosity exists between the two. It's more of a good-natured contest to see who will win my heart, affection and unconventional soul. It's a life complication I don't need.

I thank Billy for his offer of *help* and head for the parking lot. Buttercup, my ancient Toyota Tercel, is fully packed. There's just enough room for me to squeeze behind the wheel. The passenger seat includes a cat bed, and a container of kibble and cat toys. The cat is not present. His name is Thunder Paws and he lives at Nick's Sports Bar and Grill. I'm a part-time waitress at Nick's. It's also been my home for the last nine months, namely motel unit Number Ten.

Nick, my boss and owner of the pub repeatedly tells me, "Mel, you cannot move cats. They are territorial critters."

I disagree. "He's used to sleeping in Number Ten. When I'm gone, you'll be renting it out and he'll be banging on the door of complete strangers."

The big-footed tomcat doesn't demand entry by yowling. He stands on his hind legs and pounds his front paws against the door. Hence, the name Thunder Paws. My cat-moving experiment might not work, but I have to try. Otherwise, I'll be stricken with a guilty conscience as I imagine poor Thunder Paws pounding on my darkened door to no avail.

I stuff my wig and fake glasses into the glove

compartment and steer Buttercup toward my new home. My cell phone rings when I pull up into the driveway. It's Nick.

His voice sounds strained. "Hey, Mel. I need your help with something."

"You want me to come into work? I thought I was off today."

"Um, well, no. It's something else."

I wait for him to explain, but he doesn't. I want to say, "It's my day off. I'm moving. Blah, blah, blah," but I say none of these things. Nick was responsible for getting me on my feet when I arrived in 3 Peaks, Oregon with my meager possessions in a single backpack. He rarely asks for help. I owe him. Besides, he sounds so strange, my curiosity is piqued.

"Sure, I'll dump this load and be there in a flash."

When he speaks, I hear the relief in his voice. "Thanks, kid. See you soon."

Before I click off he says, "Oh, yeah, Kendra's looking for you. I let her into your room. She brought—"

The screen on my cell fades to black. Dead.

Damn, where the heck is my phone charger? Did I pack it? Is it still in Number Ten? Questions without answers make me nuts. Like, what is the deal with Kendra? Nick said she's brought...something or somebody? Kendra is Billy's sister and my best friend in 3 Peaks. We've been through a series of adventures together, some successful, some scary and some downright ridiculous.

And, while I'm pondering unanswered questions, what's up with Nick?

Chapter Two

My promise to hurry goes sideways when I step through the door. The first thing I see is a banner attached to the living room wall. It says,

"Welcome to your new home, mi hija.
May you collect wonderful memories within these
walls."

A small dining room table holds a glass bowl filled with fresh flowers and, on the kitchen counter, I spy a box filled with my favorite pastries next to the coffee pot. Bio dad Steve knows me well.

I drop my armload of cat accessories and scamper around, opening cupboards, closets and drawers. After living in a motel, basically one small room and a bath, I feel like Marie Antoinette in Versailles.

Reluctantly, I lock up, head back to Nick's and park in front of Number Ten. The door opens and Kendra steps out. She greets me with a wave and beckons me into the room. A pet carrier big enough for an eighty-pound dog sets in the middle of the bed. I give her a questioning look.

"It's for Thunder Paws, when you move him to your new place."

"I'll have to rent a pickup truck to haul it."

She waves a dismissive hand. "No worries. We'll make it fit. All you have to do is move the front seats forward."

"Or," I say, "We could use your minivan. We know that'll work because you brought it over."

She closes her eyes and shakes her head. "Uh-uh, no way. I'm not getting involved in a cat-moving venture. *Huge* potential for disaster. I can't afford to lose an eye. I have small children who depend on me."

"Speaking of which, who's watching the kidlets? Aida?"

She opens her eyes and nods. "I'm *so* loving the mother's helper concept. And since Aida loves babies, it's a win-win. Right?" She holds out a fist for me to bump.

"Absolutely," I say. "She's happiest when she's knee-deep in babies."

Aida, originally from Kazakhstan, is married to my Uncle Paco, aka, the head honcho of the Los Habañeros motorcycle gang and heavily involved in a don't-ask, don't-tell business. Paco adores Aida and her baby Larissa. Larissa is the result of an evil human trafficking, baby-selling scheme.

"Now," Kendra continues, "I'll have more time to help you with your cases, like when you look into a sketchy soul and decide more investigation is called for."

I choke back a snicker. "Great, as soon as we move the cat, we'll get started."

Her eyes widen. "Seriously? You have something in mind?" Kendra fancies herself a master of intrigue, complete with disguises.

I'm stringing her along because I have an agenda. I point at the carrier. "After the cat transfer."

She rolls her eyes and curses under her breath. "Okay, let's get it done."

"I have to talk to Nick first. He needs help with something."

She grabs the TV remote and flops down on the bed next to the pet carrier. "No hurry. I'll enjoy a little me time."

I see the girl when I walk to the back door of the pub. She's sitting on the back steps, elbows resting on her knees, chin braced in the palm of her right hand. Her hair is dyed black, the ends tinged in pink. Her jeans are fashionably ragged. Her dark hooded sweatshirt is emblazoned with an image from a popular Goth band, the outline of two faces, their big sad eyes looking to the left, both adorned with bright red lips. Men's platform boots complete the outfit.

She glances up as I approach. Her eyes, heavily lined with kohl, are an unusual shade of brown and flecked with amber. A light sprinkling of freckles on her nose tells me her natural hair color is much lighter. She doesn't hold my gaze long enough for me to peer into her soul.

"Hi." I smile and step around her to reach for the back door.

Her response is a muffled, "Yeah."

When my hand hits the doorknob, a throaty *rowr* signals the arrival of Thunder Paws. He bounds past the girl and rubs against the back of my legs. The message is clear. *Feed me now or you'll be sorry.*

I bend down and scratch behind his ears, taking care to avoid his squinty-eyed glare. "You'll have to wait, pal, so chill."

The girl on the stairs doesn't bother to turn around, apparently disinterested in human-cat interactions.

I find Nick in his office, slumped over his desk in a

pose not unlike the girl on his back stoop and plop down in a chair next to his desk. "There's a Goth girl sitting on the steps. Know anything about her?"

He heaves a huge sigh. "Yeah, she's my daughter and the reason I called you."

I gasp in surprise. "You have a daughter?"

He rubs his bristly chin. "When she was four, her mom and I got divorced. My ex moved to Minneapolis, took the kid with her. I had visitation rights, twice a year. It worked for a while. When she got older, she didn't want to come out here. I should have insisted, but I took the easy route and let it go. What did I know about raising a kid? Especially a girl. The pub was brand new then. I was spending hours here, trying to make a go of it." He pauses and shakes his head. "Big mistake on my part."

I take a moment to digest the information. "Looks like she changed her mind."

"Her mother changed it for her."

"Because…?"

Nick sighs again. "She got kicked out of school. Her mom said she can't deal with her anymore, that it's my turn to step up and be a father."

I know Nick is guilt-ridden, but what the hell is wrong with the girl's mother? She suddenly decides it's too much trouble to be a parent, so she throws the kid under the bus and says, I'm all done. You fix her. "What do you want me to do?"

"Damn." Nick lifts his hands in a helpless gesture. "You're closer to her age than I am and, of course, you're a girl, so I thought maybe you could hang out with her, maybe do some girl stuff. Aw, hell, I don't know."

"How old is she?"

"Sixteen."

"Have you enrolled her in school?"

"I tried, but it's March and the middle of a semester. She'll have to go to an alternative program until next fall. Then, if her attendance and grades are okay, she can go to a regular high school." He pauses and rubs his temples. "From what of I've seen of her grades, that scenario doesn't look promising."

I feel a pang of empathy for the kid on the back steps. Sounds like she's a complete disaster, not unlike myself at her age. I say softly. "Does she have a name?"

With a ghost of a smile, Nick stands and strides out of the office. I hear the back door open and a muttered exchange of words. He returns, herding the girl in front of him like she's an errant sheep returning to the flock. Nick says, "This is my daughter, Ziggy."

I rise and hold out my hand. "Nice to meet you, Ziggy. I'm Mel."

She doesn't grip my hand, just gives it a little swipe before jamming both hands into her pockets. "You his girlfriend or something?"

Nick is normally unflappable, but a flush rises in his cheeks.

I step in quickly. "No, I'm a waitress here. Your dad helped me when I first moved to 3 Peaks and didn't have a job or a place to live."

She leans against the wall and casts a sideways glance at Nick. "Goody for him."

I try to keep my irritation from showing. "Actually, it was good *of* him. Otherwise, I'd have been homeless."

She shrugs like she doesn't care. I wait her out. Finally, she lifts her head and gazes into my eyes. Exactly what I hoped she would do. Her soul is a kaleidoscope of colors, indicating the emotional distress she's experiencing. I see no sign of an evil nature. She's just a mixed up teenage girl who doesn't know which way to jump. After an uncomfortable silence, I say, "Ziggy is a very unusual name. Where did it come from?"

The corner of her mouth twitches, like she's trying to hold back a grin. "It's actually Zelda Ignatius." She points at Nick. "He can tell you all about it."

Nick chuckles. "Finally, you're asking me a question I can answer. My ex wife is Greek and a big time reader. She insisted on naming our daughter Zelda, because she liked the author F. Scott Fitzgerald. Ignatius is the Greek word for fiery one. Early on, we shortened it to Ziggy." He pulls a wallet from his back pocket, opens it and withdraws a picture. He slides it across the desk. "Check it out. It explains the Ignatius part.'

The photo is tattered around the edges and the colors have faded. But, it's obviously a younger Nick, smiling broadly and cradling an infant in the crook of his arm. An infant with fiery red hair.

I look over at Ziggy. "So, you're a red head. Cool."

She narrows her eyes at me. "Ya think so? How about when you get called Agent Orange, Trusty Rusty, Bushfire or Chucky? Is that cool?"

I ignore the attitude. "Actually, I dyed my hair red when I was about your age. Guess we're never happy with what we're born with."

"Whatever."

I give up on trying to bond with the sullen teen and turn to Nick. "So, is Ziggy all settled in your place? What's next?"

Nick pushes his chair back and stands. "Um, I need to talk to you about that. In private."

Ziggy rolls her eyes again. "Okay, I get it. You want me outta here so you can talk like grownups, even though this Mel person looks like she's about my age."

"For your information, I'm twenty-three years old which, in case you're not good at math, is seven years older than you."

She mumbles, "Whatever," again, pushes off the wall and leaves the office.

I'm feeling a little guilty for my hostility. Also worried. "Shall I follow her? Maybe she'll run."

Nick pulls a battered suitcase out from under his desk. "She won't leave without her stuff. Cell phone. Purse. Laptop. Clothes."

"What do you want to ask me?"

"Well, um, since you're moving out of Number Ten, shall I move her in?"

I can't believe what I'm hearing and catapult to my feet. "A motel room? Are you crazy? She's sixteen years old! Doesn't your place have two bedrooms?"

He avoids my gaze. "Well, yeah, but I thought maybe she needed her own space, being a girl and all."

I blow out an exasperated sigh. "Nick, stop with the girl thing. She's just a mixed up kid who needs parental guidance." The minute I utter the phrase *parental guidance*, I'm horrified. As a teen, whenever I was invited to a party, my mother, Sandra's default question was, "Will there be parental guidance?'

When did I turn into my mother?

Chapter Three

After Ziggy is settled in Nick's apartment above the pub, I enlist her, along with Kendra, to participate in cat removal. Nobody on my team is enthusiastic. Because of Nick's negativity, I make him promise to provide Thunder Paws with a cathouse in case the move doesn't work out. He reluctantly agrees.

Ziggy is sitting on the front stoop of Number Ten looking sulky as I launch my plan. The pet carrier is on the pavement next to Kendra's minivan, loaded with an open can of tuna. Albacore, not the cheap stuff. Kendra and I stand nearby, trying to act casual, even though we're ready to spring into action. Thunder Paws is tempted, but wary. He sneaks up on the carrier, his body slinking low.

"Get ready," I whisper.

The cat places a tentative paw inside the carrier, then stops and glances over his shoulder at us, his eyes narrowed in suspicion.

"Nice kitty," I murmur.

He bares his teeth in a snarl and backs away from the carrier.

Ziggy says, "That cat hates you. Why are you trying to move him?"

"He doesn't hate me," I say indignantly. "He's just not very affectionate. All I want to do is give him a good home."

Kendra says, "He's an alley cat. He recognizes a trap when he sees one. Otherwise he wouldn't have survived all these years. Maybe she's right. Maybe you should just let him be."

I recognize the truth of her statement, but once I embark on a plan, I have to carry it through. "New plan," I say. "Billy offered to help me move. Shall I call him?"

Kendra gives an evil chuckle. "Yes, I like this idea. If anyone is going to get scratched, it should be Billy."

Ever since Billy and I broke up last fall, Kendra has been ticked off at him. Long story. Ancient history.

"Who's Billy?" Ziggy says. She plunges a hand into the pocket of her hoodie, extracts a cigarette and lighter. She fires it up and inhales deeply.

Kendra and I exchange a glance. I'd like nothing more than to slap the cigarette out of her mouth, but decide the issue can wait until another time. Like when we bond and she learns to love me. Like when hell freezes over and pigs dance the polka.

Kendra, however, chimes in. "My car is a smoke-free zone, so you'd best smoke it down fast."

Ziggy gestures at the cat. He's stalking away from the trap. "Looks like I've got plenty of time unless you think that guy can catch him. Whoever Billy is."

I pull out my cell phone.

He answers on the first ring. "Hey, Minnie, what can I do for you?"

I don't mention Thunder Paws. "Guess I need a little help after all."

"At your new place?"

"Number Ten."

"Be right there."

I don't mention Kendra or Ziggy because I know the words *Number Ten* evoke a certain response in Billy the Kid. It's no different for me. Billy was my first love and, within the walls of Number Ten, we explored each other's bodies with the heated passion of a brand-new relationship. Until it wasn't new anymore and, like Snow White, Billy drifted. But the memories linger on.

He drives up in an unmarked city car. The driver side door opens. Billy steps out and removes his jacket, revealing a department-issued gun in a shoulder holster. He's looking studly in pressed blue jeans that cling to his lean, muscular body and black dress shirt with a couple of the buttons undone. His badge is fastened to his belt. The sunlight catches the auburn glints in his hair. His hazel eyes gleam with anticipation.

Ziggy's eyes widen. She drops her cigarette and mashes it out with a boot. "He's a cop? You called a cop to help move the stupid cat?"

Billy grins at me. "Do I need my gun?"

Ziggy nods.

Kendra says firmly, "No guns required."

Billy unbuckles the shoulder holster and places it on top of his jacket. He steps around the car, grabs me with his left hand, Kendra with his right and wraps us up in a big hug. He lowers his head and nuzzles my ear, whispering, "Who's the kid?"

I step away from his embrace, trying to ignore my body's response to his touch. I nod toward Ziggy and make the introduction. Billy looks surprised to hear Nick has a daughter but murmurs, "Nice to meet you, Ziggy. Spending some time with your dad, huh?"

Ziggy grunts, "Whatever."

Billy ignores her snarkiness and turns to me. He

bows from the waist. "How may I be of service?"

Kendra smothers a giggle. "Go ahead and tell him, Mel."

I explain the situation using all of my limited charms. A dimpled smile. A friendly punch to his shoulder and then the biggy. "Do this for me and I'll owe you."

Never one to turn down a challenge and/or a promise, Billy says, "Okay." He crouches low and calls, "Here, kitty, kitty, kitty."

Yeah, like that will work. I'm about to inform him of his wrong-headed thinking when Thunder Paws bounds across the parking lot and flops down in front of Billy. He rolls over on his back, exposing his manly tomcat parts. Billy rubs his tummy. Thunder Paws waves his paws in ecstasy, purring loudly. Billy scoops him up, tosses him into the pet carrier and closes the latch. He loads the carrier into the back of Kendra's van and brushes the cat hair off his black shirt.

"There you go, Minnie. Anything else, or are we done?"

My mouth drops open in amazement. Kendra's expression is the same as mine. We're speechless, an uncommon state of existence for us both.

Ziggy's face lights up in a genuine smile. It totally changes her appearance. The tough-down-to-the-toenails juvenile delinquent vanishes. A light-hearted, carefree teenage girl appears. It doesn't last long, but gives me hope for the future.

She says, "You should see your faces. Hilarious."

"What the hell, Billy," Kendra says. "Are you some kind of a cat whisperer?"

Billy ducks his head modestly and lifts his hands.

"Just one of many talents. Actually, it's a man thing. The cat knows I'm male, so he automatically bonds with me."

Kendra says, "You are so full of shit."

He turns to me with a mischievous grin. "I seem to remember you said something like *I'll owe you.*"

"That's when I thought the task was going to be a bit more challenging."

He puts his hands on his hips and fake frowns. "You're going back on your word?"

I flap a hand at him. "Of course not. I'm working tomorrow night. Stop by and I'll buy you a beer. Not the cheap stuff. A good one from a local brewery."

He covers the distance between us in two long strides. "I've got something else in mind and it won't cost you a penny."

Before I can react, he sweeps me into his arms and strides to his car.

"Hey," I protest.

He sets me on the hood of the car and slides his hands up my arms until he's cupping my face. "Just one little kiss for your ex-boyfriend and we'll call it even. Sound good, Minnie?"

I'm incapable of speech. How do I get myself in these situations? Finally I murmur, "As long as it's just a friendly kiss, not, um, you know, the other kind."

Part of me wonders what Kendra and Ziggy are thinking. I haven't heard a peep from either of them, and Billy's gaze is drawing me in. His soul looks pretty darn spiffy compared to earlier, when he was suffering the ravages of PTSD from his multiple deployments in the Middle East.

He lowers his head until his lips are just a few

inches from mine. "I promise it will be super-friendly."

He tilts my head back and brushes his lips across mine. He draws back and looks into my eyes. "That was just a warm-up."

My breath hitches in my lungs. "Billy," I warn. "Dangerous territory."

"Shhh," he says.

I open my mouth to protest further, to say something like, "Remember my boyfriend? Remember Mick?"

I don't get a chance, because his mouth is on mine, demanding, tempting. My body remembers his in so many ways. His hands go to the back of my head and he deepens the kiss. His assault on my senses suspends my ability to think straight and I lean into him, totally enjoying the moment.

Finally, my brain catches up. I push him away and slide off the hood of the car. "I think you went slightly beyond friendly."

He looks smug. "You always said I was a good kisser."

I brush imaginary car dust from the back of my jeans. "Are we even now?"

"Sure, unless you have another task for me. Something a little more challenging."

I totally get what he's saying and, from his knowing look, he knows I get it. Something more challenging would involve another payment and it would likely require more than a kiss. I feel the heat rise in my cheeks. He winks at me.

"No." I make an effort to get my overactive imagination under control. "We can handle it from here."

"You sure about that?"

"Positive."

I turn and look at Kendra and Ziggy. "We can handle it. Right, girls?"

Ziggy is staring at me, wide-eyed, mouth agape.

Kendra beams a delighted smile. "I had no idea Billy could be so helpful. Maybe he should follow us over to your new place and unload the cat."

I know her game. She'd like nothing better than for Billy and me to get back together.

"No," I repeat again, firmly. "I'm sure Billy has to get back to work."

Billy looks disappointed, but gives in gracefully and heads for his car. Dazed, I watch him pull out of the parking lot. What just happened here? I'm at a loss for words.

Ziggy is not. "I can't believe it. You were totally making out on the hood of his car. Is he your boyfriend?"

"Ex," I mumble.

"No way! I thought you were going to do it right here in the parking lot."

I rake her with an offended look. "It was just a friendly kiss. For old times' sake."

Kendra snickers. "Wait until she meets Mick."

"Who's Mick?" Ziggy says.

"Never mind," I say. "Let's go. We have a cat to move."

We pile into the van and Kendra fires it up. Thunder Paws is making ominous sounds, ranging from deep, throaty growls to high-pitched yowls.

Ziggy claps her hands over her ears. "Jesus, that cat is really pissed."

I assure her it will be a fast trip, a scant half-mile from the pub. Before we pull out of the parking lot, a one-ton pickup with the Rockin' R symbol drives in. Rick Rathjen is behind the wheel, his son Riley riding shotgun.

Riley spots me in the van and hops out. He opens the minivan door and gives me a big hug. "Hey, girl, I've missed you. We need to talk."

A little voice from the back seat whispers, "Oh. My. God. How many hot guys does she know?"

Chapter Four

Since we're clogging up Nick's parking lot, I ask Riley to follow us. Thunder Paws grows increasingly angry, his decibels increasing to a painful level as we inch through slow traffic. Ziggy, in the back seat, bears the brunt of it. She zips the window down and pokes her head through the opening.

Kendra, ever safety conscious, snaps, "What's wrong with you, girl? Do you want to get beheaded? Roll up the window immediately or I'll pull over to the curb."

Ziggy pouts, but complies.

When we arrive at our destination, we all burst out of the car like it's about to erupt in flames. The Rathjens pull in. I make the introductions and notice Ziggy is checking Riley out. Hmmm. Food for thought.

We sweet-talk the Rathjens into unloading the pet carrier. They place it in the middle of the living room. I make sure the front door is shut and fill his feeding bowl with yesterday's special at Nick's, tuna casserole.

""On the count of three, I'll release the cat. Assume your positions." I don't want anyone injured, so they all have pre-arranged spots, hopefully out of Thunder Paws' line of fire.

Rick Rathjen chuckles, "Damn, Queenie, you're bossy. He's just a pussycat. Not a mountain lion."

"Did he just call you Queenie?" Ziggy asks. "I

thought your name was Mel. And, that Billie guy called you Minnie. Do you have multiple personality disorder?"

"Later," I snap. "Get ready." I crouch next to the carrier, my hand on the latch. "One. Two. Three." I fling the door open, expecting Thunder Paws to spring out and look for someone to punish.

Instead, he stretches out a paw and places it on the carpet. His upper body emerges. He turns and blisters me with a slitty-eyed glare. His lips curl back revealing big, sharp, yellow teeth.

"Nice kitty," I murmur.

He hisses and walks out of the pet carrier to his feeding bowl. He polishes off the food in three gulps and makes a beeline to the front door where he stands tall and pounds the door with his front paws.

Rick reaches for the doorknob. "He wants out."

"No!" I yell.

Rick shrugs. "Maybe he has to go potty. Does he have a litter box?"

I admit he does not and realize I haven't factored in some pertinent details. Thunder Paws has always been an indoor-outdoor cat, coming and going as he pleases. He definitely likes the great outdoors for his bodily functions. "Guess I'd better put it on my list."

The cat continues pounding the door, adding a series of yowls and hisses.

"Oh, for Christ's sake," Rick says and opens the door.

Thunder Paws shoots through and the last I see of him is an orange streak heading north, toward the pub.

"Oops," Rick says.

Ziggy laughs. "Best thing that's happened all day."

Suddenly, I'm supremely annoyed. Hands on hips, I turn to Ziggy and give her the stink-eye. "Best thing? All day? Do you remember what we went through to get Thunder Paws into the trap? And, now he's gone. He may even be dead. Squashed flat by a car."

She sobers quickly and mutters, "Whatever."

"Yeah, whatever," I repeat.

Since my cell phone is dead, I borrow Kendra's.

Nick picks up after the first ring. He doesn't bother to say hello. "Let me guess. Thunder Paws took off and you want me to buy a cathouse."

The fact that he's been so right about moving the cat ticks me off even more. I take a deep breath and force myself to speak calmly. "Better wait to see if he shows up." I pause and glare at Rick. "He could be lying dead in the gutter as we speak."

Nick says, "No way. He's street-smart. He'll either come back to your place or he'll turn up here."

"I hope you're right. See you later."

"Hold on, I need to talk to Ziggy."

I hand the phone to Ziggy. She answers in her usual charming fashion and snarls, "Yeah?"

She listens for a while, interjecting an occasional "Uh huh" or "Yeah," and then hits the *off* button and hands the phone to Kendra.

"Well?" I prompt.

"He wants you to drive me back to the pub. He made an appointment at some lame school." She waits a beat before saying, "Hey, how about you call back and tell him I need to help you unpack and stuff."

I think about how unhelpful she's been, but decide not to go there. I point at Rick and Riley. "I've got plenty of help."

Kendra says, "Come on, Ziggy, I'll take you back."

On her way out, Kendra tells the Rathjens, "Nice to meet you guys. I've heard a lot about you."

I know she's dying to know why they're here. So am I. She gives me a pointed look and mouths the words, "Call me."

Rick waits until the door shuts behind her before speaking. "Sorry about the cat, but he really wanted to go out. Are you mad at me, Queenie?" He holds out his arms, inviting me in for a hug.

Last fall, I took riding lessons from Rick and earned the nickname Lil' Queenie because of my bad, but imperious attitude. Let's just say my equestrian skills are not stellar. I fake punch his arm and give him a brief hug.

"My turn."

Riley's megawatt smile melts my heart. I step from one pair of Rathjen arms to the other. I became involved with the Rathjen family last fall when Yasmin, Riley's Muslim girlfriend, was found dead close to their ranch in Red Ridge, a small community north of 3 Peaks. Because of my special ability at detecting lies, and my connection with Homeland Security, I arranged a series of riding lessons in order to determine whether or not the Rathjen's were involved in her death. They weren't, but the tragedy totally changed the family dynamics. Even though they may have other issues, Rick is all about family. He underwent an attitude adjustment and gave up his bigoted blog, Americans First. Instead of railing against brown-skinned immigrants, he focused on his son. Riley was drowning in grief. The family is still struggling, but the healing has started.

Riley squeezes me tight and holds on a little longer than necessary. He smells like teenage boy and fresh air. Nice. When he doesn't release me, I think, *Really, Riley? Remember our "I'm not a cougar," conversation?* I pat his cheek in what I hope is a sisterly fashion. "Hey, I have a real home now, complete with coffee and pastries. Follow me."

I clear off the table and chairs and fire up the coffee pot. I feel a little guilty about not sharing the goodies with Kendra and Ziggy. Kendra, I regret. Ziggy? Not so much. I live by a certain set of rules. You have to earn your doughnuts.

We settle in around the table. Riley is squirming a little. Rick slurps coffee and chomps down a maple bar.

Looks like I need to kick start this conversation.

"It's great to see you guys again. Any special reason for your visit?"

Riley glances over at his dad. "Just ask her."

Rick wipes his mouth with the sleeve of his shirt.

Note to self: buy napkins.

"Well, we were hoping you'd take a little field trip with us, up in the mountains to a place called New Dawn."

Riley jumps in. "It's like a military compound where a bunch of heavily-armed people live with their families. They also go by the name National Freedom Alliance."

"Sounds like a bunch of nuts. Why do you want to go there?"

Rick says, "The guy running the outfit, Ken Hitchcock, came to the Rockin' R to buy hay for their animals. He talked about my blog, Americans First." He leans across the table, fixing me with an intense gaze. "You know I stopped writing it, right?"

I nod.

Rick continues, "I didn't tell him I'd closed it down. I wanted to hear what he had to say, so I let him believe I still had my previous attitude."

Riley takes over. "This guy told Dad they needed more people like him in their group, people who believed our only hope is to get ready for when the shit hits the fan."

"Wow," I murmur. "What does it have to do with me?"

Rick says, "You tell her, son."

Riley gives me his most impressive smile. "There's a meeting today, and we're hoping you will come with us."

I'm still puzzled. "Why would I want to visit some batshit bonkers military compound?"

"Because, Riley says you can read this Hitchcock guy's soul. See if he's evil or, as you said, 'just batshit bonkers.' "

Rick bows his head and rubs his temples. When he looks up, I see sadness and regret in his soul. "It's not just curiosity on my part. I need to make up for my past. If they're bad dudes, they need to be stopped. If they're people who choose to live apart from society, so be it."

I think about all the Rathjen family has been through, how they've finally emerged from the darkness, braver and stronger. How can I say no?

Chapter Five

It's four-thirty in the afternoon and I'm in the back seat of the Rockin' R pickup. We're bouncing along the rutted dirt road leading to the New Dawn complex. Winter still clings to Central Oregon in early March. A brisk wind stirs through Lodgepole pines bordering the road. Dirty patches of melting snow dot the landscape. A puny sun slinks behind the mountains to the west, casting no warmth. I think about poor homeless Thunder Paws and wonder where he'll sleep tonight.

The twisty road takes a strong pitch upward. The pickup lurches into four-wheel drive. I give an involuntary grunt as we hit a deep pothole.

Riley glances back at me. "You okay back there?"

"Just dandy," I mutter. "Forgot to tell you guys I get carsick on curvy roads."

Rick hits the brakes. "Want to change seats with Riley?"

"How much farther?"

"Less than a mile."

"I'll be okay, just slow down on the curves."

We proceed at a snail's pace. The road bends sharply to the left. That's when we see the sign.

STOP AND TURN AROUND. TRESPASSERS WILL BE MET BY OUR GREETERS, SMITH AND WESSON.

"Maybe this isn't such a good idea," I say. "I'm too

young to die."

Riley says, "They're expecting us."

"Me too?"

Rick turns and gives me a reassuring smile. "No worries, Queenie. We'll think of something."

My stomach gives an ominous lurch. "They're not expecting me?" My voice is shrill. Maybe I'm a little anxious.

Riley reaches over the seatback and pats my knee. "We take care of our own."

Another curve, this time to the right. Just ahead, we see a high chain link fence topped with razor wire and pull to a stop in front of a large metal gate padlocked shut. Two men dressed in camo and carrying extremely large guns approach the gate.

My heart kicks up a notch. "Are we about to meet Mr. Smith and Mr. Wesson?"

Riley turns to his dad. "Are those AK-47s they're carrying?"

Rick nods. "I think Smith and Wesson have been replaced."

I lean forward. "Should I be officially scared shitless now?"

"You're fine," Rick says. "I'll handle it."

The guards unlock the gate, crack it open and step through. Rick zips his window down.

"Please remain in your car, sir."

Both men are unshaven with dark, scruffy facial hair. A blossoming potbelly hangs over the belt of the older man. The younger guy is lean, muscular and looks to be around Riley's age. The family resemblance is strong. Probably father and son.

The older man goes to Rick's window, the younger

one to the passenger side and motions for Riley to lower his window. Both men observe my presence in the back seat.

Guy number one asks Rick, "Your name, please?"

"Rick Rathjen, and this is my son, Riley. A fella named Ken Hitchcock invited us here. For some kind of a meeting he's got going."

Guy number two says, "We know about you two. Who's the female in the back seat?"

The way he says female makes me feel dehumanized, like I'm a heifer or brood mare. I puff up a little, but since they have the big-ass guns, I keep my mouth shut.

Rick says, "She's my daughter, Melanie Rathjen."

"Her name is not on the list. We'll have to check with the boss."

The young guy whips out a cell phone, takes a few steps away from the truck, makes his call, then turns to the other guy and nods.

"You guys carrying any weapons?"

Rick says. "Took the shotgun out of the rack."

Not willing to take Rick's word, we're asked to step out of the truck for a pat down. The young guy gives me a crooked grin and tells me to hold out my arms and spread my legs. I want to tell him to go to hell, but I comply, vowing silently to never again return. I'm getting a little pissed at Rick for dragging me along.

My pat down is more thorough and invasive than Rick's and Riley's. Finally, I've had enough and say through gritted teeth, "Take my word for it, buddy. I'm not concealing a weapon anywhere on my person."

The kid stands behind me, groping the inside of my

thighs. "Nothing personal. It's just that women have more places to hide stuff than guys. Like in their panties and bra or in a more personal space."

He's now crossed the line. The hell with his big gun. I turn, put my hands on his shoulders, shove him away and snap my legs together. "Damn it, I *told* you, I'm not carrying a gun. I don't own a gun. I don't even like guns. If that's not good enough for you, I'll wait out here while the guys go inside and you all do your *man* thing. Is that okey dokey with you?"

His eyes widen in surprise. It makes me wonder if, in his young life, he's ever been chewed out by a *female*. He straightens up and scowls at me before turning to the other guy. "She's clean."

"As a newborn babe," I add.

The men open the gate and motion us through.

I scoot to the edge of the seat so I can speak directly to the back of Rick's head. "What the hell, Rick? That kid was groping me. And, now I'm your daughter, Melanie Rathjen?"

"Sorry, kiddo. I didn't realize there would be a pat down. I figured the only way to get you inside was to say you're family."

I mutter some choice words under my breath before declaring, "Whatever you want me to do, it will have to be today, because I'm never coming back here."

"Gotcha, Queenie."

Once through the gate, it's surreal, like we've entered a time warp and stumbled upon a movie set for an old time Western movie. Other than the chain link fence and a number of above ground propane tanks, the landscape is dotted with a variety of buildings, all constructed of rough-hewn logs. Most look like individual family dwellings with kids' toys and stick-built furniture on tiny front porches. Smoke curls from chimneys and rises into the towering pines before dissipating in cold, crisp air.

We are directed to park in front of the largest building. The sign over the door says, New Dawn Community Hall. A group of men is clustered on the wide front porch. They make no effort to hide their curiosity. The door to the hall opens. An imposing figure steps out.

"That's Hitchcock," Rick says. "The guy I told you about."

"The guy whose soul you want me to read?"

Rick nods. "If possible."

The group parts like the Red Sea to allow the man through. Clad in a long-sleeved camo T-shirt and black jeans, Hitchcock is a big man, well over six feet, with dark hair going gray. His upper lip sports a bushy gray mustache. No potbelly on him. He's broad across the shoulders, lean across the middle. Unhurriedly, he walks down the wooden steps, approaches the truck and offers a hand to Rick. His hand is huge, like a catcher's mitt. Looks like he could strangle a giant bear with one hand tied behind his back. The image frightens me.

"Welcome, my friend," he says in a gravelly voice. "Sorry about the hassle. We were not informed a female would be accompanying you."

That word again. I narrow my eyes at him. It's wasted effort because he doesn't bother to look at me.

Rick says, "Is it a problem?"

"Only if she makes it one. Females are not allowed in our forums. She'll have to wait for you outside."

Rick stiffens, as if he's expecting a barrage of

indignation from the back seat. There are so many things I want to say, but this is not my world. It's Ken Hitchcock's world and apparently his word is law. However, I do want to look into his eyes. It's the reason I'm here. Once accomplished, my work is done and I'll return to the real world where females are called women and girls.

I strive to make my words non-threatening. "If I may ask, is there a reason women are not permitted to attend your meetings?"

Rick's body relaxes which I interpret as *disaster averted*.

As I hoped he would, Hitchcock turns his head and gazes into my eyes. The close-up of his face reveals a scar I'd been unable to see until now. It originates high on his left cheekbone and terminates with a crease through the corner of his upper lip. I suspect the mustache was grown to help disguise it. The scar causes his upper lip to retract a bit, resulting in a permanent sneer. Not an attractive look, but considering his rank as leader of this flaky group, maybe it works to his advantage. Though his body looks like that of a much younger man, the ravages of time are etched on his face. His eyes are an icy color of gray and bloodshot with billowy pouches beneath them. Maybe he doesn't sleep well. Or, perhaps he overindulges in adult beverages. Maybe both.

His soul, however, is what interests me. Strangely, it mirrors his eyes, which, in my experience, is rare. His soul is predominantly pale gray with red streaks. It tells me he's a stone- cold dude with anger issues. But, there's something else as well. A wavy blue line snakes across the bottom.

He bares his teeth, possibly his version of a friendly smile. "At New Dawn, every person has a specific role. While it's true our governing body consists entirely of men, we value the female role, that of wife and mother, and offer them our protection. It works for us."

I wonder if the word *us* includes the perspective of New Dawn females. I decide not to rock the boat, but smile sweetly and try to keep sarcasm to a minimum. "Very gentlemanly. I'm sure female input would muddy the waters with unseemly emotion. Probably works best when each gender knows exactly what's expected of him or her."

Rick stiffens again. Did I not try hard enough to tamp down the sarcasm?

Hitchcock's fake smile disappears, although the unfortunate sneer remains. His brows draw together as he tries to untangle the nuances of my statement. He chuckles and slaps the side of the truck. I levitate several inches from my seat.

"Well said, young lady. I believe we've come to an understanding. You're welcome to remain inside the compound until our forum is finished."

Wow, I'm now a young lady, not a female. I grab my down jacket as we exit the truck. Rick and Riley follow Hitchcock into the building. I settle into a chair on the wide porch, a front row seat as a stream of men and boys file into the hall. I'm the recipient of curious glances. Perhaps *females* are not allowed to set foot on this bastion of masculinity.

I think about my introduction to Ken Hitchcock, about his reaction to me. I've seen his soul. The coldness. The anger. But there's something else as well.

The wavy blue line tells me he should not be underestimated. He's smart and canny. An involuntary shiver crawls down my spine. I can't wait to leave this place.

Chapter Six

A few minutes later, the last of the stragglers enter the hall. I notice one man in particular. His fair hair and sturdy build speak of Scandinavian heritage. He's gripping the hand of a little boy with blond hair and bright blue eyes. The man stops at the top of the stairs, gives me a fleeting glance and calls over his shoulder, "You wait here for us, girl. Don't go wandering off."

He and the boy enter the hall. I stand and look for the person he spoke to. It would be nice to indulge in girl talk while I'm waiting. So far, I've seen none of my gender. Are they all hiding inside their log cabins? Down at the creek scrubbing dirty clothes on washboards? Kneading homemade bread?

My peripheral vision catches sight of a sudden movement. I walk down the steps and turn right until I reach the edge of the building. I peek around the corner and see a little girl pressed against the rough siding. Her dark hair is braided. Her jeans and jacket are too big and look like boy clothes. Her gaze is fixed on the ground. Her thumb is in her mouth. She clutches a stuffed rabbit.

I take a step toward her and smile. "Hi. Are you waiting for your dad?"

She nods.

I take a step closer, trying not to spook her. "I'm Mel. What's your name?"

Without removing her thumb, she mumbles something unintelligible.

I take a step close and squat down until we're eye level. "I didn't quite get your name. Maybe if you take your thumb out of your mouth it will work better."

She lifts her head and I'm looking into eyes identical to those of the little blond boy. Bright and blue. My heart breaks when I look into her soul. Streaked with pale blue accents, it's a soft shade of pink and bisected with a jagged black line. This little girl has experienced severe trauma.

"I think I saw your dad and brother go into the hall. Am I right?"

She nods. The thumb comes out of her mouth. "Papa and Gunner."

"Can you tell me your name again, sweetie?"

"I'm Kimber."

"Do people call you Kim?"

She shakes her head. "Nope. People call me Kimber, 'cause that's my name."

"Got it," I say. "How about you keep me company until the meeting is over. I've got nobody to talk to and I'm lonesome. We could go sit on the stairs and wait together."

"Not there. No females. We can sit on the bench, though."

She takes my hand and leads me to a rickety bench a few yards in front of the porch railing. We sit in companionable silence for a few minutes. I'm dying to know more about Kimber, but don't want to bombard her with questions.

"This is Blossom Bunny," she offers, thrusting the stuffed rabbit in front of my face.

Blossom Bunny is not attractive. Her fur is dull gray and splotchy. Her long, floppy ears droop down to her skinny legs. Black, beady eyes peer straight ahead atop a little pink nose.

"Very nice," I lie.

"I love Blossom Bunny. She has zippers in her ears. I keep important stuff there." She lays the bunny across her lap, lifts one of the floppy ears and points out the zipper.

"Very cool. It's good to have a place to keep important stuff."

She nods solemnly, unzips one of the ears and pulls out a stubby pencil, a little rubber ball and a hair ribbon. Seeing her sparse array of treasures makes me sad.

She pats the sleeve of my down jacket. "Your coat is pretty."

"Thanks." I look at her thin denim jacket. "Are you warm enough?"

"No."

I unzip my jacket, slide my left arm out, wrap it around her, pull her close and zip us up in it. Her little body is chilled. I want to bitch-slap her father.

"Now we're like two snug bugs in a rug," I say.

She giggles. "You're funny."

"How old are you, Kimber?"

"Five."

"And your brother?"

"Gunner's five too."

"No way! You're twins?"

"Uh huh. But we don't look alike 'cause he's a boy and I'm a girl."

"Your eyes look exactly alike."

"People say that all the time."

"Guess what?" I say.

"What?"

"I'm a twin too."

I pull the twin heart pendant from the neck of my sweater, a gift from bio dad, Steve. "See the two hearts, how they're linked together? It means your heart will always be connected to Gunner's heart."

"Really?" She touches the pendant with her index finger. "Is your heart connected to your twin?"

The innocence of her questions makes my eyes fill with tears. "Yes, we're still connected."

"Does she live with you?"

"She lives in my heart."

She persists. "But where does she really live?"

How do I explain death to a five-year-old girl? How do I tell her about Hope, about our soul connection? I can't think of a way, so I chicken out. "She lives far away." Not exactly the truth, but not exactly a lie either. Call me the queen of denial.

I still have questions, like why is she out here in the cold, instead inside a snug cabin warmed by a wood-burning fireplace. Does she go to school? She's old enough for kindergarten. Are New Dawn females allowed to go to school, or will Gunner be the only educated twin? "I'll bet your mom is getting dinner ready. Are you hungry?"

"Hungry."

I dig around in my pocket and find a cereal bar I'd stashed a while back. I hand it to her.

She looks up at me with those incredible eyes. "I'll share with you."

I shake my head. "Not hungry. You eat it." My

stomach growls loudly.

When she smiles, her eyes crinkle at the corners. "See, you are too hungry."

She breaks off a piece and hands it to me. I sense it would be rude to refuse. I'm still fishing for answers. "What are you having for dinner tonight?"

"Whatever Papa cooks. Usually beans and deer meat. Don't like beans. They make Gunner fart."

"Bummer."

Apparently Gunner and Kimber are motherless. Is that what the jagged black line indicates?

She takes her time with the cereal bar, savoring each bite. When she finishes, she brushes the crumbs from her thin little legs. "My mama's dead."

I pull her closer and murmur, "I bet you miss her."

"Not so much. It was a long time ago."

"So, it just you, Gunner and your daddy?"

She nods. "Sometimes ladies come to visit Papa. He teaches them how to shoot guns. It's one of his jobs. Maybe he'll get a new wife some day.""

"Your daddy gives shooting lessons?"

"Yes, on the days he doesn't do blinds."

Now, I'm confused. "Are there blind people here? Does your Papa work with them?"

She giggles again. "No, silly. People make the blinds for windows. Papa loads them in a big truck and takes them to people." She wiggles free of the coat, turns and points at the community hall. "See?"

I stand and look where she's pointing. Each of the windows in the front of the building is fitted with tightly closed, slatted blinds. They looked to be constructed of cheap vinyl material. This strikes me as an odd fit for a building constructed entirely of logs.

Not that I'm an expert on interior decorating, but shouldn't the blinds be constructed of wood to match the rustic setting?

Kimber wants to make sure I understand the whole *blinds* concept. She whirls around and points at a cluster of nearby cabins. "See, more blinds. On the windows. Not blind people."

"Yeah, I get it. People here make the blinds and your daddy delivers them in a big truck."

"Exactly," she says. "When he's not shooting guns."

"I guess a lot of people here shoot guns."

"Yes, they do. Do you shoot guns?"

"No, I don't know how."

"My daddy can teach you. He's teaching me."

I get a sudden, horrifying vision of little Kimber mowing down a herd of elk with a gun larger than herself and I'm at a loss for words.

It's almost dark now and the wind picks up. Once again, we wrap ourselves up inside the down jacket, two lone females, waiting for the males in our lives to reappear. When the meeting breaks up, we stand and wait at the bottom of the stairs. Kimber clings to my hand. When her father and brother appear, she drags me over to them.

Her eyes are bright with excitement. "Papa, I have a new friend. Her name is Mel and she's a twin, like Gunner and me."

He looks down at his daughter and then at me. His eyes are blue, but a different shape and color than those of his children. They register a bit of suspicion as he checks me out. Unsmiling, he greets me with a curt nod. "I'm Jacob Gunderson, but people call me Jake or

Swede."

I murmur something polite—my mother would be proud—and see Rick and Riley heading my way. I squat down and give Kimber a hug. "I'm glad I got to meet you, Kimber. Maybe we'll see each other again."

She throws her arms around my neck and whispers. "You better come back or I'll be sad. Blossom Bunny too."

Her words cling to my heart as I join the Rathjens and we head for the pickup.

Rick starts the engine. "Sorry I made you come, Queenie. I didn't know you'd be locked out. I bet you're mad at me again, huh?"

He puts the truck in reverse.

"Wait," I say. "There's something I need to do."

I climb out of the truck and hurry after the Gunderson family. "Mr. Gunderson," I call. "I want to learn how to shoot. Can you teach me?"

A smile blossoms on Kimberly's thin face. "See, Papa, I told you she'd be back."

Chapter Seven

We're traversing down the deeply rutted road in the dark. The truck's high beam headlights flicker erratically off thick stands of pine. Since Rick is afraid I'll hurl on his back seat upholstery, I'm wedged between the two of them in the front seat. I'm chilled to the bone. Riley turns the heater on full blast. He throws an arm around me until I'm pressed against his warm body.

"Not necessary," I protest.

"Best way to warm up," he says. "Body to body. I learned it at a Boy Scouts of America meeting. Scouts' honor."

Rick snorts. "Sure you did, son. Do you buy that crap, Queenie?"

I shake my head, no.

"So you're going back to the batshit bonkers place, huh?" Rick says. "Sudden change of heart? Shooting guns doesn't seem like your thing. Kinda like riding horses isn't your thing."

"Did you see the little girl? Her name is Kimber and she has a twin called Gunner."

Riley says, "Kimber and Gunner, huh? I guess it's a big deal now, naming your kids after guns."

"Isn't Kimber a nickname for Kimberly?"

"No, Kimber's an American gun company. They manufacture high quality pistols and rifles."

"Oh," I say in a small voice.

"She got to you, didn't she?" Rick says.

"Her mother is dead. Her dad shoots guns and delivers the blinds they make at New Dawn. Did you know they make window blinds?" I don't wait for an answer. I sigh and admit, "Yeah, she got to me. Poor little thing, dressed in boy clothes. And she doesn't even have a proper coat. Her dad made her wait outside in the cold all by herself."

Riley says, "We heard about the blinds. I guess it's how they make their money, so they can buy guns and protect themselves when the angry hordes storm the gate. Just a matter of time, according to Hitchcock. He seems certain it will either be a gang of criminals or the government. He's leaning toward the government."

"Is he looking to recruit you guys?"

Rick says, "Probably. He invited us back."

I tell them what I'd observed in Hitchcock's soul. "If I had to guess, I'd say the man is incapable of loving. The only emotion evident in his soul is anger. But, he's highly intelligent and that makes him a scary dude."

After I deliver my report, my eyes grow heavy as the chill leaves my body. The rhythmic whirring of the heater fan and the rocking of the pickup have a lulling effect. My chin drops to my chest. I stop fighting it and wrap my right hand around the twin pendant. Riley adjusts his body so my head is against his chest. As I always do before sleep overtakes me, I evoke the spirit of Hope. I ask her to come to me.

When I close my eyes, I feel the warmth of her presence, and see her beautiful face, not as she was as a child, but as another version of myself. It's hard to explain. We're identical twins and one would think it's like looking in a mirror, but it isn't. According to our mother, Sandra, our eyes were slightly different. Our smiles too. It's how she could tell us apart.

She'd say, "Okay, you two, give me a smile."

Then, she'd laugh and say, "Honor, it's your turn to take the garbage out."

When Hope comes to me, her eyes are luminous, as if backlit by a starry night sky. Her smile is exuberant and filled with joy. I hold the pendant tighter and ask for her help. Before I drift away, her heart whispers to mine. "She needs you. They need you."

****

I awake with a snort, completely disoriented. Rick and Riley both crack up laughing.

Rick says, "Damn girl, you snore like a grizzly bear."

I rub my eyes, feeling a little crabby. "How do you know grizzly bears snore? You sneak inside their cave?" I look around and see we're in Nick's parking lot.

When his laughter subsides, Riley says, "We figured you'd want to come here, because that piece of crap you call a car is parked outside Number Ten."

"Hey, don't dis Buttercup. She might hear you and get mad." My car is a putrid shade of yellow, but she keeps on chugging. My motto is, live long and prosper, Buttercup, at least until I can afford something better.

Rick says, "You want us to follow you to your new place. You look groggy."

"I'm okay. I need to talk to Nick and see how Ziggy is doing."

Riley opens the door and hops out. "Let me know

45

when you have your shooting lesson. I'll drive you. Trust me, Buttercup can't handle the road."

As I slide out of the truck, I think about navigating the narrow mountain road in my old clunker and know he's right. I give him a noisy smooch on the cheek. "Thanks. I'll let you know."

Nick's pub is packed. It's Friday night and a lot of folks just got paid. Nick is in his usual place behind the bar. I spot Ziggy. She's wearing a Nick's Place pink T-shirt and jeans with a black apron tied around her middle. She's heading for the kitchen carrying a plastic tub filled with dirty dishes and cutlery. Instead of pushing it open with her shoulder, she gives it a vicious kick.

I walk over to Nick. "I see you put Ziggy to work bussing tables."

He rolls his eyes. "And she hasn't stopped bitching about it."

"Did you get her enrolled in school?"

"The best we could do was a work-study program until the end of the semester. She'll get credit for working here, plus she has a couple of classes at the school on Tuesdays and Thursdays."

"Is she okay with that?"

"Oh, hell no." He rubs his temples. "She's ticked about everything."

I pat his arm. "Welcome to parenthood."

He lifts his head and gives me a quizzical look. "Why are you here? It's your day off."

"Long story, just thought I'd check on Ziggy."

He blows a huge sigh. "Thanks. Might have to ask you to drive her to school once in a while if I'm busy here. I'll pay for your gas, of course."

"Sure, no problem."

"Did you check the back steps?"

"No. Why?"

"Thunder Paws is back."

"At least he's not dead. Remember your cathouse promise." I push away from the bar. My new bed in my new home is calling to me.

"Hold it," Nick says. "Look around. See if there's anybody you know."

All I want to do is leave and he's making me inventory the customers? "I'm sure I know a lot of people here. Can I go now?"

He shakes his head. "Nope. Not until you look around."

Well, damn. He's my boss and I need to stay on his good side. To humor him, I turn and scan the crowd. I see a few people I recognize in the main seating area of the restaurant and wave. Then, I peer into the section we call the Corral. It has two pool tables and usually attracts a rowdy crowd of drinkers. I take a step closer, so I can see the tables in the alcove next to the pool tables. Four big dudes all wearing black T-shirts and faded jeans are hunkered down over their drinks. One guy sits with his back against the wall. His chair is tilted back. He's wearing a dark blue ball cap with the brim pulled down over his eyes. His brawny right arm sports a full sleeve tattoo. I know that tattoo.

I look over at Nick. "Why didn't you just tell me?"

He chuckles. "He told me not to. He said if you showed up, he wanted to see if you recognized him."

My Homeland Security boyfriend, Mick, is in the house.

Chapter Eight

When last I saw Mick, he had spiky black hair and facial piercings. He was lean, almost skinny, hoping to pass himself off as a druggie. Apparently it worked. He got his man. He usually does.

I saunter into the Corral and head to his table. He lifts the brim of his hat and I look into eyes as clear and blue as a Norwegian fjord. His soul looks much the same, although it's picked up some etches and markings common to those involved in law enforcement.

I strike a pose, one hand on my hip, and flutter my eyelashes. Not a natural flirt, this seems silly to me. I lick my lips. "Why, hello there, handsome. You're drinking Grey Goose vodka and you look like someone I knew a very long time ago, but slightly different. Is it possible we've met before?"

His hand snakes out and grabs my wrist. He kisses the back of my hand. I hold back a snicker.

"My *maylsh,*" he says in a sexy growl. "I didn't fool you after all?"

Mick is Russian born. In the past, we've gone through a number of Slavic endearments. Most of them reference pussycat or kitten. After my strong objection, we settled on *maylsh,* the Russian term for baby. It's not all that great, but it's better than pussycat. In my humble opinion, it's not worth fighting over.

48

He scoots his chair back and pulls me onto his lap. I lift his cap to check out his hair. It's pale blond and growing out from the spikey do.

He says, "Is it true blonds have more fun?"

"You get to decide."

He leans and whispers, "Believe me, I will."

Heat spirals through my body, settling deep into my belly. I want to grab him by the hand and drag him out to my car. Have my way with him. Until I see Mick, I don't realize how much I've missed him. But, this is not the time or place. I push away and stand. "Are you going to introduce me to your friends?"

I suspect they are fellow officers. Not that he'll tell me.

Instead, he says, "This is Mel."

He points at the men and identifies each one by first name only. Now I know for sure they're his work buddies.

I say, "See you around, guys. Enjoy your evening."

Mick looks a little panicked. "Hey, wait. I'll see you later. In Number Ten. Right?"

Now, it's my turn for payback and I love it.

"Wrong." I walk away.

"At least leave bread crumbs."

I hear a hint of desperation in his voice and return to the table. "You're Homeland Security. Remember, you have no rules. I'm sure you'll figure it out, big guy. Bye, bye."

His buddies burst into laughter as I sashay away.

****

He found me. Was there any doubt? His lips are on my belly, moving lower. It's late. I'm totally satisfied, happy and tired. Ready to go night-night. He's not. I reach out, take hold of his ears and tilt his head back. "Question. Have your ever heard of New Dawn?'

"Hmmm?" he says.

"It's a paramilitary group in the mountains, also known as the National Freedom Alliance. I was up there today."

He rises up until his face is level with mine, bracing himself on his elbows. "Yes, I've heard of New Dawn. What the hell were you doing there?"

I explain the Rathjen connection, how Rick wanted me to read Hitchcock's soul. Mick has always taken my soul reading ability seriously.

"What did you see?"

"From what I saw, he's not a warm and fuzzy guy, but he's smart. Plus, he's really pissed about something and has access to a bunch of guns. Big guns."

He mulls over my words. "I assume you won't be going back."

Should I share my plan with Mick? I worked undercover for Homeland Security last fall when the Rathjens were under suspicion. The potential for danger existed back then and Mick trusted I was clever enough to take care of myself. I know I've piqued his interest, so I dive in.

"Actually, I am going back."

He narrows his eyes. "Why?"

I take a deep breath and the words spill out. The whole story. The Gunderson twins, especially little Kimber. The shooting lessons with her father. I know I'm talking too fast when I see his look of puzzlement.

He sits back and makes the timeout sign with his hands. "Let me get this straight. You're taking shooting lessons from some guy because you're worried about his little girl? If she's not being abused, I think it falls under the category titled *none of your business*? If you want to learn to shoot, I can teach you."

Okay, I'm wrong. He totally heard everything I said, but doesn't understand. I need to convince him. I sit up and wrap my arms around his neck. The twin heart necklace presses against my heart and his heart as well. I rub my cheek against his. "You know I really don't like guns, so it's not about the shooting lessons. It's hard to explain, but I have to do this, Mick." I draw back and gaze into his eyes. "Remember when I told you Hope comes to me sometime? I thought you'd laugh but you didn't."

He nods.

"Your willingness to accept something that sounds so crazy is important to me."

"Slow down, baby. I understand Hope visits you. What does that have to do with New Dawn?"

"I felt a connection to Kimber. A soul connection. She's a twin. I'm a twin. I fell asleep on the way home. Just before I dozed off, Hope came to me and whispered, *She needs you. They need you.* I have to go back."

His expression hardens. "I can't stop you, but I think it's a bad idea, Melanie."

When he calls me Melanie, I know he's not happy. I respond in kind. "Mikhail Petrov, you've made that crystal clear."

After a long silence, he says, "So, you've set up shooting lessons. Then, what? Do you have an end goal? Plans to spy on the family? Report them to child services? Have the children put into foster care?" He has an edge to his voice like he's interrogating a criminal.

"Of course not," I say indignantly. "It's hard to explain, but the little girl needs me. Maybe her brother does too. At least I can check out their situation, bring them some things, like clothes, or coloring books and crayons." I'm totally aware my so-called plan is lame, and I can see it in Mick's eyes. "Actually," I add, with a touch of spite in my voice. "I don't need your permission, so let's just drop it."

Mick flops down on his back and stares at the ceiling as if looking for divine intervention. Finally, he sighs, wraps me up in his arms and pulls me close. "I know how you are, *maylsh*. When you're on a mission to right a wrong, there's no way I could stop you. But, promise me you won't go to the compound alone."

He pauses until I cross my heart and promise.

"In the meantime," he continues, "I'll try to track down information about the group. I hear they have a shooting range. Did you see people packing guns?"

"The guys guarding the gate were armed."

"Can you describe the guns?'

"Big, dangerous-looking rifles." I think back to Rathjen's conversation. "I think Riley said they were AK-47's."

"Kalashnikovs."

"Excuse me?"

"It's a Russian semi-automatic assault rifle. Did you ever see the movie *Rambo*?"

"Yes, it's one of Paco's favorites."

"The rifle Stallone uses is an AK-47. It's capable of mowing down lots of people. I wonder what else they have in their cache."

I turn in his arms and kiss his cheek. "Maybe I

could find out if Homeland Security wants to hire me again."

Surprisingly, he takes time to consider it. "My inclination is to say no, since the risk involved at New Dawn is much greater than what you did for us last year."

I choose my words carefully. "You had no problem sending me to the Rockin' R ranch when you suspected one of them might be a murderer." I slide my hand down his chest, trail it across his belly and wrap my hand around his growing erection. "Maybe I can convince you."

He catches his breath and rolls onto his back. "Maybe I'll let you."

Chapter Nine

It's still dark when I'm awakened by the sound of rain pelting the windows, driven by a gusting wind. I'm warm and toasty, curled into Mick's solid body. He loves to spoon. I've always been a lone sleeper. When I was with Billy, he had nightmares, so I learned to stay well away from him and his flailing arms. Often, he was caught up in a battle known only to him. I learned to respect the distance between our bodies. Consequently, spooning is new to me, but I'm getting used to it.

For a moment, I'm disoriented, thinking I'm still in Number Ten. Then, I remember I'm in my new home, with a separate bedroom, kitchen and living room. I smile, proud of my accomplishment. Along with the wind and rain, I hear another sound. I stiffen in Mick's arms. Is someone trying to break into the house?

Mick jerks awake. "What is it, *maylsh?*"

"I heard a noise, like someone's trying to get in."

Mick rolls out of bed. The sound of metal scraping across the bedside table tells me he's picked up his gun. I follow him down the hall and through the living room. The thumping sound continues. The front door has a peephole for safety.

Before I can peer through, Mick orders, "Stay back."

He parts the drapes covering the front window and

peeks through. Laughter rumbles deep in his chest. "Go ahead. Take a look."

I peer through the peephole. At regular intervals between the thumps, a familiar cat face appears in my line of vision. I open the door and Thunder Paws stalks through. His fur is wet. His ears are flattened against his head. As usual, he's one pissed-off cat. He marches over to his feeding dish. Finding it empty, he stalks down the hall toward the bedroom.

Mick wraps an arm around my shoulders. "I believe your pussycat has returned. Let's go back to bed. It's early."

I veto the idea when I find the sopping wet cat curled up on my pillow, looking smug and purring loudly. Hands on hips, I glare at him. "I should have kept my whereabouts secret." Disgusted, I throw on some clothes. "I'll make coffee."

Cat or no cat, Mick's getting ready to crawl back into the sack when his cell phone buzzes. He picks it up, walks into the bathroom and closes the door.

Secrets. Always secrets. I know it's the nature of his job, but I can't deny I'm bothered by it. One either trusts the person he's in a relationship with, or he doesn't. I believe I've proved I'm trustworthy. I wander into the kitchen, turn on the light and fire up the coffee pot. I haven't had time to grocery shop, but when I peer into the cupboard and fridge, I see Steve has thoughtfully provided healthy snacks. Thank God, a few doughnuts remain in the box.

I'm on my second cup of coffee when Mick appears, newly shaven and clad in fresh clothes from the small overnight bag he always carries with him. He pours a cup of coffee and joins me at the table.

"Gotta go. We'll talk soon."

I glance at the clock on the microwave oven. "It's five-thirty in the morning. And, you just got here last night."

"I know, I know. So sorry. It's not what I want." He downs his coffee in a couple of gulps and snags a doughnut. "I'll call you soon."

I shouldn't, but say it anyway. "Why do I feel like a one-night stand?"

He stands and places his hands on my shoulders. "You know that's not true. Sadly, we all have people we must answer to."

Don't be a whiny bitch, Mel. I nod, fighting back an angry response.

He tucks a finger under my chin and lifts it until I look into his eyes. "I have something very important to talk to you about the next time I'm in town."

"How about right now?"

"I have few things to clarify first."

"Like what?"

"Later." He takes my hands in his and kisses the back of each one. "Remember your promise. You'll not go to New Dawn alone."

"I keep my promises."

"Don't be mad at me, *maylsh*. It makes me sad."

I stand and give him a hug. "Not mad. Just miss you, that's all."

He picks up his bag and turns to leave.

"Hold it," I say.

He pauses. "Yes?"

I summon a smile. "If you see your mother, tell her your girlfriend says hi."

He blows me a kiss and salutes. "I will."

When Mick and I first got together, I asked about his mother. Was she still alive? Living in Russia? Perhaps somewhere in America? I could hardly believe it when he said it was classified information. Ever since then, it's been our way of saying goodbye.

Before he steps through the door, he says, "Charge your cell phone."

I toy with the idea of going back to bed, but decide to look for the cell charger first. After emptying a couple of boxes, I find it cradled inside my sports bra. I have no memory of putting it there. At the beginning of the move, I was super organized, labeling each box as to its contents. Toward the end, it turned into chaos. I tossed the mismatched remnants of my life into a couple of boxes, regardless of category. Hence, as I unpack, it's like a treasure hunt. After finding my charger, I open another box and find a bottle of catsup, a curling iron, a manila envelope containing my bank statements, a lone apple, and my winter boots.

I plug my cell phone into the outlet next to the bed and climb in, taking care to stay on the dry side. Thunder Paws is over his snit. Still purring, he crawls to my side of the bed and nudges me with his head until I give his tummy a tickle. My phone chirps to life with a series of pings, indicating unread and unanswered text messages. May as well face the music. Sleep can wait. I leave it plugged in so I can scan the messages.

My mother:

—Did you get moved? Want me to come up and help you?—

Kendra:

—How did it go with the Rathjens?—

Uncle Paco:

—Hey, little girl. Call me. I have news.—

He includes an emoji. It looks like a half loaf of bread and something else I can't identify.

Billy:

—Call Candy Talbot.—

Bio dad Steve:

—Candy Talbot needs your assistance.—

Candy Talbot:

—Damn it, Mel, don't you ever answer your phone. I've got Dwayne's girlfriend scheduled for tomorrow and I need you to do your thing. Okay? Call me ASAP.—

Nick:

—Cowboy Jim's Grandma Edie died. He's depressed and needs a new dance partner. I said, 'How about Mel?' and he said, 'Yes, indeedy, but she'll need some lessons.' So, how about it, kiddo? Are you willing to help the poor guy out?—

Cowboy Jim. He's of an indeterminate age, tall, skinny and bow-legged. I've never seen him in anything but jeans, a plaid shirt, cowboy boots and a Stetson. His grandmother, Edie, was a tiny little woman with permed white hair and dressed exactly like her grandson, minus the hat. When they came into Nick's, usually on a Sunday afternoon, we'd move the tables and chairs so they had room to dance. Nick would crank up the music and, despite the disparity in height, they would glide across the floor in a waltz or a two-step. Once they got limbered up, they'd teach the crowd a new line dance. If you've never seen a room full of drunks trying to line dance, you've missed a real treat.

And now Nick is guilting me into becoming Cowboy Jim's new dance partner. It would be unfeeling of me to refuse. If I turn him down, I'm an uncaring, self-centered ass hat.

My cell phone will be charged in a couple of hours. I'll deal with my messages then. I snuggle under the covers and try to fall asleep. I can't. It's way too quiet. I find the silence unnerving. My new home is located in a safe neighborhood, but bad things can happen in good neighborhoods. Last October, I was going for a run in a quiet neighborhood not far from here and had a near-fatal run-in with a giant SUV. I banish the image from my mind.

I've spent the last year living in a motel. It's noisy, despite the sign *Quiet hours from ten p.m. to seven a.m.* posted in each room. I'm accustomed to the sound of couples engaged in a yelling match, a fumbling, confused drunk trying his key card in my door and cars revving their engines. Factor in my exhaustion from working ten-hour shifts, and it's no wonder I slept like a baby, even though Kendra says that particular adage is far from the truth. "Babies love to wake you up every two hours, just for spite."

I start to doze off and then jerk in surprise when the furnace roars to life with a series of clicks and hisses. The warm air blowing through the registers causes the vertical blinds on the window to bump together. I pull the covers over my head. My eyes refuse to close. You just drank two cups of coffee, dummy. Finally, I stop trying and unpack the rest of my boxes.

Two hours later, my panty drawer is organized. The catsup bottle is in the fridge. The apple is next to the coffee pot, looking lonely. My winter boots are stashed in the closet next to my only pair of stilettos. My one good dress is on a hanger. The sum total of my worldly goods is pathetic.

Cell phone charged, I text my mother.

—Help not required. All settled. Will call soon.—

I'll catch Kendra later. Morning is a busy time for her. Since three of the text messages reference Candy Talbot, I go straight to the horse's mouth, so to speak.

She answers on the first ring. "About time you called me back. Judy Moss, icky Dwayne's girlfriend, will be here at eleven, providing you'll be here. Otherwise, I'll postpone it."

"I'll be there."

"Good," she says and clicks off with saying goodbye. Candy is not known for her social graces.

Chapter Ten

I'm back in Detective McKenzie mode, blond wig firmly in place. Judy Moss is a busty, overweight, multi-tattooed fake redhead. We're engaging in small talk while Candy fetches bottled water for the three of us.

I have my work cut out for me. Judy has exceptionally small eyes. One might call them beady. Small eyes I can deal with. But she has another habit and therein lies the problem, soul-reading wise. Her gaze darts nervously around the room like a trapped butterfly looking for an escape route. Her arm is in a sling and one side of her face sports a yellowing bruise, the injuries she claims were inflicted upon her by ex boyfriend, Dwayne.

I'm trying to get her to look at me. I point at the safety pin piercing her right eyebrow. "Oh," I exclaim. "Is that a real safety pin?"

Her eyes widen a bit at my sudden interest in her unusual choice of jewelry. She leans over the table so I can get a better look. "Yes. It's made of titanium. Less chance of an allergic reaction."

"Hmm," I say, feigning interest.

I manage to get a glimpse into the basic landscape of her soul, an important part of my procedure. People's souls are unique and normally maintain a fairly static balance as they progress through life, even though certain events leave marks. In Judy's case, her soul is remarkably bland. Predominantly beige with a muddy brown border, I'd be willing to bet she's not a deep thinker and, more than likely, a couch potato. I should be able to spot a lie flash across her soul if I can get her to look at me.

Candy pops through the door and distributes the water. Judy removes the cap and chugs half of it down. Dry mouth from nerves?

I lean back in the chair and cross my arms, our pre-arranged signal indicating I've successfully peered into Moss's soul.

Talbot says, "As you know, Ms. Moss, we've interviewed your boyfriend, Dwayne."

"Ex-boyfriend," she corrects. "Why the hell isn't he locked up?"

Talbot attempts to deliver a friendly smile. It looks more like a shark baring its teeth. Exactly why she needs me.

"A very good question," I say. "I would totally feel the same way. I mean, what the hell? If my boyfriend slept with my mother, I'd do anything to lock the bastard up."

"Anything?" Her brows draw together in a puzzled frown. She so wants to believe me, but a glimmer of doubt remains. "He told you about my mother?"

"Actually," I say. "He seemed rather proud of it."

"Bastard," she mumbles.

Talbot steps in. "How's your broken arm?"

Moss's eyes dart to and fro before connecting with mine, the friendly cop. I give her an encouraging smile.

"Getting better every day."

"Oh my God," I say. "How did he break your arm?

I bet that really hurt."

She glances over at Candy before her gaze returns to me. "He threw me down a flight of stairs."

The bold-faced lie flashes across her soul like strobe lights at a rave. Not even a challenge. I decide to push a little harder. "Really? That's awful! Did you call 911?"

"I decided to go directly to the cops to get the asshole locked up.

I lean back in my chair, ready to deliver the nail in her coffin. "Here's the deal, Judy. Dwayne swears up and down he never laid a finger on you. He says your broken arm is fake and you whacked yourself across the face to implicate him."

Her eyes widen in outrage before going into darting mode. "I-I-well, that's ridiculous. Who would do something that crazy?"

It isn't easy, but I manage to track her eyes long enough to see the lie. I turn to Candy and nod.

Talbot says, "Then, I guess you won't mind taking off your sling so we can take a look at your broken arm."

Judy Moss jumps to her feet. "Screw you! Both of you! I'm so outta here."

I look at Candy. "Wanna nail her for a false police report?"

Candy rubs her temples. "Aw, what the hell. Let her go."

Moss wastes no time. In a flash, she's through the door and down the hall, moving fast for a woman her size.

I glance over at Candy. "Another one bites the dust."

She picks up the file folder and stands. "Thanks, Mel. Don't forget to turn in your time so you can get paid."

I glance at my cell phone. It's almost noon and I'm due at Nick's for the lunch crowd.

"Tomorrow," I say. "Gotta run."

As I dash across the parking lot, I whip out a quick text message to Nick. "Running late. On my way."

Billy pulls in next to Buttercup. He steps out of his car. "I need to talk to you."

"I'm late for work. Later." I unlock the door and slide behind the steering wheel.

Billy grabs the door before I can close it. "Mick called me. He said you've got something going at New Dawn. He's worried about you and I agree. You need to re-think it, Minnie. There are some pretty bad characters up there."

I bite back a snarky reply, knowing it will make things worse. Something like, "Gee, Mick is only in town for twelve hours, manages to get me in the sack and he still has time to talk to you?" Instead, I say, "Thank you for your concern. I'll take it under advisement."

Billy shakes his head. "Yeah, sure you will. Don't say I didn't warn you."

I start the engine. "I won't."

Before he shuts the door, he leans in close. "Take care, Minnie."

I look into his eyes and see it again, floating across his soul. I catch my breath, because I know what it means and it shocks me. "Thanks, Billy. I will."

I arrive at Nick's along with the lunch crowd. The other waitress, Helen, gives me a dirty look. "About time you got here."

I ignore her and get busy taking orders and delivering food. When the action dies down, I notice the tables are cluttered with dirty dishes. Nick pitches in to help.

"Where's Ziggy?"

"School. I dropped her off this morning."

"Did you walk her in?"

"She didn't want me to."

I remember my rebellious teenage years and how adept I was at cutting classes. "Did you see her go into the building?"

He says, "A bunch of kids were across the street from the school, smoking. She walked over to them and bummed a cigarette, because I threw her smokes in the garbage. I stayed in the car and watched. A few minutes later, the bell rang and they all went inside."

He cocks his head to one side, looking quizzical. "Why are you giving me the third degree? You think she skipped out?"

"Maybe," I say. "She wasn't too thrilled about going to school."

"Damn!" he says, vigorously wiping a table down. "How about you pick her up at three? See if she'll talk to you. She sure as hell won't talk to me."

"I'll pick her up, but here's my disclaimer. She doesn't like me all that much."

Nick mutters, "She probably likes you better than me."

****

I leave Nick's in plenty of time to be at the school at three, but didn't factor in late afternoon traffic. It's five minutes after three when I pull up in front of the school. I spot Ziggy across the street with her new friends. All are clad in black. Cigarette smoke wafts through the air.

I lower the window. "Hey, Ziggy. Your dad sent me to pick you up. Hop in."

She's standing next to a tall, skinny guy with a bright green Mohawk and multiple piercings. She calls, "Benny's giving me a ride."

"No, Benny's not giving you a ride. Let's go."

Benny drops his cigarette and grinds it out with his unlaced shoe. He flips me off, grabs Ziggy's hand and they take off running.

"Aw, shit!" I put the car in gear.

The designated smoking area is across the street from the school in a vacant lot, flanked on both sides by rundown houses with an alley behind. Ziggy and her new boyfriend hit the alley running, take a quick right turn and disappear behind the houses. I stomp on the accelerator and zip down the street. After a quick left turn on the next street, I pull to a stop next to the alley and spot them immediately. Benny has a long-legged lope and is practically dragging Ziggy along behind him. They see me, make an abrupt left turn across a private back yard and disappear around the corner of the house.

Still cussing like a sailor, I drive to the intersection, just in time to see them pile into an old junker car with primer on both sides and a flaking tan vinyl roof. As I turn the corner, Benny fires up the engine and peels out, laying a patch of rubber. I press the gas pedal to the floorboard. Buttercup shudders and tries valiantly to keep up. Benny doesn't slow down at the stop sign and makes a quick right turn. I figure he's heading for the expressway. There's no way I can catch the kid. Since I'm sure he has no intention of taking Ziggy home, I go back to the school, hoping to score some information about Benny, like maybe where he lives. I hold off calling Nick.

What would I say? Hey, Nick, I just lost your daughter.

Chapter Eleven

In my short life, I've learned some valuable lessons. Institutions, like schools and hospitals, will not give out personal information. I understand why. It's to protect their clients' privacy. Sometimes, rules are made to be broken. As I pull into the school's parking lot, I take a moment to decide how best to acquire the information I need. I choose hysterics.

After running my fingers through my hair until it's standing on end, I try to think of something sad, like little motherless Kimber at New Dawn, shivering in the cold wind. Tears well up in my eyes.

I burst through the door of the school and dash down the empty hall to the office. A stout woman with a crew cut and red-framed glasses looks up from her desk as I enter. Her nametag says, "Call me Tootsie."

I'm sobbing hysterically, barely able to get the words out. "Oh, my God," I wail. "I came to pick up my sister and she ran off with some guy named Benny. I couldn't catch them. Please, please, tell me where he lives. Maybe he took her to his house."

She stands, holds up a finger. "I'll get Principal Dan."

Principal Dan looks like an aging hippy. Long, gray ponytail, tie dye T-shirt, jeans and sandals with black socks. He leads me into his office, waves me into a chair and thrusts a box of tissues into my hands.

"Alrighty then, let's see if we can chill a little. Tell me what's going on."

I repeat my story. He asks Tootsie to deliver Ziggy's folder and I'm gratified to know Nick listed me as a relative with the power to pick up and deliver her to and from school. It makes my plea easier, once I convince Principal Dan we don't need to put out an Amber Alert. I describe Benny. I can tell by his reaction he knows exactly who Benny is.

He says, "If I give you his address, what do you plan to do?"

"First of all, I'll contact Ziggy's father and see how he wants to proceed."

Principal Dan gives me an approving nod. I have no intention of following this course of action. "Then," I continue. "We'll try to call her cell phone. If she doesn't answer, her father will contact the authorities and let them know she's underage. She's only sixteen. How old is Benny?"

He glances down at Benny's file. "He's one of our older students, here for GED prep."

"Is he over eighteen?"

"Maybe."

"It's possible he's putting a minor in danger. I'm sure you don't want that to happen."

Bottom line: I leave with Benny's address. I climb into Buttercup and call the person I know can help with my little problem. Uncle Paco.

After I explain the situation, he agrees to meet me at the address provided by Principal Dan. I shoot a quick text to Nick: *Be back soon. Ziggy and I are working something out.* It's not a total fabrication. Ziggy is trying to get away from me. I'm trying to locate her and get her into my car. I think the current situation falls loosely within the *working it out* category.

Benny lives in a sprawling, seedy-looking apartment complex, number 2D. When I pull into the parking lot, I spot the junker car. Naturally it's parked haphazardly, taking up two spaces instead of one. I expected no less from the creep who aided and abetted a runaway teenage girl. Not that Ziggy is the picture of innocence.

Paco arrives on his Harley. A huge, intimidating presence, he's clad in baggy jeans topped with his Los Habañeros leather jacket. The jacket features a habañero chili shaped like a knife and dripping blood. A blue bandana holds back his bushy black hair. A droopy Fu Manchu mustache completes the image. I step out of Buttercup and into his embrace.

He kisses the top of my head. "Haven't seen you for a while, little girl. Whose ass do I get to kick?"

"I hope we can do this without an ass-kicking, Unc, but you never know."

"So, let me get this straight. Nick has a daughter, who knew? And, instead of hopping into your car like a good little girl, she took off with a skinny ass kid and they're holed up here?"

"Yeah."

"No problem. Let's go get her." He wraps a beefy arm around my shoulders as we head for apartment 2D.

"Here's the plan," Paco says. "You try to coax her out and if it doesn't work—"

"It won't," I interject.

He smiles. "I believe I'll be able to convince her."

We pass by apartments A, B, and C without

attracting unwanted attention. Paco's appearance is scary. People have been known to call 911 when he appears in their neighborhood. We stop in front of D. The drapes on the window left of the door are tightly drawn. Heavy metal music and smoke leak out from under the ill-fitting door. I knock. Loudly. The music stops. I hear approaching footsteps. The drapes part and Ziggy's face appears. Paco is standing on the other side of the door, out of her view.

"Open up, Ziggy," I say. "Let's go home. I haven't ratted you out to your dad. We need to talk."

She says, "Screw you, Mel."

Pretty much the reaction I thought I'd get. It was my best shot. Now, all bets are off. I nod at Paco.

He doubles up a ham-sized fist and pounds on the door. It quivers in the frame and a crack appears. He puts his mouth next to the crack and bellows, "Open up now, shithead, or I'll break it down."

Benny's pale face appears in the window, mouth agape. His eyes are wide and fearful. Paco leans over the window until his face is level with Benny's. "Now."

The drapes fall shut. The door opens a few inches. Benny peeks out. I see Ziggy standing behind him. Paco gives the door a vicious kick and the two stagger backward. Paco and I step inside and close the door behind us. The place reeks of pot and greasy food.

Benny apparently thinks this is a drug bust. He points at the still smoldering joint. "It's medicinal, man. Totally legit. I have a condition. I can show you the prescription if you want."

"You've got a condition, all right," Paco growls. "It's called being an asshole and I don't think weed's gonna help."

71

I walk over to Ziggy. She's shaking and the pupils of her eyes are dilated. Even though I'm mad as hell, I can't help but feel pity for the screwed-up kid. I grip her arm. "Let's go, Ziggy. We'll talk in the car."

The fight has gone out of her. I lead her from the apartment. Paco gives Benny one last ferocious scowl and follows. The ruckus we created attracted attention. As we walk past apartment 2C, the door flies open. An elderly gentleman with a cane steps out. He peers at me through his bifocals and then catches sight of Paco. "What's going on here?" he barks. "Young lady, are you okay?"

I hold my breath and keep a tight grip on Ziggy's arm. This could go sideways quickly.

Thankfully, she says, "I'm okay."

Maybe the weed mellowed her out.

"Sorry we bothered you, sir," I say. "We had a little misunderstanding with your neighbor, Benny. We'll be going now."

"Benny." He flaps a hand and snorts, "It figures." He steps back into his apartment and slams the door.

Paco and I load Ziggy into the car. I give Paco a hug. "Thanks, Unc. That was awesome."

He bends down and looks into my eyes. "Did you get my text message? The one with the thingamajig?"

I scan my brain cells. "Oh, yeah, the emoji. It looks like a loaf of bread and something else…"

"An oven." A huge grin blossoms on his face. "Get it?"

My foggy brain attempts to connect the dots. Obviously, this is important to him. It would be crass to rain on his parade, especially after his help with my Ziggy problem. I pull out my phone, check his message and the dim bulb brightens. "No way!" I exclaim. "Aida's got a bun in the oven?"

"Yep!" He grabs me around the waist and twirls me around. When he sets me down, I stagger sideways before I get my balance.

"Wow, you guys didn't waste any time. Is Aida ready for another baby?"

"It was her idea. She wants Larissa to have a little brother or sister."

I give him a hug. "Congratulations, Paco. You're a great dad. Now, you'll have another one to love. Just don't ask me to babysit. Okay?"

After a roar of laughter, he says, "Gotta run. First birthing class tonight."

I watch him climb on his Harley and tool away, wishing I could be a fly on the wall when my gangbanger uncle and his beautiful Russian wife walk into the birthing class.

Ziggy nods off on the way home. I let her sleep.

When we pull into Nick's parking lot, she rouses. "Are you going to narc me out?"

"Here's the deal. I'm going to work. I'll take orders and deliver food. You're going to get your butt inside, put on an apron and start bussing tables. We'll talk later. Got it?"

She nods. "Got it." She climbs out of the car, pull up her hood and head for the backdoor of the pub.

I'm still ticked off and part of me wants to tell Nick the whole story. On the other hand, I now have leverage. She knows I know. Maybe she'll behave for a while. I know what I want to tell her. In her present condition, she may not remember my words of wisdom, so I'll wait for tomorrow.

Chapter Twelve

It's nine in the morning and I'm groggy. I can only imagine how Ziggy feels. Tough titties, we're going to breakfast whether she likes it or not.

I climb the stairs to Nick's apartment and pound on the door. He opens it immediately. I'd told him last night what I planned to do. He'd pumped me for information as to my motives. I gave him my default answer. "You said Ziggy and I should do girl stuff together."

He looked surprised. "Didn't know going out to breakfast was a girl thing."

I stick to my story and here I am, sleep-deprived and grumpy. Ziggy doesn't look much better. She's in her usual costume, raggedy jeans and hooded sweatshirt. The hood is pulled over her head.

She squints at me through puffy eyes and whines, "I'm not hungry. Why do I have to go to breakfast?"

I take her arm and pull her through the door. "Because you do, Sunshine. You're stuck with me. If you don't want to eat, you can drink coffee. Tell your dad goodbye."

She gives him a half-hearted wave.

If I paid attention to my budget, we'd be going to McDonalds, but I want privacy so I opt for a pricier place. We're seated in a booth with high-backed seats. The waitress brings a carafe of coffee, leaves it on the table and takes our order. I order a cheese omelet with hash browns. Suddenly starving, Ziggy has a change of heart and orders strawberry waffles and a side of bacon. I fill both our coffee mugs. I drink mine black. Ziggy loads hers up with sugar and creamer. We sip our coffee in silence.

Finally, Ziggy can't handle it. "Why am I here?"

I sigh. "Think about it, Ziggy. Do you even remember what happened yesterday? How I came to pick you up and you took off with Benny? Surely, you haven't forgotten. Or, did the fact you were stoned out of your mind wipe out the memory?"

She looks down at her lap. "I remember."

"Good, because the reason we're here is to talk about it and figure out a solution. Or, if you prefer, we can include your dad."

Ziggy knows a threat when she hears one. "This is okay."

I don't say another word. I sip my coffee and let her stew. Our food arrives and we dive in.

When we're members of the clean plate club, I begin. "When I was fifteen, I was like you. School bored me. I was more interested in partying and getting high."

She looks into my eyes. "What happened?"

"I had a mother who was a pain in the ass."

"My mother gave up on me."

I reach across the table and grab her hand. "Well, guess what? My mother is still alive and needs something to do." I look into her soul and see a flash of fear skitter across it. She snatches her hand away. My plan is working. She covers her fear by rolling her eyes as if she's supremely disinterested.

"Here's what happened to me at age fifteen," I continue. "I was cutting classes. Getting high. My mother, Sandra, chose a course of action. She drove me to school, walked me inside the building and attended my classes. Do you have any idea how embarrassing that was to a teenager?"

Ziggy shudders. "Oh, my God. What happened?"

"What do you think happened? I had no choice. I went to class."

Ziggy thinks it over. Finally, she says, "Why are you telling me this?'

I give her a smug smile and hold up my cell phone. My mother's picture is on the display. "Because Sandra has time on her hands. She really needs something to do. All I have to do is give her a call. My stepfather, Abel, owns a fleet of trucks. She could easily hop on one today and be here by nightfall. There's nothing she'd like better than to have a new project. By new project, I mean *you,* Ziggy. Does that sound like fun? You and a forty-five-year-old woman attending class together?"

"No way. You can't do that."

"Wanna bet?"

My finger is poised over the call button. "Three…two…one and—"

"Stop!" There's a tinge of panic in her voice. "What do you want me to do?"

"You will not only go to school, you will go to class and pay attention. Do your homework and turn it in. When school is out, you will be waiting for a pickup by your father or me. Is that clear?"

Her sullen expression returns. "Yeah."

I decide to throw in some extras. "In addition, you

will stop bitching about your work load. Nick is paying you a fair salary. So, shut the hell up and do your job. Got it?"

She stares at the table and nods.

I purposely don't mention Benny. Even though he's a creep, I can't choose her friends. I'll settle for school and work right now.

We drive back to Nick's in silence. When I pull into the parking lot, she bolts from the car.

I zip the window down and holler, "You're welcome. So glad you enjoyed breakfast and our little chat."

My cell phone vibrates. Riley Rathjen.

He doesn't waste time on pleasantries. "When's your next day off?"

When I tell him, he says, "How about another trip to New Dawn? You up for it?"

"Sure, I'll see if I can set up a shooting lesson. What about you? Won't they wonder why you're there?"

"They've got a shooting range and said I could come up any time and use it."

After we arrange the time, I steer Buttercup toward my favorite thrift shop. Time to do some serious shopping for the Gunderson twins. While I'm at it, it's a good time to put Mick, the missing boyfriend, out of my mind.

****

Thankfully, I don't have to submit to an invasive pat down when we arrive at New Dawn's gates. Riley let them know we were coming. I've arranged a shooting lesson with Jake Gunderson. Apparently he's not delivering blinds today, so everything seems copacetic.

The guard waves us through after a thorough visual examination of the Rockin' R pickup truck. Riley shows the guard his weapon. I'm not gun savvy, but it looks like a rifle one would use to kill a deer. Maybe Bambi. I don't ask because I really like Riley and there's no way I could kill Bambi. Remember don't ask, don't tell? It's kind of my mantra.

Riley pulls in next to the community hall and parks. As we exit the car, Ken Hitchcock appears and descends the stairs. Something in his manner seems faintly menacing.

Riley says, "Mr. Hitchcock, how are you?"

He doesn't acknowledge Riley. His gaze is fixed on me. "Your name is not Melanie Rathjen. In fact, you're not a Rathjen at all. Their daughter is named Rachel."

I open my mouth but no words come out.

Riley bristles. "You're right. She's not my sister. Mel's a close friend of the family and we asked her to come with us. Her name wasn't on the list, so my dad thought the easiest way would be to say she was his daughter."

Hitchcock is still giving me the stink eye. "I don't appreciate being lied to."

"Actually, I didn't lie to you."

He waves a dismissive hand. "You were complicit."

I'm getting a little hot under the collar. "So, what do you want to know, Mr. Hitchcock?"

"Let's start with your real name."

"I'm Melanie Sullivan and I'm here for a shooting lesson."

"With Swede?"

It takes a moment before I remember Jake Gunderson is also called Swede. "Yes. Is there a problem?"

He looks me up and down. His icy gaze crawls over me. I want to jump back in Riley's truck and lock the door. Then, I remember why I'm here. It's not to learn how to handle firearms.

He nods to Riley. "Head for the range. I'll walk Melanie to the Gunderson place."

Riley hesitates. I know he's reluctant to leave me alone with Hitchcock.

I give him a little push. "I'm fine. Go. Have fun. See you later."

He gestures toward the truck. "Don't forget your stuff."

Oh, yeah. The stuff. I go to the truck and gather up two bags of thrift store items. Hitchcock eyes them suspiciously. "Whatcha got there?"

"Just a few things for the kids."

"We don't accept charity."

I try to control my temper. "I recently moved and I'm getting rid of some things from the past. Items from my childhood I no longer need. Feel free to go through the bags if you like. Be sure to check for contraband and hidden weapons."

I thrust the bags into his hands, turn and head down the path. Since I don't actually know where the Gundersons live, I hope I'm going the right way. I sense Hitchcock's presence behind me but ignore him. Then I hear him chuckle.

"You don't know where you're going, do you? What's your plan? Knock on all the doors until you find the right place?"

I turn to face him. "Yes, if I have to."

He hands me the thrift shop bags. "Follow me."

The Gunderson place is not in the cluster of cabins I was heading for. The main path forks off in two different directions. Hitchcock leads me to the left and points at a cabin nestled against the hill and surrounded by towering pines. "That's Swede's place."

"Thanks, I can find my way back."

He doesn't get the hint and follows me onto the front porch. I double up my fist to knock, but the door flies open and Kimber emerges, Blossom Bunny tucked under one arm. Her face lights up in a delighted smile. Her brother, Gunner, stands, sober faced, in the open doorway.

"Mel," Kimber cries. "You came. I told Papa you would."

Despite Hitchcock's presence, I kneel and hold out my arms. She runs into my embrace. As I hold her thin body next to mine, my eyes well up with tears. I'm not sure why. I loosen her arms and stand. Jacob Gunderson looms large behind Gunner. He's looking over the top of my head at Hitchcock. I know what I have to do. If I want access to the twins, I have to earn the trust of both men.

Last year, my ditzy female persona worked well on Rick Riley. He now knows it wasn't the real me. I need to figure out how to deal with Jake Gunderson. I'm pretty sure it will involve lying.

And if there's one thing I know about, it's lying.

Chapter Thirteen

Not that I'm proud of it, but I'm very good at lying. It's a learned skill. Because I'm paid to do so, I've become very adept at identifying liars. It's not simply what I see in their souls, although the flash signaling a lie seals the deal. When people lie, certain physical mannerisms occur. A delayed response to a question is a telling sign. Others include lifting hands to cover mouth or closing eyes tightly. Throat-clearing, obvious swallowing, biting or licking lips, adjusting hair or clothing or even nodding yes when saying no.

Therefore, I know not to do these things. Goodie for me. Still, I feel some guilt when I lie. Chalk it up to my upbringing. Sandra. Need I say more?

Now, confronting Jake Gunderson, I have to use everything in my toolbox, so to speak. I take Kimber's hand and step closer to the Jacobson males. I smile up at Jake. "Thanks for working me into your schedule."

He acknowledges my comment with a nod.

Hitchcock says, "A word, Swede, and then I'll leave you to it."

Jake gestures for me to enter the cabin before he steps out and shuts the door. I hear their voices rising and falling, but can't make out the words.

Kimber says, "What's in the bags? Is it for us?"

I nod. "Let's wait for your dad."

While we wait, I look around the cabin. The walls

are lined with framed, beautifully rendered pen—and-ink sketches. A doe with ears cocked forward, with a speckled fawn at her side, peer out of a thicket. A flock of Canadian geese swoop onto a pond. The largest sketch features the twins. The artist not only captured their physical appearance, but their inner spirit as well. Kimber is a step ahead of Gunner and tugging him down the path. Gunner's face is solemn. Kimber's is full of mischief. Each of the sketches is signed with the initials JG.

Kimber takes my hand and tugs me to an open door leading to a bedroom. She points at a set of wooden bunk beds. "It's where we sleep."

Next, she guides me into another room containing a single bed and a large desk cluttered with bottles of ink, pens and stacks of paper in various sizes. "Papa works here," Kimber says.

Acutely uncomfortable at invading Jake's personal space, I step back into the living room/kitchen.

A moment later, Jake returns. I point at the sketches. "Your work?"

He nods.

"They're beautiful. Have you tried to sell them?"

I'm gazing into his eyes. Hope blossoms in his soul, only to be extinguished by a shadow of dark despair. His sadness tears at my heart.

He says, "Maybe, someday."

"Absolutely," I say. "Just let me know. My dad is into art and knows people who own galleries." Not a lie.

Kimber tugs at his sleeve and points at the thrift shop bags. Her eyes are shining with anticipation. "Mel brought stuff for us. Is it okay?"

His gaze flicks back and forth between my face and the bags I'm toting. "Like what?"

Game on. I take a big breath and launch into my story. "I think Kimber told you I'm a twin. I called my mom and mentioned your kids. She dug out some things from our childhood and sent them to me via my stepfather's trucking firm. I got them yesterday. Is it okay if I give them to Kimber and Gunner?"

When he doesn't respond, I continue. "You can look them over. If you don't want me to give them to the kids, no problem. I'll donate them to a thrift shop."

From whence they came.

He glances at Kimber's hopeful face and shrugs. "Let's see what you've got."

I set the bags on a rough-hewn table and extract a pink down jacket, similar to my own. Then I root around until I find the canvas camo jacket in Gunner's size. I set them side-by-side on the table. Kimber quivers with excitement. Gunner's gaze travels from the camo jacket to my face, like he can't believe it.

Jake says, "Judging from the clothes, looks like your twin is a boy."

"More like a tomboy,' I say. "Shall we see if they fit?"

Both kids grab the jackets and slip them on.

Kimber is over the moon. "It looks like your coat. Now, you and me are twins!"

Gunner is more subdued, but he can't hide his smile. He ducks his head. "Thank you, miss."

"You're welcome, and call me Mel, not miss. Okay?"

He looks up at his dad for permission. Jake nods.

After I offload two packs of crayons and a stack of

coloring books for the twins, they settle in at one end of the table and get to work. Kimber opts for Cinderella. Gunner goes for Birds of the World.

Jake clears his throat, obviously uncomfortable. "Guess we better get started."

"Are we going to the range?"

"We'll start here. You're not ready for the range."

I'm not?

He points at the unoccupied end of the table. "Have a seat."

Kimber, still wearing her new jacket, chirps, "She can use my gun, Papa. Okay?"

He nods, unlocks a metal gun safe and removes a black handgun. He sets the gun on the table, the muzzle pointing away from the twins and me.

"This is a Glock19. It's a nine millimeter pistol with a customized grip to fit smaller hands. It's the gun Kimber uses and, since you're, um, well, petite, I think it will work for you too."

"Okay. So, now are we going to the range so I can shoot it?"

Kimber giggles. Gunner rolls his eyes. Apparently I'm funny and don't know it.

I lift my hands "What?"

Kimber says, "First you gotta know the rules. Then, you gotta learn the parts of the gun. Then, you get to shoot. Right, Papa?"

I pinch my lips together to keep the words from leaking out. Words like, "Aw, shit, what have I gotten myself into?"

Jake says, "Kimber's right. First things first. What does she need to learn, kids?"

Kimber and Gunner chorus, "The twelve golden

rules for safe gun handling."

They take turns rattling off the twelve rules starting with Kimber who begins with number one. "Always treat the gun as loaded."

Gunner finishes with last one. "Be aware of your surroundings when handling guns, so you don't trip or lose your balance and accidentally point or fire the gun at anyone or anything."

"Wow," I say. "I'm impressed you guys know all the rules."

Jake says. "Now, it's your turn."

"Me?"

"Yeah, you."

Not to be outdone by a pair of five-year-olds, I tear a page from the Cinderella coloring book, snag a black crayon and ask the kids to recite the rules again. I take notes and pace the floor while I memorize. Jake Gunderson looks annoyed and offers coffee, which I gratefully accept. After thirty minutes, I'm ready. I manage to regurgitate all the rules, even though they are out of order. At least, I thought I covered them all.

Kimber says, "Pretty good but you forgot number eight."

I search my brain for number eight and come up blank.

Gunner looks disgusted. "Geez, it's only the easiest one. What goes in the gun so you can shoot it?"

The light bulb in my brain flickers on. "Number eight. Always use proper ammunition."

Kimber and Gunner clap for me. Jake is unimpressed, but mutters. "I guess it'll do."

"Now, do I get to shoot?"

Gunner says. "Now you gotta learn to field strip

the Glock and clean it."

This time, I can't stifle my groan. I pick up the gun by its grip, taking care to point it at the wall. Rule number two—always keep the gun pointed in a safe direction. I run my finger over the barrel. "It looks pretty clean to me. No dust or anything."

The kids try to hide their amusement.

Jake Gunderson crosses his arms and sighs. "Inside, not outside."

Kimber abandons her coloring book. "Want me to teach you?"

"Sure."

Jake fetches the cleaning kit and hands it to Kimber. She chatters non-stop as her little hands disassemble the gun, pointing out the major parts, which I discover are the slide, the barrel, spring recoil receiver and frame. I try to focus, knowing I'll be tested later.

After she gives it a thorough cleaning, she pops it back together and grins up at me. "Now, you do it."

An hour passes before I'm able to accomplish the task a small child did with such ease. The embarrassment factor looms large. I'm itching to know when I'll get to fire the gun I've become intimately acquainted with, but hesitate. Jake Gunderson is not a man to be hurried. It's possible I may have more to learn before I actually pull the trigger.

Fortunately, I'm not above manipulating a child to gain information. When Jake leaves the table to put the cleaning kit away, I whisper to Kimber, "Ask your dad if I get to go to the range now?"

She gives me a thumbs' up, scampers over to Jake and tugs at his pant leg. In a loud whisper, she says,

"Mel wants to know if she can go to the range now?"

Busted. Serves me right for using a five-year-old.

Jake places a hand on Kimber's head and levels his gaze at me. "Oh, she does, huh?"

My cheeks heat up. "Um, unless you don't think I'm ready. Or, maybe you don't have time." I know I'm babbling but can't seem to stop.

Gunderson glances at his watch. "I've got time if you do."

I rise and slip on my jacket. "I'll check with my ride. See if he can hang out a little longer."

Actually, I need to get out of the cabin and away from Jake Gunderson for a few minutes. The intensity of his steely blue gaze confuses me and makes me acutely uncomfortable. I'm not sure what I'm seeing. Is it lust? As Kimber suggested, is he looking for a wife to care for his motherless children? Suspicion? After all, I am a *female.* Maybe he harbors deep mistrust toward the fair sex. Or, does he have another agenda?

Even though I see no signs of evil, wispy shadows flicker across his predominately dark red soul. That particular shake of red is an indicator of strong masculinity. The shadows tell a different story. I'm quite certain Gunderson has deeply guarded secrets.

As I head for the door, Kimber says, "Can I go with her, Papa?"

I turn and lock gazes with Gunderson. Does the man ever smile? Without looking away from me, he nods.

"Go on ahead. I'll be there in a few minutes."

Kimber skips across the floor, rips a page out of her coloring book and prints her name. She hands it to me. "For you."

"Gunner," I call, "Do you want to go?"

He glances over at his dad and then down at his coloring book. "Nah, I'll stay here and finish my picture."

Kimber, beside herself with excitement, drags me to a path that winds through the cabins and behind the community hall. From this new perspective, I see things I hadn't noticed in my previous visit. The hill rising up behind the encampment bristles with several satellite dishes. A long, windowless building nestles at the bottom of the hill.

I ask Kimber. "Is that where they make the blinds?"

She shakes her head, swivels around and points out a two story industrial-sized building with a metal roof and a loading dock. We watched as a truck backs in and a couple of guys jump out.

I remind myself of one of my mother's favorite sayings, curiosity killed the cat, but ask anyway, "What's the other building for? The one without windows."

Kimber's face grows solemn. "It's where the females work."

I should bite my tongue, but it's not my style. "By females, you mean women and girls. Right?"

Her jaw juts out. "Papa says, s'posed to be called females."

I know when I'm fighting a losing battle. "What do the females do there?"

Kimber looks around to make sure nobody is listening. "Talk on the phone."

So, I gather this is some sort of a call center. Interesting. Are they calling to sell their blinds?

I feel a little guilty about pumping Kimber for information, so decide to change the subject. I hold up the picture she gave me. "It's awesome you know how to write your name. Do you think your daddy would mind if I brought you some ABC books?"

Kimber is not good at hiding her emotions. At first, her eyes light up with excitement. Then, the gleam in her eyes dims and the corners of her mouth turn down.

She says, "I would like that *so* much, Mel. But, Papa doesn't like people to give us stuff. And Gunner, well, I'm trying to teach him the letters, but he'd rather play outside."

"Who taught you how to write your name?"

She points at a wooden structure a bit larger than the cabins. "School. Miss Anna taught me."

"But not Gunner?"

"Gunner doesn't like school. He'd rather shoot guns and go with Papa when he delivers blinds."

This new bit of information throws me off kilter. With Hitchcock's attitude toward *females*, I'd assumed education would be a low priority for them. Obviously, I'm wrong since Kimber is sucking up knowledge like a little sponge while Gunner prefers doing man stuff.

Kimber trots ahead of me. "The range is this way."

Actually, I could have found it myself by following the sound of gunfire, but Kimber is taking her job as guide seriously, frequently glancing over her shoulder to make sure I'm following. The path turns sharply to the left and Riley appears. Kimber slams to a stop, ducks behind me and pops her thumb in her mouth.

I wrap my arm around her shoulders and pull her close. "It's okay, sweetie. He's a friend of mine."

Riley drops down to her eye level and smiles. "Hi,

I'm guessing you're Kimber. I'm Riley."

She clings to my leg. I wonder why she's so afraid of strangers.

Riley says, "Gotta go, Mel. Dad called. He needs me to help with something. Sorry."

Kimber looks up at me, tears welling in her eyes. "Don't go, Mel."

I pull her into my embrace. "I'll be back."

"Promise?"

"Yes, I promise."

Chapter Fourteen

Riley is quieter than usual on the drive home. I tell him about my first gun-handling lesson. "And I didn't even get to shoot the damn thing."

He doesn't respond.

"How did it go at the range?"

He glances over at me. "The shooting part was fine."

"And, the non-shooting part?"

"Hitchcock is seriously weird. He showed up at the range and stood behind me the entire time. When we were here before, he asked if I would be coming back and if Dad had any thoughts about joining New Dawn."

"What did you tell him?"

"I wanted to say hell no, but I know you need me to drive you. I said Dad's thinking about it."

I place a hand on his arm. "Look, Riley, you're under no obligation to bring me here. I can always borrow Nick's pickup."

He grins at me. "And miss out on the bitching and moaning?" He loses the grin quickly. "Here's the weird part. He asked about Yasmin. He knew she was my girlfriend and that her body was found close to our ranch. He asked if anyone had been arrested for her murder."

Okay, now I know what's troubling Riley. Yasmin, the Muslim girl he loved was killed and dumped in Red

Ridge. A small group of people, myself included, knows the real story and have arrived at a place of peace and forgiveness. There's no way Hitchcock could discover the truth. The fact he mentioned it to Riley makes me furious. Riley and his family are trying their best to move past the tragic events of last fall. They don't need Hitchcock stirring the pot. "I hope you told him it was none of his damn business."

Riley turns away from me. He swipes at his eyes and takes a shaky breath. "I didn't know what to say. He kept looking at me with those creepy eyes, like he was trying to read my mind. And, how did he know she was my girlfriend? My mom and dad didn't even know until after she was killed."

Truthfully, this is bothering me too. "He was probably fishing for information. I think Hitchcock is a guy who's skilled at ferreting out secrets and files them away to use as leverage. Don't tell the nosey old bastard anything."

Riley pulls to the side of the road and stops. I offer him a tissue. He blows his nose and tries to give it back to me.

I tuck my hands under my butt. "It's all yours, buddy."

The light comes back into his eyes.

With a ghost of a smile, he says, "I didn't tell him anything. I just shrugged and he walked away."

"Good."

He pulls into my driveway. "How's the kid doing, the girl with the black and pink hair?"

I roll my eyes. "She's a piece of work." I go on to explain the whole chasing down Benny and Ziggy scenario.

"Bring her out to the ranch. We'll put her to work shoveling shit out of the stables. Maybe throw in some riding lessons. Worked for you. Right?"

I burst into laughter. My lack of equestrian skills is a huge source of amusement for the entire Rathjen family. And, Ziggy is basically a city kid. Then, I remember she was checking Riley out. Benny? Riley? No contest. "Great idea. I'll talk to her dad." I give him a sisterly smooch on the cheek and tell him I'll stay in touch.

I'm barely through the door when my phone rings. Kendra.

She doesn't bother with a greeting. "Hey, what's happening at the cuckoo compound?"

I fill her in on my first gun handling lessons. When I start to recite the twelve golden rules of safe gun handling, she rudely shuts me down. "Yeah, yeah, I don't need to know all that. Get to the juicy stuff. Any cute guys there who want to jump your bones?'

"Kendra," I say sternly. "I'm not there looking for cute guys. I told you about the twins. Their dad, Jake, is my instructor."

"Single?"

"Very. But not my type."

"Hmmm," she says. "Mick still gone?"

I know what she's implying. "Yes, but I'm not looking for a new boyfriend."

We chat for a while. I tell her about the call center and the building where they manufacture blinds. Probably a mistake.

"Hey," she says. "How about I order blinds so I can check out Jake Gunderson. You obviously need a second opinion."

"Do you actually need blinds? Trust me, these are cheap-looking vinyl blinds, not fashion blinds. I don't think you'll want them in your house."

"Basement," she says.

"What about Craig? He doesn't mind you spending the money?"

She chuckles. "Craig likes to keep me happy. Happy wife. Happy life."

Once Kendra is on a mission, there's no deterring her. I promise to put her in touch with Gunderson, as long as I can be present when he comes to her house to measure the windows.

"Yay," she says and clicks off.

My plan to go for a run is put on hold when I receive an urgent text from Nick.

—*Cowboy Jim is here. Wants to give you a dance lesson.*—

Aw, shit. No rest for the wicked.

I jump in Buttercup and head for Nick's. When I arrive, I find Cowboy Jim bellied up to the bar, hunched over a Budweiser pounder.

His eyes are bloodshot and sad, but he brightens when he sees me. "Hey, girly! Thanks for showing up on your day off. Ready to learn the two step?"

"I was born ready," I say with a grin.

It's between lunch and dinner so the place is pretty empty. The crowd mainly consists of early drinkers and late lunchers. Nick takes care of the music and plays Cowboy Jim's favorite song.

He slides off the bar stool and holds out his arms. "Alrighty then, let's do it."

After my embarrassing fiasco learning basic gun handling rules, I'm worried I'll screw this up too.

No problem.

"First, we assume the position," Jim says, placing my left hand on his shoulder, his right hand on my upper back and clasping my right hand in his left. "Now," he says. "Relax and feel the music. The steps are easy. Slow. Slow. Quick. Quick. All you have to do is follow my lead. I'll do the hard part."

Following Jim's firm but steady lead, I shut down the part of my brain that tells me I'm doing it wrong. I feel the music, move to the rhythm. Soon, the music carries me away and I'm flying across the floor, first in closed position and then, side-by-side. By the end of the lesson, I'm twirling under Jim's outstretched arm, giddy with dizziness and unfettered joy. We even receive a smattering of applause from Nick and two hardcore whiskey drinkers peering in from the Corral. High praise, indeed.

After teaching me a simple line dance, Cowboy Jim hydrates himself with a brewski. "Next week? Same time?"

"I'll be here."

Out of habit, I exit through the kitchen where I spot Ziggy. She's sitting at a table reading a book.

She glances up at me. "Lame."

"What's lame?"

"That kind of dancing. It's dorky."

"Actually, it's fun. You should try it sometimes."

"As if," she says, returning to her book.

I think about my last conversation with Riley. "Hey, Ziggy, remember Riley? The cute kid from the Rockin' R ranch?"

She closes her book and gives me her full attention. "What about him?"

"If you're interested in taking on another job, he's got one for you at the ranch."

"Doing what?"

I take care not to mention the term *shoveling shit.* "Oh, just this and that. He said they could use another ranch hand. Have you ever been around horses?"

Her eyes widen. "They have horses?"

"Well, duh, it is a ranch. So, what do you think?"

She rolls her eyes. "Well, duh, of course I'll do it. Like, Riley is hot."

I quickly add, "You still have to do your job here. Got it?"

She heaves a put upon sigh. "Yes, Mel. I've got it."

"Talk later," I say and sidle out the door, wondering when I made the transition from sullen teenager to semi-adult. It feels like ages.

Chapter Fifteen

It's three days later and I'm at Kendra's house. It's nine o'clock. Early times for me since I worked until Nick's closed last night at two a.m. I guzzle coffee while Kendra sorts out various and sundry kids. Destiny and Andrew are in side-by-side highchairs with Toasty O's and sippy cups of milk on their trays. Occasionally, Andrew snags one of Destiny's Toasty O's. She slaps his hand and screeches, "No! Mine!" Three-year-old Aaron makes car noises as he pushes a toy dump truck across the floor. Kendra hands him a piece of peanut butter toast, which he stows in the truck bed.

She pours herself a cup of coffee and joins me at the table. "Aida will be here soon to watch the kids so I can focus on the blinds guy. You know, in case this turns into a big deal and you need help."

"Define help."

She thinks for a minute. "Like when we pretended to work for the catering company and you snagged the zip drive with all the incriminating stuff on it. Like that."

"I don't think disguises will work at New Dawn. I just want to stay in contact with the kids."

Her eyes brighten. "You need to seduce Jake Gunderson. Then, he'll trust you and let you be around his kids."

I roll my eyes. "I bet he likes mommies, so maybe

you should seduce him."

She, stands, places a hand on her hip and cops an attitude. "Hey, girl, I could do it if I wanted to."

"No doubt in my mind."

Aida arrives with baby Larissa. After we hug, I look her over. Her face is pale and she has dark circles under her eyes. So much for the glow of pregnancy.

"Not feeling so good?"

Her mouth draws down into a frown. She thrusts Larissa into my arms and points toward her tummy. "Never sick with girl baby. Damn Paco! He put boy baby in belly."

"You sure about that?"

She glares at me. "Of course I'm sure."

I stare at her, speechless. Sweet Aida, always so happy and good-natured, has turned into a snarling beast, like her head spun around and an entirely different person now occupies her body.

I recover quickly. "Paco seems happy."

"Yes, big, um, whippersnapper is happy. He's not having sickness in the morning. Just me." She sighs. "My own fault. I tell Paco I want another baby."

Kendra fakes a coughing fit to disguise her laughter evoked by the term whippersnapper. I try to keep from snickering, because I can tell Aida is proud to demonstrate her knowledge of American slang. It's not my job to tell her she sounds like a crotchety old man describing a smart-ass kid.

Kendra takes Larissa from me, puts her arm around Aida and leads her to the table, stepping over Aaron and the peanut butter toast deposited from his toy dump truck. "Sit. I'll fix you a cup of peppermint tea. You'll feel better soon."

Therefore, Kendra is helping her mother's helper when the box truck from New Dawn rumbles into the driveway. Jake Gunderson steps out, carrying a clipboard. Just Jake. No twins. I wonder who's looking after them.

Over the din of crying babies, Kendra hollers, "Take him to the basement. I'll join you in a sec."

"Which windows?"

She throws up her hands. "I don't care. Pick whatever you want."

When I open the front door, Jake's eyes widen in surprise. He glances at the clipboard and then at me. "You live here?"

I launch into a convoluted explanation, closing with, "And since my friend Kendra mentioned she wanted new blinds for the basement, I told her about New Dawn."

He stares at me while he thinks it over. "Okay, let's take a look."

I lead him down the stairs, unfamiliar territory since I've never been in Kendra's basement. It runs the full length of the house with a couple of bedrooms, a full bath and a rec room. Along with a sliding glass door to the back yard, there are six windows, none of which are covered. I'm totally out of my depth, not knowing the extent of Kendra's budget.

Jake follows me from room to room. "Does she want all the windows done?"

Damn Kendra! Like I'm supposed to know? I say, "Maybe you should start with the windows in the rec room. Once she gets things under control," I point upward, "I'm sure she'll join us."

Jake whips out a metal tape measure and strides

toward the glass slider. I offer to help but he turns me down. He presses a button and the tape measure shoots out to the top of the slider. He measures the height and width, making notations on the clipboard.

The noise from above subsides. Kendra clomps down the stairs. With a dimpled smile, she walks to Jake and offers her hand to shake. "So happy to meet you, Jake. Mel told me all about you, and your darling twins. I'm Kendra."

When Kendra is at her charming best, she's hard to resist.

Jake sets his clipboard down, wipes his right hand on his jeans and gives hers a squeeze. He ducks his head and says, "Pleased to meet you, ma'am."

With a trill of laugher, she says, "Ma'am? Isn't that term for older ladies? I'm not quite over the hill yet, so please call me Kendra."

Jake's cheeks flush, but a rare smile appears. "Sure thing, Kendra."

Whoa. I should have gone to charm school.

As the talk turns to windows, my cell phone rings. I glance at the display. It's Mick, my absentee boyfriend. Note to self: Don't act like a needy girlfriend. Dial down the resentment.

I wander away from the others to answer. "Hey there."

"Baby," he says. "Coming your way."

"What happened to *maylsh*?"

"So you prefer Russian terms of endearment? We can always go back to *kotik*. Or, maybe *zaichik.*"

"That's my only choice? Pussycat or bunny?"

A rumble of laughter. "How about we discuss it in person. Like maybe, tonight?"

While we banter back and forth, I'm catching bits and pieces of conversation between Kendra and Jake. Kendra is following him from window to window, peppering him with questions. She's moved into the personal realm, quizzing him about Kimber and Gunner. Much to my surprise, he responds. I only catch a few of the words, but they don't include *none of your damn business*. My admiration for Kendra's interrogation skills is growing by the minute.

Before we sign off, Mick again mentions he has something important to tell me. I get no hints from his tone, so it could be anything from revealing the whereabouts of his mother or a new recipe for *Syrniki,* a Russian delicacy he knows I love. If I've learned one thing about men in the past year, it's this: they're damn poor communicators.

I join Kendra and Jake who's just finished measuring.

He tells Kendra, "I'll work out the details and call you with an estimate."

"Super," she replies, bouncing up and down with excitement. In my opinion, her enthusiasm is a bit over the top considering the circumstances. But, what do I know?

Jake looks at me. His expression grows serious, as it always does when we interact. "Another shooting lesson soon?"

"I'll check my work schedule and give you a call."

He nods and heads for the door.

After he leaves, Kendra looks smug. "He's hot for you."

"Give me a break. He can hardly look at me."

"He's shy."

I do an eye roll worthy of Ziggy and don't reply.

Finally, Kendra can stand it no longer. "Guess what I found out?"

"Enlighten me."

"Jake is not the father of the twins."

Chapter Sixteen

"Of course he is," I counter. "They call him Papa and he takes care of them. Would he do that if he isn't their father?"

"You have daddy issues," Kendra says. "Because your dad bailed out on your mom before you and Hope were born, you're not a good judge of fatherhood material."

I feel the need to defend Steve. "There were extenuating circumstances. He's trying to make it up to me."

Kendra sighs. "Mel, this isn't about you. It's about the twins. Are you willing to listen?"

Kendra, being totally serious, rarely happens.

"Sorry," I mumble.

She pulls me over to a couch littered with toy trucks, sweeps them onto the floor and pulls me down beside her. "When the twins were two, they turned up at the compound with their mother who, according to Jake, was in bad shape. Strung out on drugs is what he called it. He said the twins were filthy and underfed. Apparently the guy in charge of New Dawn..." She pauses, trying to come up with the name.

"Hitchcock."

"Yeah, Hitchcock. He took the woman and her kids to Jake's cabin and said it was his duty to take care of them."

"His duty? Those were Jake's exact words?"

"Yes, Mel. I don't have short term memory loss yet."

"Sorry," I murmur again. "It just sounds strange, like something out of the Bible."

Kendra shrugs. "You said the place was like stepping into a time warp."

"But why Jake? Surely there were other families willing to take them in."

"Maybe Hitchcock was doing a little matchmaking since Jake's a single guy."

"Maybe," I say, trying to make sense of the story. "If so, it didn't work. Kimber told me their mother is dead."

"I asked Jake about the kids' mother. I could tell he didn't want to talk about her. He mumbled something about her running off and leaving him with the twins."

"But, he didn't say she was dead?"

Kendra shakes her head. "Nope. Then, he changed the subject."

I grin at her. "Even though you gave it all you got, charm-wise, he clammed up?"

"No worries, girlfriend. I figured full wattage charm might scare him, so I held back a little. I'll get the rest of the story the next time I see him. Actually," she says, looking me over. "Since he's lusting after your cute little bod, you could try charming him yourself."

"In case you've forgotten, I have a boyfriend who, by the way, is on his way to 3 Peaks as we speak."

"Oh?" she says, one eyebrow shooting upward. She lowers her voice to a conspiratorial whisper. "Have you two done it in your new place yet?"

I mock-punch her. "None of your beeswax."

She turns serious. "You know Billy wants you back."

"I'm aware."

She takes my hand and squeezes it. "He's changed, Mel. The PTSD counseling really helped him work through his issues. He knows he screwed up. He loves you and I know you love him. You two are meant to be together. Just think about it. Okay?"

Damn Kendra! Like my mother, she always knows how to push my buttons. When I speak, my voice is hoarse with emotion. "Did Billy ask you to tell me that?"

"No!" Her hands fly up in denial. "But I'm not blind, Mel. I can see what's going on in his life and in yours. Mick is a great guy, but he's rarely around. Am I right?"

As they say, whoever *they* are, the truth hurts. And, I've had all the truth I can deal with right now. I rise from the couch. "Gotta go. Thanks for your help with Jake. I'll be in touch."

****

Mick strolls into the pub shortly after the dinner crowd dissipates and wraps me up in a bear hug witnessed by Ziggy, whose eyes widen in surprise and then sparkle with evil intent.

"New guy, huh?" she says, her glance sweeping over Mick who has returned to bad boy mode. Scruffy five o'clock shadow, hair dyed black again, tats prominently displayed.

I extricate myself from his embrace and make the introductions. I think the image Mick is projecting is right up Ziggy's alley. As it turns out, I'm not mistaken.

"Wow," she says, fluttering her lashes at Mick. "Guess you don't know about Mel's other guy. He's a cop and they were totally making out in the parking lot."

Mick's laser blue-eyed gaze swings over to me. "Guess you missed me, huh *maylsh.*"

I take his hand. "Pay no attention to the child. She likes to exaggerate."

Ziggy draws herself up and huffs, "Did you just call me a child?"

Obviously, she doesn't know she's messing with a pro. We've arrived at a teachable moment. "When you behave like a child, that's what you'll be called. Oh, by the way, have you filled your dad in on our little adventure the other day? The one involving Benny, the drug dealer?"

Her face loses color and she glances over at her dad who's in his usual spot, behind the bar. Safe in her belief he's not overheard our conversation, she puts her hands on her hips and sputters, "You don't play fair, Mel."

I smooch Mick on the cheek. "Best you should keep that in mind and we'll get along fine." I point at a table littered with dirty dishes. "Ziggy, don't you have tables to bus? Busy hands are happy hands."

"God, you are such a pain in the ass," she mutters and stomps away.

Mick gazes down at me. "What was that about?"

"Nothing important."

"Was she talking about Billy?"

What the hell? I have nothing to hide and decide to go with the truth. Who knows what Mick does when he's undercover? He could have a dozen girlfriends for all I know. I tell him about Billy's help moving the cat and how he wanted a kiss as payment. He listens with a furrowed brow. I know he's not happy, but all he does when I finish is give me a curt nod along with a noncommittal, "I get the picture."

I zip my lip and wait.

Finally, he cups my face in his palms and brushes his lips across mine. His voice is husky when he says, "Nick says you can leave early."

This is what bugs me about Mick. He tries to micro-manage my life. This is *my* workplace, not his to manipulate so I can devote my time and energy to meeting his needs when he decides to pop into town. I bite back an angry reply and push away, heading for the bar. "Nick," I say. "If you need me here, I can stay. No problem."

He waves a hand. "Nah, take off. We're not super busy. Consider it your reward for spending time with my bonehead daughter."

I pat his cheek. "She's smarter than you think. Don't give up on her."

"If you say so," he mutters.

I deliver a round of drinks to the guys in the Corral before I take off my apron and join Mick at the bar.

Ziggy, holding a tub of dirty dishes, sidles up next to me. "Hey, what about the job at the ranch where the cute guy lives? This job really sucks."

I'm still a little ticked about her snarky comment to Mick. Perhaps spending time cleaning out box stalls might result in an attitude adjustment. "It's not one or the other, Ziggy. You still have to do your job here. Understand?"

She pouts, looks over at her father's stern

expression and then nods.

I decide to let her stew for a while. "I'll call Riley soon and let you know."

"Can't you call him now?"

I glance at the clock. "He's probably out with his new girlfriend."

This has the desired effect. She pinches her lips together and stomps into the kitchen. Her dad offers me a high five.

Mick slips his arm around me and nuzzles my ear. "Power tripping?"

"Whatever it takes. Gotta stay ahead of the kid."

Mick follows me home. I wonder if this is another one-night stand. If he has something important to say, I want to hear it while we're still wearing clothes.

Thunder Paws is on my tiny front porch, looking irritated as usual. When he notices I'm not carrying a box of leftovers, he hunches his back and hisses. I avoid eye contact and step carefully around him to unlock the door.

Mick leans over and scratches him behind the ears, murmuring to him in Russian. Thunder Paws flops onto his back, purring in ecstasy. The big tomcat is definitely into male bonding. Once inside, he checks out the feeding bowl, discovers it contains only kibble and demands to be let out.

I close the door behind him. Mick grips my shoulders, spins me around and presses me against the door with his muscular body. I catch my breath and, unbidden, my arms curl around his neck. My good intentions slip away.

"My *maylsh*," he murmurs, feathering kisses along my neck while his hands slide under my shirt. I gasp with pleasure at his touch, unable to find my voice. Still pinning me to the door, he deftly unzips my jeans and then slides down my body, his lips trailing a path of heat down my belly. When the warmth of his mouth envelops me, when his tongue flicks over my vulnerable center, I'm lost in sensation, unable to speak or even think. Soon I'm deposited on the bed, his body covering mine.

So much for conversation while clothed.

Chapter Seventeen

Later, we're at the table. Mick sips Grey Goose.

My eyelids droop, but I fight off fatigue as well as annoyance. I need answers. Mr. Sensitivity doesn't get the picture, so I resort to a bit of nagging. "Twice, you've mentioned you have something to tell me, yet here you sit with a look of satisfaction on your scruffy face, saying nothing."

It came out a little harsher than I intended.

He reaches across the table, takes my hand and kisses it. "Forgive me, *maylsh,* when I see you, my brain ceases to work as other body parts take over."

I can't help it. I snicker. "Tell me something I don't know." I look into his eyes, mesmerized by his beautiful sky blue soul. I've always loved Mick's soul. Sure, he has secrets he can't share, but nevertheless, his soul glistens with integrity. When I'm with him, I feel safe and, for me, that's a big deal. The words *with Mick* are important. When he's gone for days, sometimes weeks at a time, doubts slither into my mind like snakes creeping into a garden. Yes, it sounds needy and I don't like it. In all fairness, one might say I'm a bit conflicted about my feelings for him.

He squeezes my hand. "I know you are aware I work hard in my job. I've taken every shit assignment that comes along without complaining, hoping my superiors will take notice."

I nod, waiting for the other shoe to drop.

A dark cloud of sadness flickers across his soul. "I'm not sure whether to be happy or sad about what I'm about to tell you."

My forehead wrinkles as I try to grasp the meaning of his words. Seconds later, a lightning bolt of understanding flashes through my sleepy brain. "You got a promotion!"

When he fails to answer, I prompt, "Am I right?"

He nods. "Here's the bad part. It's in Boston."

In my mind, a colorful map of the United States appears. 3 Peaks nestles in the mountains of Central Oregon, less than one hundred fifty miles from the Pacific Ocean. Three thousand miles to the east, Boston clings to the opposite shore. The Atlantic Ocean. My gaze drops to the table. "Oh."

He tucks a finger under my chin and tilts my head back. "Look at me, Mel. Here's what I've been waiting to ask you. I want you to come with me. I'll always take care of you."

Overwhelmed, I can't seem to form words.

"You don't have to decide right now. Think it over."

Suddenly, it's important to know how long I have to think it over. "When do you leave?"

"I have to report April first."

"Twelve days from now."

He nods. "I could get you work there, *maylsh*. Many law enforcement agencies would love to access the unique skills you have."

I think about my life here. Steve, my newly discovered biological father. Our business together. Uncle Paco. Aida. Their little bun in the oven. Kendra, her family. Billy the Kid. Nick and the pub customers who've become my extended family. My mother and stepfather, Abel, in San Bernardino. Though I'm trying hard not to think about them, Kimber and Gunner nag at my consciousness. I can almost feel Kimber clinging to my hand and hear her cry of delight. "You came! I told Papa you would."

What will happen to them if I move to Boston and never show up in their lives again?

I gaze into Mick's hopeful blue eyes, willing myself not to say something that will cause him pain. "I'll let you know soon."

Mick has never been able to hide his feelings. But he also is attuned to mine. Disappointment flashes across his soul.

He releases my hand. "I think I know the answer, but I will hope for the best."

Even though I'm tired, sleep eludes me. Cradled in Mick's arms, I feel his chest rise and fall in steady rhythm as I gaze into the darkness, unable to turn off the images in my mind. Images of those I would leave behind if I moved across the continent with Mick.

When he leaves the next morning, I promise I will call him soon with my answer. My throat is choked with tears as his car pulls away from the curb. It feels like farewell.

This dark state of mind leads me to a decision I know I will regret. I call my mother, Sandra. When she answers, I recite a long, rambling, disjointed account of my current situation with Mick.

She listens carefully before declaring, "Honor Melanie Sullivan, are you crying? Do you want me to come to 3 Peaks? I'll hop on one of Abel's trucks and be there by nightfall."

"No, no, that's not necessary," I protest. "I just need someone to talk to, preferably someone of the female persuasion. Kendra has her own agenda, so you're next on my list. All you have to do is listen. Actually, I feel better already. So, I'll hang up now. Okay?"

No way am I getting off that easy.

Sandra takes a deep breath and blows it out. "Hold it. I have questions for you. Do you have a ring on your finger?"

I admit I do not.

"Did Mick ask you to marry him?"

"Uh-uh."

"No brainer. Stay in 3 Peaks."

Her advice is hardly surprising since my biological father impregnated her with twins and then returned to his native Spain with nary a goodbye kiss. Later, we would learn of his difficult issues, namely an arranged marriage and finally, the fact that he's gay and waited until his parents' deaths to come out of the closet. I've been able to forgive him, but Sandra is still bitter, even though she's married to Abel, a wonderful man who is my second father.

Still, she's my mother and cares about my welfare. Sometimes a girl just needs her mother. However, my independent streak asserts itself. "Thanks, I'll think about it.."

"I'll be waiting for a text from you."

What have I done? Her last statement translates to, "I will be nagging you with non-stop texts until you make a decision."

"Love you, bye!" I click off.

****

Two days later, I arrange a shooting lesson with Jake Gunderson to get my mind off the Mick situation. I also have another agenda. Ziggy will go to the Rockin' R Ranch with me and begin her second job, cleaning box stalls. I've made the arrangements with Riley and Ziggy is beyond excited. Riley's dad, Rick, will drive me to New Dawn while Riley supervises Ziggy. Win-win situation. Or, so I thought.

First, I undergo an interrogation by Ziggy as we drive to the ranch.

"Did Riley break up with his girlfriend?"

Since the girlfriend is totally fictional, I say, "Not sure. Maybe you can figure out a sneaky way to find out."

"Will he be in the barn with me or what?"

"I'm sure he'll give you instructions. You might have to do stuff on your own, though, to see if you can handle it."

She stays quiet for a while. When she speaks, she sounds like an insecure little girl. "Do you think Riley could ever like a girl like me?"

I reach over and grab her hand. "What do you mean, a girl like you? Listen to me, Ziggy. I was exactly like you and I mean *exactly*. My mother would say, 'Mel, you're a huge pain in the ass, but I'll never give up on you, so give it a rest.' You, Zelda Ignatius, aka Ziggy, have people in your life like my mother. Give them a chance. And, I'll tell you a little secret about Riley."

I pause until she leans close and whispers, "What?"

"He's not attracted to your typical airhead teenage girl. He's wise beyond his years. He even hit on me last year, until I said I was too old for him."

Her lips form a perfectly round O. Am I finally reaching this girl?

As we pull into the Rockin' R driveway, Riley emerges from the barn and waves Buttercup into a parking spot. Ziggy checks herself out in the rearview mirror and climbs out of the car, casting sidelong glances at Riley.

"Slight change of plans," Riley says. "I'll be driving you to New Dawn. Dad forgot he has a dentist appointment today." He beckons to Ziggy. "I'll show you what needs to be done." He pivots and walks to the barn.

Ziggy scorches me with a hateful look and hisses, "Nice one, Mel."

I lift my hands. "Hey, I had no idea, so don't blame me. Just do your job. He'll be back."

She flips me off and follows Riley into the barn. I remain outside, stunned by how rapidly our tenuous relationship had gone south. My mother's second favorite saying passes through my mind. Pride goeth before a fall.

Her first favorite saying? When something really matters, you should never give up.

I'm not done with you, Ziggy.

Chapter Eighteen

Hitchcock stands in front of the community building after we're waved through the gate.

Riley mutters, "Oh, great. My guard dog is waiting for me."

It's not Riley he's waiting for. After Hitchcock sends Riley to the shooting range, he turns to me. "I'll walk you to Swede's."

"He told me to meet him at the range."

"Change of plans."

He clamps a hand on my shoulder and points me toward the path leading to Jake's cabin. His hand feels heavy and intrusive, as if I'm now under his control. I don't like it and pull away, putting some space between us. He continues walking beside me.

"I know the way. You probably have something important to do," I tell him.

After a brief, humorless smile, his gaze travels over my body. "Honor Melanie Sullivan," he says. "That's your name. Right?"

I stop and turn to face him. Is this a new game we're playing? I gaze into his squinty bloodshot eyes and see malevolence in his soul. A chill runs through my body. "Yes, why do you ask?"

"I know a lot about you, Ms. Sullivan."

So he knows my full name. Big deal. A lot of people do. I bite back the Goodie for you, I'm longing to say, knowing it will get me nowhere. Instead, I say, "What is your interest in me, Mr. Hitchcock?"

I hold my ground as he takes a step closer and says, "I thoroughly vet everyone who comes through our gate. You have a very colorful past, hence my interest in you."

I can tell he's dying to elaborate and try to think of a way to deflect him. "I'm just here to learn how to shoot." I dig around in my tote bag, pull out my cell phone and check the time. "Speaking of which, I'm late. So, if you'll excuse me…"

He takes hold of my arm. "Let me finish."

Once again, I pull away.

He lifts both hands and backs away. "Hear me out. There's a reason we're called New Dawn. We welcome those who have made mistakes in their lives and want to start over. This is a place of refuge. All we ask is that they contribute in some manner."

"How does that concern me?"

"Because," he says with a forced smile, "I thought you might like to join us. You connected with Jake's twins. If you lived here, you could be with them every day, see to their needs."

Before I can open my mouth to protest, he says, "I know your secrets. You murdered a man in San Bernardino. You tried to kidnap a baby at the hospital. But your past is of little consequence here. We protect our own."

I'm livid with rage, but know I need to tread carefully, if I ever want to see Kimber and Gunner again. Be cool, Mel, I tell myself. Though I'd rather not, I stare directly into his eyes. "Thank you for your offer, Mr. Hitchcock, but I have to decline. As for my supposed crimes, if you dig a little deeper, you'll find the so-called murder was ruled an accidental death and I fulfilled my obligation to the court. As for the baby snatching, I never left the hospital. Maybe you need to be more thorough in your research."

Hitchcock is unfazed. He shrugs as if my comments mean nothing. "I'm aware of your involvement with the Rathjen family. I understand you knew the Muslim girl Riley was dating. As I remember, her murder remains unsolved."

He pauses and waits for me to respond. When I don't, he says, "I also know about your unique ability to read souls."

I shrug. "Not exactly a secret since it was mentioned in the newspaper last summer."

"What do you see in my soul, Ms. Sullivan?"

There are so many ways I can answer his question. I decide to take the high road while dishing out a dollop of truth. "As I'm sure you already know, my dad is also a soul reader. We have a business together called CyberSecure Plus and we usually charge for our services. But, since you asked and I'm on your home turf, this one's for free. When I look into your soul, I see a man who is highly intelligent, but has anger issues."

His eyes widen in surprise before his face settles into its usual stoic expression. "Sometimes anger is a good thing. It enables you to accomplish goals that may otherwise be out of reach."

"If you say so."

"You don't agree?"

"Do you care what I think?"

His lips part in a facsimile of a smile, revealing

yellowish teeth. "Yes, because if I have my way, you'll be part of New Dawn one day."

I shake my head. "Thanks for the offer but I'm perfectly happy living the way I do."

"We'll see," he says. "Since you know the way, I'll leave you now. Enjoy your shooting lesson. Enjoy your time with the twins. Who knows when you'll see them again?"

He pivots and trudges back down the path without a backward glance, leaving me frustrated and a little pissed off. If there's one thing I hate it's a bully and Hitchcock is the living embodiment of the word. He uses his power to threaten or intimidate in order to get what he wants. And what he *wants* is for me to be part of New Dawn. I'm pretty sure his interest is not based on my charming personality.

How clever the man is. He totally zeroed in on my attachment to Kimber and Gunner and uses it as leverage. It's also obvious he'd like to use my soul reading abilities to further his cause. Whatever his cause may be. Who better to learn from than Jake, the pretend father of the twins?

I try to calm down before I reach the Gunderson cabin, taking deep breaths and talking to myself. When I tap at the door, it flies open revealing Gunner. He peers up at me with a shy smile and steps back so I can enter. With a squeal of delight, Kimber scampers across the room and wraps her arms around my legs. I reach out and pull Gunner into a hug as well. He stiffens at first and then snuggles close.

Pressed against my body, Kimber's voice is muffled. "Told you, Gunner. Told you she'd come."

Gunner pulls away and scowls. "Females always

think they're right."

Kimber puts her hands on her hips and glares at her brother. "That's 'cause I *am* right."

Even though I'm longing to, I know better than to address the *female* issue. Instead, I change the subject. "Where's your dad? Already at the range?"

A chair scrapes across the floor and Jake appears in the doorway of his bedroom/office. He has dark circles beneath his eyes. His fingers are ink-stained.

"Hi Mel. I have a little work to finish before we shoot. How about you and the kids go pick up the mail. By the time you get back, I should be done."

"No problem. Doing another sketch?"

His gaze darts away from mine and back. "Special order."

I'm not close enough to look into his soul, but his body language tells me he's hiding something. He turns and shuffles back into his workspace.

I hold out my hands. "Let's go, kids."

Clutching Blossom Bunny, Kimber immediately takes hold of my right hand.

Gunner, still pouting from his sister's put-down, hesitates. He says, "She takes that stupid bunny everywhere. Papa and I call it My Bunny because if anyone touches it she yells, *My bunny!*"

"Not stupid," Kimber says.

I ignore Gunner's attitude and grab his hand. "Will you show me where the post office is?"

"I can!" Kimber crows.

Gunner tugs me through the door. "She asked *me* to show her."

Crisis averted, we head for the post office.

Chapter Nineteen

Knowing she'd love to dart ahead of her brother, I keep a tight grip on Kimber's hand. Gunner leads us down the path. When he glances over his shoulder, his bright blue eyes sparkle with glee, thinking he has bested his sister.

Gunner points at a low-slung cabin with a wide porch. "Mail lady lives here."

I want to say, Really? She lives at the post office? I don't utter the words, because nothing is normal about this place. Perhaps she has a cot nestled between stacks of incoming mail.

Gunner takes my free hand and hauls me through the door. A horizontal interior wall divides the cabin in half. Centered in the middle of the wall is an open window. A woman with iron gray hair stands behind the window. Her eyes are black and only half visible due to wrinkled drooping lids. She doesn't look happy to see us.

Gunner points at the woman and announces, "Agnes. She's the mail lady."

I greet her warmly. She gives me a brief nod and turns away. She rummages through a pile of plastic grocery bags, looking for Gunderson mail. This is not a high tech operation. Silently, she hands two bags bulging with mail to Kimber and Gunner.

"Wow, you guys get a lot of mail," I say.

Kimber says, "That's because it's mail day."

"So, it doesn't come every day?"

"Nope," Gunner says. "Just on mail day."

The twins each take a bag and head for the door. I thank the taciturn Agnes. She gives me a sniff of disapproval and turns away.

After exiting the cabin, I say, "I don't think Agnes likes me."

Kimber chirps, "She doesn't like anybody. Papa says some people are born unhappy."

She grins up at me, swinging the bag of mail back and forth as we head back to their cabin. She still clings to my hand like it's a lifeline and she's afraid I'll disappear if she lets go. Halfway down the path, she swings the bag a little too vigorously and the contents spill out over the pine needle-covered ground.

"Oops," she says.

Gunner turns and glares at his sister. "You're supposed to be careful with the mail."

Kimber retorts, "Shit happens."

Gunner sets his bag of mail down and gives her a disapproving scowl. "That's a man word. It's not for females."

Kimber looks at me for help.

I channel my inner adult. "Actually, you're both too young to be swearing."

A sudden gust of wind swirls through the trees, scattering the envelopes. This puts an end to the bickering as we scamper after the errant mail, most of which is addressed to Kimber and Gunner. Bank statements. Mail from the U.S. Treasury Department. Others with only a post office box as a return address. Even stranger, most of the envelopes have been slit open, leaving me with a multitude of questions. Why would five-year-old twins receive this volume and type of mail? Why have they been opened? Is mail fraud on of New Dawn's specialties? A chill sweeps over me.

I hold out the bag as the kids fill it. "You guys must be important to get this much mail."

Gunner gives me a measured look. "Papa says we're special."

"I agree with your papa."

Back at the cabin, Jake meets us at the door, takes the mail and stows it in a closet.

"You ready?" He asks me.

I nod.

He unlocks the gun safe and removes the Glock.

Gunner says, "Can we go, Papa?"

"Not this time. Miss Anna wants you two in school."

Gunner grumbles under his breath. Kimber's face lights up. She grabs Gunner's hand. "Come on, silly boy. I'll help you with your letters."

She starts to tug him out the door, but stops suddenly and turns. "Will you be here when we get back?"

"I'm not sure, sweetie."

She runs to me and holds up her arms for a hug. "See ya," she says.

"Not if I see you first."

She giggles. "Silly!"

The twins disappear down the trail and I'm alone with Jake.

Jake is quiet as we walk to the range. No big surprise. I decide to kick start the conversation. "Kendra said you're not the twins' father."

"I'm not their *biological* father."

I stay silent as we continue walking down the trail. Finally, he takes hold of my arm and stops. I turn to face him.

His expression is grim. "Their mother Cassie turned up here when the kids were two. All three of 'em were dirty. Half-starved. She was strung out on drugs. Hitchcock brought them to my place, told me to take them in, so I did. Cassie had no idea who fathered the twins. When she couldn't get her drugs here, she took off. Read in the paper later, she died from an overdose. I've taken care of them ever since. I do the best I can."

His words are so heartfelt, I blink back tears. "You're the only papa they've ever known. They love you."

He nods and propels me forward. I assume, correctly, he's through talking.

We arrive at the range. I wave at Riley who's blasting away with a lethal-looking long gun. Hitchcock is there too, watching.

Jake shows me the correct shooting stance and supplies me with protective earmuffs. He stands behind me, guiding my shooting hand. "You're gonna feel a little recoil, a kick, so brace yourself."

I take careful aim at the paper target and pull the trigger. Even though I'm braced, the recoil takes me by surprise and I stumble backward. Jake steadies me. I peer at the unblemished target.

Like Kimber, I say, "Oops."

Jake chuckles. "You'll get better."

Surprisingly, I do. Jake wraps both arms around me to help absorb the recoil. I actually hit the target a few times.

We take a short break and Hitchcock, apparently bored to tears, wanders away. Another guy takes his place, but is absorbed in his cell phone.

Jake glances at the guy and then leans close and lifts the muff on my left ear. Under the guise of giving me shooting directions, he whispers, "I need to talk to you. I'll call your cell tomorrow. Just shake your head yes or no."

I nod once and take careful aim. Holy shit! I hit the bull's-eye.

When Riley and I get back to the Rockin' R, Rick emerges from the barn pushing a wheelbarrow full of straw and horse poop. No sign of Ziggy.

Rick says, "Your girl's not here. Some kid with green hair came tearing down the driveway in a piece-of-shit car. She jumped in and they took off."

"Aw, crap on a cracker." I groan. "Now I have to go find her."

Riley says, "I'll go with you."

I try to talk him out of it but he insists. I fire up Buttercup and Riley follows me to Benny's apartment complex. We see his car and climb the stairs to 2D. I'm glad Riley is with me. Who knows what kind of a mess Ziggy is in? As before, the drapes are tightly drawn and the music is blasting, bass notes rattling the windows.

I double up my fist and pound on the door. "Open up, Benny. If you don't, I'm calling Paco. You remember Paco, right? The big Mexican guy who wanted to kick your ass?"

The door opens a crack, just enough for Benny's face to appear. "She ain't here."

I'm close enough to peer into his soul and look for the flash that indicates a lie. Hard to believe, but he's telling the truth.

Riley braces one hand against the doorjamb. "Where is she?"

"She was pissed off, man. She hung out here for a while and then asked me to drop her at Mojo's on Franklin."

Riley's expression hardens. "Let's go get her."

"This isn't your problem, Riley," I say.

"Don't argue. I'm making it my problem. Leave your car here. We'll take my truck."

Mojo's is a coffee place not far from Nick's. Ziggy is not inside. We cruise slowly down Franklin and spot her walking down the sidewalk. Her hands are thrust into her pockets, hood pulled up, partially obscuring her face.

Riley pulls up beside her, zips the window down and barks, "Get in."

Ziggy's head swivels toward us. Her eyes widen in surprise when she spots Riley. She saves her surly look for yours truly. "I'd rather walk," she says.

"Fine," Riley says. "We'll drive slow and tail you all the way to Nick's. How does that sound?"

I stifle the laughter bubbling up from my chest. This is Riley acting all grown-up. This is Riley dealing with a semi-delinquent teenage girl. Who knew?

Ziggy gives us a sidelong glance. Her cheeks are fiery red, probably from embarrassment. Riley is the reason she wanted to take the job at the ranch, and now he's itching for a confrontation. She stops and looks directly into my eyes. Confusion blooms in her soul. I feel a bit sorry for her.

After a long moment, she snaps, "Oh, all right. I'll get in."

She climbs in next to me. Riley does a quick U-turn.

"Where are we going?" Ziggy asks.

"I'm taking Mel to her car and then, we're going back to the ranch. We've got stalls to clean and horses to feed. You said you wanted the job, but ran away like a spoiled brat. If you're not willing to work hard, tell me now and I'll take you home. Otherwise, we'll give it another shot."

Ziggy gnaws on her lower lip and thinks it over. "I want the job."

Chapter Twenty

Back in the sanctuary of my home, I take a moment to check my messages. Three from Sandra, asking if I've made a decision about Mick. Two from Kendra, curious about my trip to New Dawn. One from Billy saying, "Call me. We need to talk about Nick's kid." Nothing from Mick.

Billy first. I plop down on the couch and punch in his number. Thunder Paws, who'd been waiting on my front porch, curls up next to me, purring loudly and kneading my denim-covered leg with his claws. He likes me today, but only because I put leftover tuna casserole in his bowl.

Billy picks up on the first ring. "You home?"

"Yeah."

"I'm off today. Coming your way."

He clicks off before I can ask if he needs the address. Apparently, he has sources.

A few minutes later, the unmistakable sound of a Harley Davidson rattles the windows. When I open the door, Thunder Paws scampers out. Strangely, a red balloon is attached to the bike's handlebars. Billy unties the balloon and greets Thunder Paws who welcomes him by twining his furry, orange body around and through his legs. Billy grins, tucks him under one arm and steps into my living room.

He hands me the balloon, sets the cat down and

looks around. "Nice place. Talked to your dad today."

Hence the red balloon.

I wave him into a chair and remain standing, arms folded while I gaze down at him.

"Why did you talk to my dad?"

"We have a job for him."

"One I'm not suitable for because I have two X chromosomes?" Yes, I'm being snarky, but can't seem to stop myself.

Billy, not at all perturbed by my bad attitude, chuckles. "This particular job involves getting next to a guy who belongs to a private men's club. You might stand out a little in an all-male environment?"

Well, damn. My lips pinch together in annoyance.

Billy stands, takes hold of my shoulders and looks deeply into my eyes. "Minnie, lighten up. You'll get your chance. I'll make sure."

What I see in his soul impresses me. Actually, it's what I don't see. For many months, his soul burned with a smoldering fire caused by PTSD from his Middle East deployments. Now his soul is crystal clear and untroubled. Billy is in a good place.

I should step away from him, but the warmth of his hands on my shoulders creates a sizzle in my blood. It spirals through my body. My feet feel glued to the floor. I may not see fire in his soul, but my body reacts to his as it always has. I want to deny it, but I know the old attraction is still there, alive and burning hot.

Then I see it. It floats lazily across his soul. Imagine a full-blown crimson rose tumbling through the air, caught by a gentle gust of wind. I blink and it's gone. I'd seen it in Billy's soul previously and asked my soul-reading father what it meant. His answer surprised me.

Finally, I gather my wits and return to the couch, letting the balloon slip through my fingers. It sails upward, directly over my head and bumps against the ceiling. I point at the balloon. "I guess Steve told you about the balloons. Blue for me. Red for Hope."

"He says it's a reminder to let your sister into your life."

Even though my life is full of men who think I can't survive without their guidance, I have to admit Steve is usually right when it comes to matters of the soul.

"Thanks," I say with a smile. "Now, what's this about Ziggy who, by the way, is making me crazy?" I fill him in on her latest act of rebellion.

Billy looks thoughtful. "The Rathjen kid might be good for her. He needs a project after what he's been through."

"Problem is, she's got a major crush going. I'm not sure Riley's ready to handle it."

"Not your problem."

"Actually, it is. Because Ziggy and I are both of the female persuasion, Nick thinks Ziggy will listen to me."

"And does she?"

"Most of the time, no."

His gaze is intense. "If you move to Boston with Mick, Ziggy's dad will have to step up."

His words surprise me although they shouldn't. News travels fast in law enforcement circles. I decide not to give anything away. "Yes, I guess he will."

Billy leans forward, arms braced on his knees. "So, you are moving to Boston?"

"I'm thinking it over."

"For what it's worth, I hope you stay in 3 Peaks. Your dad's here. Your friends are here." He pauses and takes a deep breath. "I'm here. What I'm trying to say is, *I* want you to stay and hope you'll give me another chance.

We've had this conversation before. Billy has a cocky, competitive nature and when he sets his sights on a goal, he's like a heat-seeking missile. In this situation, I'm the target.

I gently remind him, "I'm with Mick now."

He gives me his full-out mischievous Billy the Kid grin. "Boston's a hell of a long way from 3 Peaks. You know what they say about long-distance relationships."

I know he's trying to wear me down. "It won't be a long-distance relationship if I'm in Boston."

"Aw, damn it, Minnie, you don't play fair." He stands, a smile tugging at his lips. "I dare you to come over here, close enough so I can touch you, and tell me you feel nothing."

I'm *so* tempted, but shake my head. "Not going there, Billy. Now, about Ziggy?"

Billy sits, but is far from defeated. "I know you want to. I see it in your eyes. We're not done and you know it."

"Ziggy," I remind him, even though his words take root in my heart.

He leans back. "Yeah, Ziggy. I saw her with a guy who's bad news."

"Does he have a green Mohawk?"

"I know the kid you're talking about, but it's not him. He's Paul Moen, probably in his thirties. Clean-cut looking and dresses nice. He has a consulting business we think is a front for prostitution."

An involuntary shiver scampers down my spine. "And you've seen Ziggy with him?"

"Vice is checking him out. I just happened to see them at Mojo's coffee shop. They were at a corner table. She didn't see me."

Mojo's. Where Ziggy asked to be dropped off. I say, "Is there a connection between Moen and Benny, the green-haired kid?"

"Not sure. I'll see what I can find out. In the meantime, you might keep a close eye on her."

"Which means, I stop living my life and follow Ziggy around twenty-four seven. Hey, you want to share the duties? Take the night shift?"

He narrows his eyes. "What's with the crappy attitude? I'm trying to help."

Now, I feel bad. "Yes, and I appreciate it. I have a lot on my plate right now."

He nods. "Nick needs to take some responsibility."

"I'll talk to him, but he panics when it comes to fathering a teenage girl."

"Gotta go." He crosses the room and points at the red balloon. "Talk to Hope. I think she wants us to get back together."

This strikes me as so ludicrous, I smile. "So now you're communicating with my dead twin?"

He looks totally serious. "I know she wants you to be happy and, I promise, I will make you happy." He bends down and cups my face in his hands.

Again, I feel his heat, the magnetic pull of his body. I close my eyes to fight it. I stifle a gasp as his lips brush across my cheek in a feathery touch.

"See ya, Minnie."

When I open my eyes, the door is closing behind

him.

Later that night, I take my break and look for Ziggy. I find her in the kitchen, loading the dishwasher. "How did it go at the ranch?"

She straightens ups, winces a little and limps over to me. I'm pretty sure I know what her problem is.

She says, "It was okay. Riley showed me what to do. I thought he'd help, but he didn't."

Sometimes I forget how young she is. I point out the obvious. "It wasn't a date, Ziggy. He's paying you to do the job. Why would he help?"

She rolls her eyes dramatically and shrugs. "Anyway," she continues, "I knocked on the door when I was done. He checked out the stalls and said I did a good job. Then, he gave me a riding lesson."

I chuckle. "How's your butt?"

"It hurts. Damn, those saddles are hard."

"Hang in there, it will get better."

She bends forward and reaches behind to massage her buns.

As I turn to leave, I spot the diamond bracelet around her wrist. Previously tucked beneath the sleeve of her shirt, it's now exposed, sparkling in the illumination of the overhead light. "Nice bracelet. Is it new?"

She flushes and looks away. "My mom sent it to me."

Later I mention it to Nick.

He shakes his head. "I get the mail. Her mom hasn't sent her anything. Maybe she saved her money and bought it herself."

I know how much she gets paid and doubt she can afford such a pricey bauble. Somebody gave it to her.

Green-haired Benny? I doubt it. The older guy Billy mentioned? Scary thought. I need more information before I get Nick fired up. However, he's the dad. I need to say something.

"You need to keep a close eye on her."

His eyes widen in surprise. "I talked to the school. She's doing okay."

Since I hadn't filled him in on the Ziggy/Benny chase scene, I'm in a bit of a bind. Tact is not my strong suit. I blurt, "She's got some sketchy friends. Just make sure you know where she is when she's not in school."

"Good luck with that." He throws up his hands in frustration. "She's a truly gifted liar."

Don't I know it.

Chapter Twenty-One

It's eight-twenty in the morning and I'm in a deep sleep after working until closing time. When my cell phone rings, it's a relief since I'm trapped in a disturbing dream. I'm chasing Ziggy through a corn maze. I see her ahead of me, sunlight bouncing off the diamond bracelet. I'm trying to run as fast as I can but it feels like my shoes are made of concrete. Periodically she stops, turns to face me and allows me to catch up before laughing and darting away. I fight through foggy layers of sleep until I'm semi-conscious and reach for my phone. I open one eye and recognize the number belonging to Jake Gunderson. "Hello," I croak.

I hear the sound of a car engine and rapid breathing.

"Jake? Are you okay?"

"Yeah, I'm heading for 3 Peaks. I've got a serious problem and need to talk to you. Can I come to your place?"

Fully awake now, I sit up. "Sure." I give him the address and ask, "Are the kids okay?"

"That's what I need to talk to you about. There's stuff going on here."

"At New Dawn?"

"Yeah," he says, a note of panic in his voice. "Stuff I don't want to be involved in. I need to get away for a while, but I can't take the kids with me and I don't want

135

to leave them here."

I listen to my heart, not my head. "I'll take them."

"Thanks, Mel. I'll fill in the blanks when I get to your place."

I wait for hours, but Jake doesn't show up. His phone goes directly to voice mail. Considering the circumstances, I'm uneasy about leaving a message. I grow increasingly anxious as the day goes on. By two in the afternoon, I can't handle it. I put the cat out, hop in Buttercup and head for New Dawn.

I'm nervous about driving my junker car up a narrow, mountain road, but don't want to impose upon the Rathjens for a ride. The weather is decent for March. With an altitude of just under four thousand feet, spring in 3 Peaks can be iffy, with temperatures in the sixties one day and a blizzard the next. Today, the sun peeks out from behind white scudding clouds driven by a brisk wind. Dark, ominous clouds hang over the mountains that give 3 Peaks its name. With any luck, I'll be home before the storm clouds close in.

Buttercup cooperates fully for the first part of the trip, chugging happily along the straight ribbon of a road heading west. It's a different story when I veer off the main highway and start to ascend the twisty, two-lane road leading to New Dawn. As the uphill grade gets steeper, she coughs and sputters like something is caught in her throat. Poor Buttercup. Like me, she's a city girl. I contemplate turning around, but my worries about Jake make it impossible.

I pull over and give her a little rest. "Sorry, old girl. We gotta keep going. Do it for me. Okay?"

I ease out onto the road and keep the speed at thirty, even though it's posted at forty-five. A huge one-ton pick-up truck looms large in my rearview mirror, riding my bumper. I hold steady at thirty. We come to a straightaway. He pulls up beside me, flips me off and hits the gas, roaring past me. Before disappearing around the bend, I see a big chocolate Lab in the truck bed.

I pat Buttercup's dashboard. "Road rage. Don't take it personally. We'll keep plugging along like the tortoise and the hare. Okay?"

Comforted, Buttercup responds. Her engine smooths out and I push the speed to thirty-five. At this rate, I should make New Dawn before nightfall. Fortunately, I don't have to work tonight.

Ten miles ahead, speed or lack thereof becomes a moot point. I see a line of stalled vehicles and flashing lights. I pull behind Mr. Road Rage, stop and put my window down. The door of his truck flies open and the driver steps out. He's a big, burly guy clad in baggy jeans and a flannel shirt. He walks toward me, flashing a conciliatory smile. His ball cap proclaims his love for titties and beer. He looks harmless and there's a butt load of people around, so I don't zip my window up.

He leans down and peers at me. "Hey, pretty lady, sorry about the obscene gesture. I was in a hurry, but it looks like we're stuck here for a while."

"No problem. What's going on?"

Eager to please, he says, "I'll go check and let you know."

He hitches up his baggy pants and saunters past the line of cars, a man in search of the truth and possibly some chips and dip. Five minutes later he returns. He crouches down next to my open window and allows his gaze to roam over my body before he speaks. "Hey, I think I know you. You work at Nick's. Right?'

I try not to encourage him. "Yes. What's going on? Was there an accident?'

He takes his cap off and holds it over his heart. "Yep. Some dude missed the curve and went over the side. He's deader than a doornail. They're waiting for the coroner to show up."

My heart kicks up a beat. I grip the steering wheel until my knuckles turn white.

"You okay? You're lookin' a little pale."

I turn my head and look into his eyes and, by extension, his soul. I see kindness and realize I've unfairly judged him. "Thanks for your concern. I appreciate it. Do you know who got killed? I've been waiting for a friend of mine to show up in 3 Peaks and, when he didn't, I decided to drive up here."

He shakes his head. "Oh, man, that's the shits. I'll see what I can find out."

On a mission, he trots away, heading for the gaggle of law enforcement gathered at the scene. When he comes back, he's walking slower, like he's afraid to deliver bad news. He lowers the tailgate of his truck. The Lab jumps down and follows him to my car. He says, "I'm Clayton and this here," he gestures at the dog, "is Whizzer."

I reach through the window and shake his hand. "I'm Mel."

Right on cue, Whizzer lifts his leg and pees on Buttercup.

"Damn it, Whizzer. Look what you did to the lady's car."

"It's okay," I say. "What did you find out?"

"They wouldn't give me a name, but I heard it was

a guy from New Dawn, the whacko compound up the mountain. Ya think it's your friend?"

I gnaw on my lower lip, not sure how to answer. Finally I choke out a few words. "Not sure. Guess I'll have to wait to find out."

He pats my arm. "Ya want me to, ya know, give you some support? I can sit with you if you want."

"Thanks for the offer, but I think I'll head home. Wait and see. Hope for the best."

"All righty, then. Nice to meet you, Mel. See ya at Nick's." He tips his hat and starts to walk away, the dog trailing behind him.

"Hey, Clayton," I call.

He turns.

"Do you love your dog?'

"Sure do. Why?'

"Then let him ride up front with you. It's not safe for him in the back of your truck. If he sees a cat, he might jump out, break a leg or get hit by a car."

"He likes it back there."

"I'm sure he does, but who's smarter, you or the dog?"

He looks puzzled for a minute like it's a hard question. "Yeah, I see your point."

As I crank the wheel and do a U-turn, Clayton opens the door of his pick-up and Whizzer scrambles in. My good deed for the day.

Chapter Twenty-Two

I'm almost to 3 Peaks when my phone pings. I glance at the screen. Mick.

—*I'm heading your way.*—

I know why he's heading my way. He'll be pressing me for a decision. Am I going with him or not? Since my mind is now frantic with worry over Jake Gunderson and the twins, my decision-making ability is severely handicapped. I don't want to think about it right now.

Driving down the mountain, I reflect on the information delivered by Clayton. He said some guy from the compound had been killed in the wreck. He mentioned nothing about other passengers. In his phone call, Jake asked if I could look after the twins for a while. I agreed. What if he decided to bring the kids with him today? My imagination runs amuck. I picture Kimber and Gunner's terror as the truck misses a curve and flies off a cliff, landing in a mangled heap on the rocks below. I fight tears and grip the wheel to stop my hands from shaking.

The road flattens out and I find a place to pull over. First, I call Kendra, fill her in on Jake's request and tell her about the accident.

"Oh, my God, were the kids with him?"

"Hopefully not." I swallow hard. "Did Jake get back to you after he measured the windows?"

"No, I was going to call him today. But, listen, Mel. There's no positive ID yet. Maybe it's not him. If the road's closed, there's no way he can get to town."

I want to believe her, but my heart tells me Jake's soul has flown away. "He would have called. His phone goes right to voice mail."

"Maybe Billy can get more information."

I promise to keep her in the loop and punch in Billy's number. It too goes to voice mail. I leave a message asking him to call me as soon as possible.

Anxiety and worry are my constant companions for the rest of the journey home. To my relief, Mick has not yet arrived. Mick could get the information I need, but then I'll have to tell him the rest of the story. When he discovers I was heading to New Dawn by myself, he'll be ticked off. Remember when I promised one of the Rathjens would be with me? Breaking my promise would surely kick him into his frowny-faced, disapproving, I-know-better-than-you mode.

I make coffee and pace the floor. The waiting becomes unbearable. I decide to go in search of Billy. Just as I jump into the car, he calls.

"In a meeting. Phone was off. What's up, Minnie?"

Without actually revealing I was on my way to New Dawn—he's kind of hyper protective as well—I tell him I heard there was an accident and could he please find out the name of the person killed.

He's quiet for a long moment. "I assume you have a good reason for wanting to know."

I assure him I do. "And could you please find out if he was by himself?"

"I heard you've been going up to New Dawn. Kendra told me about the kids."

Of course she did. Kendra has always confided in her brother, especially when it comes to their mutual acquaintance, *moi.*

Since I'm already busted, I give him the edited version of today. "The kids' dad, Jake, called this morning, said he needed to see me about something important. He never showed up and didn't answer his phone. Then, I heard there was an accident and somebody was killed."

Billy's sigh is rife with irritation as it bounces off the cell towers and into my ear. "Minnie Mouse. I know you're not telling me the whole story. But, if this is important to you, I know a state patrol guy who probably knows what's going on. Are you at home?"

I exit the car. "Yes."

"I'll stop by later."

Now I have a dilemma. Mick is on his way. In all likelihood, he'll be here when Billy stops by and Mel will be busted all over again. I want to tell Billy he doesn't have to deliver the info in person. But he's doing me a solid and it would be incredibly crass to say, You don't have to come over, just call me. Instead, I say, "Thanks, Billy. I owe you."

Oops, just remembered what happened the last time I said those words.

He chuckles. "Good, now I'm motivated."

Mick shows up shortly after. He's in business attire. Suit and tie. I've never seen him dressed thusly and it throws me off my game. I stiffen in his embrace like he's a stranger.

He says, "Something wrong?"

I push away and give him a thorough visual examination. "Why the change in wardrobe? You don't look like the Mick I know."

"Gotta dress for the part."

"And, the part is,,, ?"

"Administrative."

"So, you're not in the field anymore?"

He hedges. "Mostly no, but who knows? I might miss it and want to get involved."

There's no *maybe* about it. He'd miss the action like he'd miss oxygen if he couldn't breathe.

I take his hand. "Mick, I have a lot going on right now. I can't move to Boston with you. Please try to understand."

I gaze into his eyes, see a cloud drift across his extraordinary blue soul and I'm swamped with sadness and regret. I'm the source of his pain and he doesn't deserve it. I lean in and wrap my arms around him. "I'm so sorry, Mick. I can't do it. Please forgive me."

He leans down and presses his cheek against mine. "Nothing to forgive. It's the answer I expected. It's just that you are so special. I can't bear the thought of not having you in my life."

Tears spill from my eyes and roll down my cheeks. "Can't we still be in each other's life? Maybe not romantically, but as friends?"

His expression hardens. "Not sure. Maybe."

We're still locked in an embrace when Billy rolls up on his bike.

I swipe my eyes and whisper, "It's Billy. I called him about something that happened today. It has to do with New Dawn and you're not going to like it."

He grips my shoulders and stares into my eyes. His gaze is steely. "You're involved?"

"Yes. It's the twins. I can't walk away."

He opens the door and steps through as Billy approaches. They exchange a few words. I'm not close enough to hear, but Mick maintains a steady course to his car.

I stand in my front yard, my heart aching as I watch him walk away. He didn't even say goodbye. When he gets to his car, he stops and turns.

Needing something more, I run after him. "Don't leave like this, Mick."

He takes a couple of steps closer and then stops. "If I had a ring to offer you, would it make a difference?"

I don't even hesitate. "No, of course not. It's not just the twins. It's my family, my friends, my job. I can't leave it all behind. Try to understand."

He nods and smiles. "I do understand. Your loyalty is like nothing I have ever seen. Goodbye, my *maylsh*. You will always be in my thoughts."

He holds out his arms. I step into his familiar embrace, wrap my arms around his body and breathe in his familiar scent, reminiscent of fresh air and crystal clear waters. He drops a kiss on the top of my head and gently pushes me away.

Tears streaming down my cheeks, I watch until the car disappears from sight. I take a couple of shuddering breaths and swipe away tears with my sweatshirt sleeve. Determined not to look like a basket case, I re-enter the house and find Billy standing at the window.

"Looks like goodbye," he says. "You're not going with him?"

Not trusting my voice, I shake my head.

He holds out his arms. "Need a hug?"

I walk past him and sit on the couch. "Rain check."

He takes the chair opposite me and studies my

face. "The name Jake Gunderson mean anything to you?"

At that moment, I know the intuitive feeling I sensed earlier is right. Jake's soul has flown. "He's the New Dawn guy who was giving me shooting lessons. I think you're here to tell me he's dead."

"He missed a hairpin turn and landed in a ravine. It took a while for the guys to get to the wreckage, but Gunderson probably died on impact."

Now, the question I'm almost afraid to ask. "Was he alone?"

"They only found one body."

I don't like the answer. "Does that mean there could be more?"

Billy rises, crosses the room and sits next to me. "Maybe you'd better tell me the whole story. Start at the beginning."

I let it all pour out. How I said I'd never return to New Dawn. How I changed my mind after meeting the twins. How I embarked on shooting lessons I had no interest in because of them. I ended by sharing my concerns about Jake. "He was in trouble and worried about the kids. He asked if I'd look after them for a while."

Billy listened without interruption but his expressions were easy to read. Puzzlement. Disapproval. Amusement when I mention the twelve golden rules of gun safety.

When I finish, Billy says, "So, you're afraid the kids were with him."

"Yes."

"I really doubt it, Minnie. Unless they were pinned under the truck…" He stops when he sees me wince.

"There was no mention of other, um, victims, so put that thought out of your mind."

"You'll let me now if you hear anything more?"

"Of course."

"What next?"

"Not sure, but I'll figure it out."

Chapter Twenty-Three

Before Billie leaves, he promises to look into the whole New Dawn situation, see if there's any scuttlebutt about criminal activities. He adds, "I'd tell you not to go there, but we both know I'd be wasting my breath. Anyway, looks like you're stuck until the road opens up. Do me a favor and let me know what you're up to. Okay?"

Like a little kid, I cross the fingers of my right hand, deep in my jeans pocket and say, "Okay."

With a rueful smile, he shakes his head in disbelief. "Sure you will, Minnie. Try to stay out of trouble. I'll be in touch."

Not sure what to do next, I resume pacing. What will become of Kimber and Gunner? Their mother is dead, their father unknown and now their primary caregiver, Jake, is dead. I know what I have to do. As much as I loathe the idea, I have to cozy up to Ken Hitchcock. First, I have to figure out how to reach him. Then, I remember how the hillside behind the compound bristled with satellite dishes and a cell tower. I don't have Hitchcock's cell number, but I maybe their manufacturing business has a website.

I fire up my laptop and Google New Dawn and window blinds. Sure enough, their website for custom window coverings pops up, complete with phone number.

147

I'm greeted by a recording. "You have reached New Dawn Custom Blinds. Currently, we are unable to take your call. Please leave your name and contact number and we will get back to you shortly."

Surprisingly, there's no option to be put on interminable hold and wait for the next available representative.

I dither for a moment, trying to figure out the best way to get a response and decide to go for the truth. After leaving my contact information, I add, "Please have Ken Hitchcock call me. I heard about the accident involving Jake Gunderson and have some questions. Thank you."

It's highly unlikely I'll hear from Hitchcock soon. As the head honcho at New Dawn, he's probably up to his eyebrows in red tape. I can't sit still. My brain is buzzing, overloaded with worry and confusion. In addition to my concern about the twins, I'm trying not to think about the sadness in Mick's soul as he left.

I have a couple of choices. Phone my mother? Check and see if the road's open. If it is, call Uncle Paco and ask him to drive me up to New Dawn. Pig out on junk food. Clean the house.

Sandra? No. Option two is out when I look online and find out the road is still blocked. I'm leaning toward option three until I discover only a few crumbs remain in the potato chip bag. Option four it is.

Thirty minutes later, the carpet is vacuumed, the furniture is dusted and the kitchen floor is so clean, if a piece of food were to land upon it, the five-second rule wouldn't apply.

I'm still at loose ends and need another project. Why not Ziggy?

I call Nick. "Is Ziggy working her shift?"

"Nah, she said her butt hurt from horseback riding, so I gave her some time off."

"Damn it, Nick." I can't keep the irritation from my voice. "That's the lamest excuse I've ever heard. She needs to be busy. You're too easy on her."

"Yeah, well, it's too late now."

"What do you mean, it's too late," I say. "Where is she?"

"She went to meet some friends from school. I dropped her off at Mojo's. I told her to be back by eight."

Mojo's again. Where Billy saw her with a creepy older dude.

"When did you drop her off?"

"Half hour ago."

"Mind if I check on her?"

"Hell no. I'll be eternally grateful."

If I'd arrived at Mojo's a minute or two later, I would have had missed her. As I pull into the parking lot, I see her push through the door, her backpack slung over one shoulder. She's closely followed by a guy I presume to be Paul Moen. I scramble out of the car and plant my body directly in their path.

A look of panic flashes across Ziggy's face. She's ready to bolt.

The man places a steadying hand on her shoulder. His eyes are dark and set a little too close together. His gaze sweeps over me in a dismissive glance. "Is this the little twerp you were telling me about, Ziggy?"

Though the term *little twerp* frosts my cookies, I ignore the slight because I have an agenda. I smile and step closer. "Yes, that would be me." I extend my right hand. "And, you are…?

He has to release Ziggy to shake my hand. She shrinks back, unwilling to meet my gaze.

He squeezes my hand a little harder than necessary. "I'm Paul."

No business attire today. A veritable poster boy for the expensive weekend casual look, he's rocking faded jeans and a black cashmere sweater over a buttoned down blue collared shirt. His high top running shoes are probably worth a couple hundred bucks. Black hair, combed straight back and glistening with gel completes the image.

I beam at him like a clueless idiot and stare into his soul. "Nice to meet you. Ziggy's dad asked me to pick her up. Were you giving her a ride home?"

"Of course," he says. "Where else would I take her?"

It's easy to spot the lie as it flashes across his smoky gray soul. A heavy black border and ice blue blotches tells me he's cold, calculating, and self-centered. A pulsing red blotch bounces around his soul like a Ping-Pong ball on speed. He's not only evil, he's angry. It's probably safe to assume it's currently directed at me.

I shrug. "Just asking. Let's go, Ziggy."

She plucks at his sleeve and whines, "I don't want to go with her."

Paul lifts his hands in a helpless gesture. "She doesn't want to go with you."

I lose the smile and pull out my cell phone. "How about this, Paul. Since Ziggy is only sixteen, let's call her dad and let him decide who takes her home."

His eyes narrow and he steps into my personal

space. I hold my ground. "She's all yours. Just remember, kids sometimes rebel against control freak parents."

I almost laugh. No way do the words *control freak* describe Ziggy's father. "I'll keep it in mind."

Paul pivots on his pricey shoes and strides away. He uses a fob to unlock a shiny, black Mercedes-Benz. Ziggy, looking forlorn, watches him drive away. She glances over at me. I figure she's getting ready to take off like a gut shot gazelle.

I step close and grasp her arm. "Don't do it. I can run faster than you. I can also do a leg sweep. Trust me, you don't want to kiss the asphalt and mess up your pretty face."

She pulls free but makes no attempt to escape. "You're such a jerk, Mel. Why can't you leave me alone?"

I ignore the question and lead her to the car. She opens the passenger door and angrily flings her backpack onto the floorboard. Only partially zipped, some of the contents fly out. I spot a plastic baggy of pills and snag it before she can. I stuff into my pocket and start the car. Ziggy climbs in, turns her back to me and stares out the window.

"Did Paul give you the pills?"

"They're birth control pills."

"Oh, please. You think I don't know what birth control pills look like?"

She shoots me a hateful glance. "What with all the guys you screw, of course you do."

I don't take the bait. "Unfortunately for you, this isn't about me."

I pull out of the parking lot, afraid if we aren't

moving, I'll be chasing her through the streets of downtown 3 Peaks.

We ride in silence for a while. Finally, I say, "Isn't Paul a little out of your age range?"

She turns to face me, tears welling up in her eyes. "He listens. He's nice to me. He doesn't judge me."

"And, he gives you stuff, like the diamond bracelet."

When she starts to argue, I hold up a hand. "Stop lying. I know your mother didn't send it to you."

She swipes at her eyes. "So, you're checking my mail now?"

"I talked to your dad. He gets the mail. Your mom hasn't sent you anything since you got here."

I ask again. "Did Paul give you the pills?"

She averts her eyes. "No!"

Even though I can't see into her soul, her body language pretty much tells me she's lying. Again.

We pull into Nick's parking lot. I put a hand on her arm. She shrugs it off and reaches for the door handle.

"So Paul listens to you?" I say. "Try talking to your dad. Maybe he doesn't know the right words, but he wants what's best for you."

"Oh, we talk, if you can call it that. He says, 'Did you do your homework?' I say, 'Yeah.' He says, 'I'm going to the store. Do you need any, um, feminine products?' I say, 'I'll take care of it.' Then, we have nothing more to say, because, guess what? We don't really know each other." She grabs her backpack, exits the car and slams the door.

I don't follow her in, but punch in Nick's number. "Ziggy's heading your way. She was with the guy I told you about. I'll talk to you later."

I don't mention the pills. Best to find out what they are first.

As I pull into my driveway, my phone rings. It's Ken Hitchcock.

Chapter Twenty-Four

"So you heard about Jake," he growls.

"Yes."

"I understand he called you earlier today."

The statement knocks me back on my heels. In our phone call, Jake sounded panicky, like he had to get away from New Dawn. I assumed it was top secret and had something to do with Hitchcock. So, if he knows about Jake's conversation with me, what else does he know? I proceed carefully. "Yes."

After a long silence, Hitchcock asks, "Did he tell you the reason for his visit?"

"Not specifically. Did he tell *you* the reason for his visit?"

After a mirthless chuckle, he says, "Do you think I'm stupid?"

"Quite the opposite."

"Then, stop playing games with me. I know and, I'm sure you know, Jake has grown increasingly unhappy at New Dawn. Sound familiar?"

"Possibly."

Finally, he says, "Do you have questions about his death?"

"I know he missed a turn and went over the side of the mountain."

"If you already know how Jake died, I bet I know the reason for your call."

I know he's toying with me so I don't reply, even though I have to pinch my lips together to keep from blurting, "What about the twins?"

"You want to know about Kimber and Gunner."

Bingo.

"I heard Jake was alone in the vehicle," I say. "I wanted to make sure the kids were all right."

He lets me stew awhile before answering. "They're here at New Dawn."

I can't hold back any longer. "I'd be glad to take care of them."

"Ah, there it is," he says. "It took you long enough to make your point. I know Jake asked if the twins could stay with you for a while and you agreed. It's not going to happen."

This guy is on such a power trip. It takes every ounce of my will power to hold back the flood of angry words and force myself to speak calmly. "The kids must be heartbroken. Who's taking care of them?"

His voice is without emotion. "Not your worry. We have adequate care givers."

"I'd like to see them."

He chuckles again. "Quid pro quo, Ms. Sullivan. You know what that means, right?"

"I'm familiar with the concept."

"For clarification purposes, I'll spell it out. It's an exchange of goods or services where one transfer is contingent upon the other."

"So, if I want to see the twins, I need to do something for you."

"Exactly. I'm sure you have an idea of what it is I want from you."

"Since you seem to have the upper hand, maybe

you should *spell it out* for me."

"Your unique ability, of course. I have dealings with people who are not always honest. You can help."

I can see a dozen pitfalls in his proposal. I toss one his way. "Since I can read souls and you can't, how do you know I'll be truthful?"

"My thoughts exactly. We need to meet and hash out the details."

The last thing I want to do is meet with Ken Hitchcock, much less work for him. Unbidden, I feel the rush of warmth signaling Hope's presence and, once again, hear her words. *She needs you. They need you.* I think about Kimber and Gunner, lost and alone. I know I'll do whatever's necessary to see them again. I say, "The sooner the better. I have to be at work by two tomorrow. Can we meet before then?"

"Tomorrow works for me. Be here at ten."

"I'm afraid my car can't handle your mountain roads. Can you come here?"

"I'll send a car for you."

"I'd prefer to meet at CyberSecure. It's where my dad and I work."

He's not happy with this arrangement and hems and haws for a while. Finally, he agrees. I breathe a sigh of relief. Now, all I have to do is explain the situation to Steve and hope he doesn't screw things up by going into dad mode. Maybe my new worries will crowd out the sadness I feel about Mick's departure.

****

"So," Steve says. "Let me clarify."

He's pacing back and forth across the office while I stuff a maple bar down my gullet. There's always a supply of sugary, yummy pastries in the office, just begging to be eaten.

He stops and gazes down at me. "This Hitchcock guy, who you do not trust, wants you to read the souls of the various and sundry miscreants he's dealing with. In return, you will be allowed to spend time with the little twins you're so fond of. Am I correct so far?"

My mouth is full, so I nod.

"Do we have any idea who the clientele will be? Business associates? Fellow residents at New Dawn?"

I wipe my mouth with a napkin. A cloth napkin, I might add. Steve runs a high-class operation. "I assume we're discussing the details today. It's why I wanted the meeting here. I'd like your input."

Steve folds his arms and leans against his extremely tidy desk. "You've read his soul. What did you see?"

"I'll wait until you've had a look. You often see things I miss."

"Fair enough."

He looks thoughtful and when he speaks, he chooses his words carefully. "*Mi hija*, I do not like the idea of you being in danger, but I know, full well, you are determined to follow this course of action. I'll do everything possible to help you."

His words evoke an unseemly wave of emotion. I swallow the lump in my throat. Steve, who wasn't around when I was growing up, has proven to be the loving and protective father I need in my adult years. He's bailed me out of trouble more than once.

I dig a tissue out of my jeans pocket, blow my nose and mumble, "Thanks, Steve."

The awkwardness of the moment vanishes as Hitchcock pushes through the door.

I make the introductions. The men make eye contact and shake hands. Steve waves Hitchcock into the chair next to mine and retreats behind his desk.

Hitchcock glances over at me. "Getting a second opinion from your dad?"

"Sure. Why not?"

"And, he knows about our deal?"

"He knows we're negotiating a deal."

He purses his lips in disapproval, but nods.

"You said you meet with people who may not be honest," I begin. "We'd like to know more about that."

Hitchcock turns to face me. "First, I need to explain the basic premise behind New Dawn. As I stated previously, it's a refuge for people who have no other options. Some have been falsely accused and are running from the law. Some have been incarcerated and have no jobs, or family to take them in. Some are lonely misfits, longing to be part of something larger than themselves." He pauses for a moment while Steve and I absorb the information.

"Why do I have the feeling you don't provide for these people out of the goodness of your heart?" I ask.

The corner of his mouth twitches in a suppressed smile. "I gather you know this by looking into my soul."

"Yes."

He looks at Steve. "Do you agree with her assessment?"

Steve nods.

He rubs the stubble on his chin. "You're both right. If folks want to stay at New Dawn, they have to contribute in some manner."

"How did Jake contribute?" I ask.

A flush of anger rises in his cheeks. "He took care of orphaned twins, worked in our window covering business and ran our shooting range? Isn't that enough?"

I recall the last time I saw Jake. His fingers were stained with ink. His eyes were red. He said he had work to finish. I got the impression he wasn't indulging in a hobby. But, I want to keep Hitchcock talking and therefore need to tread lightly. "I'm sure he did more than his share."

After a strained silence, Steve says, "How, exactly, will Melanie will be involved. As her father, I'm sure you understand I am concerned about her safety."

"You needn't worry. One of New Dawn's guiding principles is the protection of females within our compound," Hitchcock says.

That word again.

Steve bristles a little but doesn't respond.

"To answer your question," Hitchcock continues, "We've a number of applicants seeking refuge. I'd like Melanie to sit in on the interview, to determine if the person is being honest about his or her background, and to evaluate their ability to be a productive member of New Dawn."

"Tall order," I murmur.

He hastens to add, "To the best of your ability."

"How do you know you can trust me?"

His gaze intensifies. "You're familiar with the concept of a control group in science experiments?"

I harken back to my biology class. "Yes."

"Every now and then," he says, "I'll have a person brought in, someone known to me. I'll already know the correct answer to the questions I'm asking.

Therefore, if you tell me something different, you'll be lying to me."

Steve stiffens in his chair. "Mr. Hitchcock. You must realize soul reading is not an exact science. There are times Melanie and I have both been wrong in our assessment. Therefore, your scientific approach may not work."

Hitchcock stands and stares down at me. "I know you want to see the twins. Take it or leave it."

I stand and offer him my hand to shake. "I'll take it."

"Thought you would."

Without another word, he heads for the door.

Chapter Twenty-Five

I have one more item on my agenda this morning. The mystery pills I snagged from Ziggy. I need Billy to identify them before I go ballistic with my accusations. They may be harmless, though I sincerely doubt it.

Billy picks up on the first ring. "Hey, Minnie, what can I do for you?"

I ignore the underlying message in his response. "Working today?"

"Not 'til later. I'm home. Why?"

I explain my dilemma.

"Want me to come over?"

"I'll stop by your place if that's okay."

"I'll be here."

I have a valid reason for going to Billy's house, and it has nothing to do with the pills in my pocket. The last time I darkened his door, I got the shock of my young life. Billy had a houseguest, an extremely sexy houseguest. At the time, he was suffering with the residual effects of PTSD.

According to Kendra, he was having a crisis of faith and felt he wasn't good enough for me. Therefore, he undermined our relationship by screwing around with a cop colleague. The affair didn't last and, since then, Billy has immersed himself in counseling with other veterans who suffer from the same disorder. Kendra tells me he's now the poster boy for successful rehabilitation. But then, she's his sister and loves him dearly.

Still, as I pull into Billy's driveway, I feel the breath hitch in my lungs. Unlike the day my heart shattered into a bajillion pieces, the drapes are pulled back and Billy is standing in the window, looking out. I take a deep breath and exit the car.

Before I hit the porch, the door flies open.

Billy beams at me. "Welcome. I have coffee and doughnuts."

Oh, yeah, Billy knows what floats my boat. The maple bar I ingested at CyberSecure is history. I'll run an extra mile before I go to work.

I check the place out as I follow Billy into the kitchen. It's tidy, yet homey. He even has a sprawling ivy plant perched on the windowsill above the sink.

I point at the plant. "Didn't know you were so domestic."

"It's not like we spent much time here before..." his voice trails off.

He pours the coffee and sets a plate of pastries on the table.

A flush warms my cheeks. "You're right. We spent most of our time in Number Ten."

"Screwing our brains out," he finishes.

We make eye contact and both burst out laughing.

He says, "Like they say, hindsight is twenty-twenty. Looking back on our relationship, it was sort of one-dimensional?"

"Sort of?"

"Okay, totally one-dimensional."

We sip coffee and let the silence build. It's an easy silence, unlike the nerve-wracking, tension-filled moments I felt with Hitchcock.

Billy leans across the table and takes my hand. "I'd like to make up for my lack of, um, wooing."

Wooing. The word evokes images of women carrying parasols, strolling through manicured gardens. I visualize them in elaborate dresses and a multitude of petticoats beneath which lurks a whalebone corset that won't allow them to take a full breath. Men in top hats and tails trail behind, discussing the merits of horseflesh.

I try to hold back a snicker, but fail. "What would this wooing entail? Buggy rides? Games of whist? Drinking tea in the parlor?"

He doesn't appreciate my humor. His eyes narrow. "I'm totally serious, Minnie. I have a plan. All you have to do it give me the green light."

I pull my hand away. "The light's still red, but, at some point, it could change to amber. So don't give up."

"Fair enough," he says. "Now, show me the pills."

I hand him the baggy. He pours them on the table, picks up one and examines it carefully. "Ziggy had these?"

"They fell out of her backpack."

He shakes his head. "I'm ninety percent sure they're fentanyl, but I'll have the lab people check them out. Bad stuff."

"How bad?"

"Way more potent than heroin. Street names are China Girl, Apache, Goodfella, among others. Lots of people are hooked on it. You say she got it from Moen?"

"No proof, but she was with him when I picked her

up."

"Damn! Nick needs to lock the girl up."

"Teenage girls are tricky, Billy. I know 'cause I used to be one."

He reaches over and pats my cheek. "You may not be a teenage girl, but you're still tricky."

I down my coffee and rise. "Gotta run."

Billy picks up a sugar donut, wraps it in a napkin and hands it to me. "I'll call you."

When he calls later, I can't answer, because I'm heading for the Corral carrying a tray loaded with five sixteen-ounce beer mugs filled to the brim. Along with the pounders, I'm toting a huge plate of nachos, oozing with melted cheese and jalapeños. The potential for disaster looms large and keeps me from fishing the phone from my apron pocket.

Later, when I check my voicemail, Billy's message is brief. "It's fentanyl. Prescription grade, not the street stuff."

I'm through tiptoeing around the issue. Nick needs to act like a dad and stop putting the responsibility on me. Ziggy is avoiding me like the plague tonight, taking care to put a large sphere of distance between us. Like she thinks that will help.

Nick's behind the bar mixing drinks. I wait until he's caught up and beckon him away from the drinkers perched on bar stools. "I have something to tell you. You're not going to like it." I fill him in on the pills, making sure he knows Billy has checked them out.

His face loses color. He sweeps a hand through his hair and swears. "Aw, shit, Mel. Fentanyl is bad stuff. You know for sure she got them from this older guy?"

"She says no, but Billy thinks Moen is getting

young girls hooked on drugs and turning them out."

"You mean…"

"Yeah, hooking."

He swears under his breath and mutters, "What the hell am I going to do with her?"

I repeat Billy's advice about locking her up and add, "Look, I know that's not possible. She has to go to school. I was hoping the job at the Rockin' R would keep her out of trouble."

While we're pondering the problem, the girl in question appears from the kitchen, carrying an empty tray. She sees me with Nick. In order to keep her distance, she takes a circuitous route to the table she needs to bus. Ziggy badly needs lessons on how not to act guilty

Finally, Nick says, "I'll go talk to her. You take over the bar. I'll tell Helen to take your tables."

When she sees her dad approaching, Ziggy looks ready to run. Nick corners her, claps a hand on the back of her neck and marches her into the kitchen.

He returns twenty minutes later. No sign of Ziggy.

"How did it go?"

"Not well. She claims you set her up, that the pills don't belong to her."

I shake my head sadly. "She's a pretty convincing liar."

"She also said she'd stay away from Moen."

I think for a moment and then, ignoring my vow to butt out, I say, "Maybe we can double team her."

"How?"

"Perhaps it's time for Uncle Paco to have a chat with Paul Moen."

With a grim smile, Nick says, "I like it."

Chapter Twenty-Six

Paco is happy to comply. He squeezes into Buttercup's passenger seat, bitching about the inconvenience of my ride. Apparently Aida needed their car today, and the only other option is the Harley. He tries to fasten the seatbelt around his bulky frame. It's not long enough, so we have to endure the dinging sound for a couple of blocks. "Shoulda taken the bike," he grumbles.

"What? And forego the pleasant conversation we're having?"

"Yeah, yeah."

I suspect I know the reason but ask anyway. "Why so grumpy?"

He pounds an enormous fist on the dashboard. A crack emerges and slithers across the entire dashboard like a meandering stream. "Oops," he says. "Not sure it's fixable." He peers over the seatback and spots the towel I use to wipe up condensation, since Buttercup's internal ventilation is iffy. He spreads it out and covers the crack, muttering, "Sorry, little girl."

I pat his arm. "It's okay. What's bothering you?"

"Remember Aida, the sweet girl from Kazakhstan I married last fall?"

I glance over at him, pressing my lips together to hold back a smile.

He sighs and rolls his eyes. "She's gone. It's like

166

an alien took over her body."

"An alien *has* taken over her body. She's pregnant, Unc. Kendra says she'll feel better in a few months."

He shakes a sausage-sized finger at me. "Are you forgetting I was with her when she was pregnant with Larissa?" He doesn't wait for my answer. "Back then, she was nice. Now, she's mad at me all the time. She's just plain mean."

"Aida said this pregnancy is different because the baby is a boy."

"Yeah, I know, and she blames me."

"Well, you are the guy who knocked her up."

"Hey, she wanted to be knocked up. Can I help it if I'm such a stud I put a baby boy seed in her?"

The image of a tiny, anatomically correct baby boy sprouting from a seed tickles my funny bone. I'm laughing so hard I have to pull over to the curb.

Paco scowls at me. "Not funny."

"Actually, it is." I slug him in the arm. "Seriously, she needs you right now. She can't help it if she doesn't feel good, so chill. Think about the splendiferous result. Paco Junior."

This gets a weak smile. "Yeah, you're right. I'll give her a back rub tonight."

I shake a finger at him. "Just a back rub. Don't expect a little something in return. Got it?"

He looks disappointed. "Got it."

"Good." I pat his knee and merge into traffic. "Now let's talk about Paul Moen."

Our plan is finalized once we reach the pricey, well-appointed office of Paul Moen Consulting. I don't expect Paco to stick to the plan. He's an intimidating figure and uses it to his advantage. I just don't want things to spiral out of control, resulting in broken bones, blood, mayhem and a subsequent 911 call. He reluctantly agrees. I hope I haven't made a horrible mistake involving him in the Ziggy mess.

"So," he says, as we take the elevator to Moen's office. "You think this creep is giving drugs to Ziggy?"

"No proof yet, but that's what we think."

I don't tell him about the prostitution angle, knowing it's a hot button issue. If the evil people who brought Aida to America hadn't been busted, Paco's currently not-so-sweet wife was destined to meet the same fate. I choose not to wave a red flag in front of the bull.

An attractive blonde receptionist guards Moen's inner sanctum. When we appear on the threshold, her eyes widen in barely suppressed horror. I look fairly harmless, so I assume Paco is the reason for her alarm. He often affects people that way.

The door to Moen's office is ajar and I hear his voice. I attempt a disarming smile. "We would like to see Paul Moen."

She stands to assert her authority. "Do you have an appointment?"

"No, but I can hear him, so I know he's in his office. We'll wait."

"Name, please?"

"Melanie Sullivan. Mr. Moen and I have met."

She glances over at Paco. "And, this, er, gentleman is with you?"

"He sure is."

Paco stomps over to her and thrusts out a giant paw. "Paco Morales. And, you are…?"

For a moment, she appears to have forgotten her

name. She stands at arm's length, places a well-manicured hand in Paco's, gives it a squeeze and steps back. "I'm, uh, Angela."

I say, "Is Mr. Moen with a client?"

"I believe he's on the phone. I'll check and see if he's available."

Paco's brows draw together in a ferocious frown. "We already know he's available."

Angela is a tall, willowy girl, her height unnecessarily augmented by four-inch stilettos. She spins, teeters a bit and goes into Moen's office, shutting the door behind her.

Paco beckons to me and we stand side by side outside the closed door. When Angela emerges, I see Moen behind his desk.

Angela gives us a saintly smile worthy of her name. "I'm afraid Mr. Moen can't see you right now?" She tries to pull the door shut, but Paco's foot blocks it.

"I think we can persuade him to change his mind."

As we move forward, Angela backs up, guarding the portal with outstretched arms. As Paco brushes by her, she loses her balance, cries out and falls on her butt. Paco, who's barely bumped her, looks shocked and reaches down to help her up.

She scoots away from him on her butt. "Don't touch me!"

Moen picks up his phone. "I'm calling security. Get the hell out of here."

Paco reaches his desk in two long strides. With a wicked backhand, he whacks the phone from Moen's hand. It bounces off a wall and skitters under a chair.

"Angela!" Moen bellows.

"I'm on it." She's back on her feet, ready to dart

through the door.

I block the way. "We only need a few minutes of Mr. Moen's time. No need to call security."

After a fearful glance over her shoulder at Paco, she hisses, "Who's going to stop me? You?"

I step forward until I'm eye level with her chin. "Don't test me. I'm tougher than I look."

My threat becomes a moot point when Paco strides to Angela's desk, rips the phone from the wall and tosses it into the wastebasket.

He points at her desk chair and orders, "Sit. Stay."

Before she obeys, she turns and screeches, "This is *so* not in my job description, Paul."

Paco gives her another stern warning and leaves the adjoining door open.

To his credit, Moen doesn't appear intimidated. Glowering, he stands behind his desk, arms folded across his chest. He stabs a finger in my direction. "What's this about?"

Paco puffs up.

I know he wants to jump in. I step in front of him so I can look in Moen's soul. "It's about our mutual friend. In case you don't remember her name, it's Ziggy. I believe she acquired some pills from you. Fentanyl."

His eyes shift to the side and back. "That's bullshit. She probably got them from one of her sleazy friends."

He's lying his ass off.

"She got them from you. We'll let it go this time. Don't do it again. Ever."

Moen postures a bit, trying to save face. "If she said I gave them to her, she's lying."

"Shut the hell up," Paco thunders. He lunges at

Moen, grabs him by the shoulders and hoists him in the air. Ashen-faced, Moen dangles helplessly in Paco's grip. Paco says, "Listen up, asshole. You go near that little girl again and I'll be paying you another visit. Trust me, you'll be looking for a good plastic surgeon to fix your face when I'm done with you. Got it?"

Moen nods.

Paco says, "Say it."

"I got it."

After we exit the office, Paco and I exchange a high five.

"Thanks, Unc. At least we solved half of the equation."

"Meaning?"

"You scared the crap out of Paul Moen. I don't think the same tactic will work with Ziggy.

On the drive back to Paco's house, I get worried. "What if Moen calls the cops and says we threatened him."

Paco waves a dismissive hand. "Guys like Moen don't want to draw attention to themselves. Didn't you tell me the cops were already checking him out?"

"Yes, but he's a good liar. He could make something up."

He looks over at me with a sly grin. "You've got connections. Billy."

"Yeah, Billy."

"I hear Mick's gone. Billy's a good guy."

I pull into his driveway and park. "Six months ago, you said the exact same thing about Mick. Make up your mind."

He levers himself out of the car. "Love the one you're with, *Chica.*"

Before he slams the door, I call. "Thanks, Unc."

He leans down. "Anytime, little girl."

As I pull into traffic, my cell phone chirps. Hitchcock.

He doesn't waste time with pleasantries. "Do you want to see the kids?"

"Of course. When?"

"Tomorrow. I'll send a car for you at nine. First, you'll join me while I interview a person who wants to move to New Dawn. Then, you can see the twins. Work for you?"

Since I'm under his thumb, right where he wants me, I agree.

He clicks off abruptly, leaving me to wonder what tomorrow will bring.

Chapter Twenty-Seven

I'm seated in a four-wheel drive pick-up truck jouncing along the rutted mountain road leading to New Dawn. The damn pick-up has massively huge tires and has been jacked up so high, I needed a running start to launch myself into the passenger seat. My driver is eager to give me a boost from the rear, but I wave him off and manage to climb in, even while wearing my backpack and toting an overstuffed plastic grocery bag.

It takes a while for me to remember who he is. After I check him out, I realize he's guy number two, the camo-clad young man who so enjoyed frisking me when I went to New Dawn with the Rathjens.

"I'm Chad," he says. "I remember you. You're the feisty chick who gave me a chewing out a while back."

I shoot him an unfriendly glance. "And don't you forget it."

He grins at me. "You carrying a weapon?"

"Just my evil tongue. It's primed and ready to give you a tongue lashing if you attempt to frisk me again." After I utter the words, I think about what I said and clamp my lips together in horror. What if he interprets my statement as a veiled invitation to an explicit sex act? Oh, Mel, think before you speak!

He looks puzzled for a moment, at least until he sees my forbidding expression. "No frisking," he says. "But you'll have to give me your cell phone."

He's true to his word. We're waved through the gate without the requisite frisking. Before I hand over my cell phone, it pings. Text message from Mick.

—Arrived in Boston. Miss you. Have you changed your mind?—

I hedge my answer, texting only,

—Miss you too.—

He drops me at the community hall where Hitchcock is waiting. I thank Chad for the ride, grab my backpack and grocery bag and leap from the truck, wishing I had a parachute.

I climb the stairs and join Hitchcock. I can't resist saying, "You're actually going to let a female into the sacred portals of the community hall? Geez, who knows what might happen."

He doesn't appreciate my humor, but gives it the old college try with a fake *"heh, heh, heh."* Then, he corrects me. "FYI, females are allowed in the community hall except for the monthly meeting."

I know I'm screwing myself over but the words spill from my lips. "God knows we wouldn't want excessive estrogen screwing up a perfectly good meeting. Especially when it comes to issues concerning *all* the residents of New Dawn."

His eyes narrow ominously. "You have a very bad attitude, Ms. Sullivan."

"So I've been told."

He pivots toward the door. "Follow me."

We walk through a cavernous room where stacks of folding chairs are stowed against one wall. A few steps down a narrow hall, Hitchcock stops in front of a closed door and pauses with his hand on the doorknob. "They're in here."

They? "How many?"

"Just two. Is that a problem?"

I shrug. "Probably not, unless they refuse to make eye contact."

He pushes the door open. A middle-aged couple clad in jeans and matching windbreakers sits on one side of a conference table. Two large backpacks are stowed beneath the table. The woman glances up as we enter before dropping her gaze. Her layered brown hair swings forward, partially covering one eye. The man swipes a hand through thinning colorless hair and checks me out, his gray-eyed gaze sweeping over my body. Ick.

Hitchcock and I settle into chairs across from the couple.

Hitchcock says, "Shirley and Conrad, this is Melanie, my assistant." He points at a tablet and pen setting on the table. "She'll be taking some notes and might ask a few questions. Shall we start from the beginning again?"

Conrad's mouth twists in ill-disguised impatience. Shirley looks up for a moment. Her eyes are hazel and red-rimmed with dark circles beneath. It's a small window of opportunity, but the brief glimpse tells me she's upset and angry. Shirley will be my challenge of the day.

Conrad's attitude does not go unnoticed by Hitchcock. "Conrad," he says. "I know you've already explained your situation, but Melanie needs to be brought up to speed. "He slides the tablet and pen my way.

It's then I realize we should have made a plan. Even though I'm pretty decent at multi- tasking, I can either take notes or read souls. Since I really want to spend time with the twins, I choose the latter. I cut my eyes at Hitchcock, grip the pen and slide the tablet onto my lap. Hidden from the couple, I write, "Can't do both."

His eyes widen in surprise, but he eventually gets it. After a brief nod of acknowledgement, he looks at Conrad. "Once again, I need to verify your social security numbers. Yours first, Conrad." He pulls a small notepad from his shirt pocket, checks it out and rattles off the nine-digit number. "Correct?"

I'm staring into Conrad's eyes and see he's telling the truth. Shirley's a bit harder to read since she's staring down at the table. When Hitchcock recites the number, she nods. Hitchcock looks over at me. I'm guessing the ball is in my court.

"Shirley," I say. "We need a verbal response. Is the number correct?"

She looks up, but her gaze darts all over the place like she's looking for an escape route. After a brief glance at me, she says, "It's the correct number. Not sure why you need it, though."

Actually, I'm wondering the same thing.

Hitchcock ignores her question and tells Conrad to start at the beginning

"Like I said before," Conrad begins. "We worked for a business in Medford, or I should say we formerly worked there. Due to series of unfortunate transactions, we felt compelled to pack up and leave."

"In the middle of the night," Shirley adds, with a hateful glance at Conrad.

The two drone on for another ten minutes. Bottom line, they were skimming money and about to be arrested. They cleaned out their bank accounts and departed Medford in haste, a couple of steps ahead of the law. I pretend to scribble a few notes, but their story is pretty straight forward and I see no attempt at a cover-up, at least until we get to the money angle.

Conrad gets shifty when Hitchcock says, "Since you closed your bank accounts, you must be carrying a large amount of cash with you."

Conrad mumbles, "Not that much. We're pretty strapped financially."

Despite my reluctance to take notes, I write LIE on the tablet in big, block letters.

Hitchcock notice and sighs. He places his arms on the table and leans toward the couple. "Conrad and Shirley. The rules here are simple. If you take up residence at New Dawn, we will protect you. In return, you will turn over your assets and contribute to our community by donating your time and abilities. Our relationship must be based on absolute honesty." He leans back in his chair and lets the words hang in the air.

Shirley flushes and squirms in her chair. Conrad reaches over and covers her hand with his. She snatches it back, clenches her hands together and puts them in her lap. She's one pissed-off woman.

Conrad frowns and clears his throat. "I'd like to follow up on something you said earlier about our assets being an investment. You implied we would financially benefit at some point."

Hitchcock's gaze sweeps across the couple. "When you start being honest with me, I'd be glad to be more forthcoming." He pushes his chair back and stands. "I'll let you two have a moment while I confer with my assistant."

He claps a heavy hand on my shoulder. I resist the urge to shake it off. I'm not budging since I need more answers.

I fix my gaze on Shirley. "About a year ago, I got into some trouble and left my home in southern California. I moved to Oregon to stay with a friend. She died and I was on my own. No money. No job. I was so scared. You look like you're scared too."

Shirley lifts her head and looks at me, really looks at me. "I have nothing of my own. Conrad controls the money."

The truth is evident in her soul.

I stand. "You'll figure it out. I did. Best of luck to both of you."

Hitchcock leads me to his spacious office and waves me into a chair. He leans against a rustic pine desk. The room has a musty odor, probably from all the dead animals mounted on three of the walls. A crouching bobcat occupies a large shelf behind Hitchcock's desk and looks ready to spring. The heads of various and sundry animals stare down at us with glassy eyes.

I want out of here, so I waste no time getting down to business "I detected no lies until the question about the amount of cash they're holding."

"And their social security numbers?"

Warning bells clang in my head about his extreme interest in the couples' personal IDs, but it's not like I have a choice if I want to see the kids. "Yes. They are correct."

He pushes away from the desk. "I'll take you to the twins."

I scurry out the office, anxious to leave the hall of dead animals. Once outside, I start down the path to Jake's cabin.

Hitchcock takes hold of my arm and leads me in the opposite direction. "This way."

"They're not at home?"

"No. They're in Anna's care. I'll take you there."

I ask, "Are you going to accept Conrad and Shirley?"

"No, but there are other options."

"Like what?"

He doesn't answer. His grip on my arm tightens. "Thank you for your input today. Enjoy your time with the kids."

Chapter Twenty-Eight

The wooded trail terminates in a clearing. It surrounds a large log structure. A wide front porch spans the width of the building. A redwood picnic table with attached benches sets next to the entryway. As with the other log homes, the windows are covered with cheap mini blinds. Tire swings hang from the lower branches of the pine trees surrounding the clearing. A rope ladder leads to an elevated wooden platform next to an old fashioned Jungle Jim.

Hitchcock says, "Anna is our teacher. She lives here. The twins are staying with her."

"She lives at the school?" I can't keep the tone of incredulity from my voice. I set my backpack and grocery bag on the picnic table.

Hitchcock leads me through the door. "No school today. It's Saturday."

Once inside, all thoughts of an old-fashioned one-room schoolhouse disappear. The walls are off-white, the ceiling cerulean blue, and adorned with a half moon, planets and stars. Each planet is carefully labeled in a familiar-looking script. Sleek desks, each with a tablet computer, are lined up in rows. The walls are crowded with bookshelves and tall cupboards, overflowing with a variety of items designed to encourage creativity. A large flat screen TV is mounted on the wall over the teacher's desk. Makes me want to go back to school.

"This is nice."

"Nothing but the best for the kiddies."

Hitchcock's statement sounds so cynical, I glance into his eyes to see if he's lying. If so, I missed it. His expression is always difficult to read, since the scar on his lip transforms his smile into a sneer. Then, factor in his puffy, bloodshot eyes, the window to a truly scary-looking soul. Therefore, I'm not crazy about looking into his eyes.

"Anna," he calls.

A door leading to what are probably living quarters flies open and Kimber appears. Her thumb is back in her mouth and she has a death grip on Blossom Bunny. Still dressed in boy's overalls, she appears thinner. After a brief pause on the threshold, she sees me. "Mel! My beautiful Mel! Nobody told me you were coming."

In my entire life, I've never had a more creative, heartfelt welcome. Smiling, I start across the room, but she puts a finger to her lips and tiptoes back through the open door.

"What's she up to?" Hitchcock says.

"I think she's playing a trick on her brother."

He heaves an impatient sigh, eager to be off. Maybe he has pressing business to take care of, like shaking down Conrad and Shirley for more financial information. Or, perhaps he has a dead animal in need of skinning.

"You can leave if you want. I'll be fine," I tell him.

"After I introduce you to Anna."

Their footfalls preceding them, Kimber appears, her eyes dancing with mischief. She pops through the door, tugging a blindfolded Gunner behind her. Gunner is not a happy camper. In fact he's complaining bitterly.

"This is dumb. Why are you doing this?"

"'Cause I told you, it's a surprise, a good surprise. Remember, you like surprises, Gunner."

As Kimber drags her brother across the room, a tall, spare woman appears in the doorway. She's unsmiling and dressed in running shoes and jeans, topped off with a long-sleeved black tee. The black tee is in stark contrast to her fair hair and pale skin, completely devoid of makeup. Strangely, it gives the appearance of a disembodied head floating above her body. Her hair is pulled back tightly and secured at the back of her neck, resulting in an instant face-lift and perpetual look of surprise.

Hitchcock clears his throat and is about to make the introduction when Kimber succeeds in dragging her brother over to us.

She snatches the blindfold from his eyes. "See? I told you it was a good surprise."

To his credit, Gunner tries to work up some excitement for his sister's benefit. He gives me a tremulous smile, ducks his head and whispers, "Hi, Mel."

I'm shocked at his appearance. While Kimber appears thinner, Gunner is absolutely gaunt. His eyes are red-rimmed, his posture defeated. It breaks my heart.

I crouch down and pull the twins into my embrace, rocking them back and forth. "I'm so glad to see you guys."

"Anna," Hitchcock repeats, his tone a bit sharper. "This is Melanie Sullivan. As I told you before, she'd like to spend some time with the twins. Chad will be here to fetch her shortly."

Anna's face doesn't change expression. She simply nods.

I rise and walk to Anna, Gunner and Kimber clinging to my hands. "Nice to meet you Anna. I'd like to take the kids outside."

Her gaze on the floor, she nods again.

My stomach growls and I check the time on the big school clock. Twelve twenty. "Hey, Kimber and Gunner, it's lunch time. Have you eaten yet?"

Gunner makes a face.

Kimber says, "Anna made us a sandwich with some weird green stuff in it."

"No beans," Gunner mutters.

I make another attempt to get a response from Anna. "Okey, dokey, then, we'll be right outside."

She pivots and disappears through the door, leaving me to wonder if she is capable of speech. Hitchcock follows her. Would I love to know what their conversation is about? Yes, indeedy. I suspect it might involve yours truly.

The kids and I go to the picnic table. I can hardly wait to reveal the contents of the booty I've brought along. After speaking to my mother, she sent a huge box of kid things, not only from my childhood, but also from her friends who have male-type offspring. Her note said,

"Hi, my darling girl,

After our conversation, I can tell these kids have a special place in your heart. It sounds like they could use a little fun in their lives. I hope the items in this box will bring them joy.

Always,

Your loving mother,
Sandra"

The twins' attention is riveted on me as I pull out a blond GI Joe doll and set it on the table. Gunner's eyes widen in surprise. My old Barbie doll with long, flowing brown hair is next. Kimber is uncharacteristically speechless.

I hold Joe in my left hand, Barbie in my left. I walk Joe over to Barbie and lower my voice. "Hey there, Barbie. You're hot. Want to go for a ride in my jeep?"

Kimber giggles.

Gunner leans forward and says, "He has a jeep?"

I dig around in the backpack and place the jeep on the table. Still speaking in my GI Joe voice, I say, "Well, duh. Of course I have a jeep. How else could I take an awesome chick like you for a ride?" I position Joe in the driver's seat and bring Barbie to life, who says, "Hey, Joe, I like your cool ride. Let's go." I place Barbie in the jeep with Joe and push it around the table making car noises I learned from Kendra's son, Aaron. "Varooom, varoom, varoom!"

Gunner is instantly engaged. He reaches for the jeep. I give the vehicle to him and he takes Barbie on a wild ride with hairpin turns and screeching brakes.

Kimber joins in the fun, speaking for Barbie. "Slow down, buddy, you're messing up my hair."

While the kids are playing, I pull out a pink Barbie scooter with a puppy riding in back, plus a bunch of lethal looking miniature weapons for Joe, along with outfit changes for both dolls. Then, I add the educational stuff. Sticker books, ABC and counting books, plus Barbie and GI Joe coloring books. When they see the new stuff, both kids stop and look up at me with those amazing blue eyes.

Kimber says, "Is this for us?"

Gunner runs to me and raises his arms. I pick him up and hold him tight, shocked at the frailness of his little body. "Of course it's for you. My next question is, who's hungry?"

The twins each raise a hand and chorus, "Me, me!"

I dig around in the grocery bag, pull out a bag of corn chips and a jar of bean dip. "I think a certain somebody will like this."

Gunner's eyes light up and he digs in. Kimber wrinkles up her nose.

"No worries," I say. "I brought cheese dip too."

I'm not sure if the kids have ever had junk food in their lives, but in my humble opinion, it's about time. When Chad comes to pick me up, every bit of the food is gone and they are licking their fingers.

Before I leave, I pull them close for a hug and whisper, "You need to start eating more. Please."

Kimber says, "Anna's nice but we don't like her food. She says it's healthy, but it tastes icky."

Gunner says, "When are you coming back?"

"As fast as I can. I love you guys."

Gunner pulls me close and whispers in my ear. "I love you too."

When I try to leave, Kimber clings to my legs and starts to cry. "Don't leave, Mel. Blossom Bunny misses you."

"I'm sorry, Sweetheart, I have to. I'll be back as soon as I can."

I tell Chad to take me to Hitchcock.

"He might be busy."

I give him my death stare. "I'll take my chances."

He lifts his hands in surrender. "Whatever you say, lady."

I march into the sacred testosterone-laden community hall and stand outside the meeting room. I hear voices inside, my cue to pound on the door. It flies open. Hitchcock is glaring down at me. I glare right back.

"We need to talk about the twins," I say, a little too loudly.

He glances over his shoulder and pulls the door shut. "I'm in a meeting."

"Wonderful," I say. "You go right back to your oh-so-important meeting while Kimber and Gunner starve to death."

He puts a finger to his lips and goes, "Shhh."

"Don't shush me," I say. "Did you take a good look at those kids? They're not only grieving for their dad, they're not eating whatever it is Anna is serving up."

His brows draw together. "Anna is very healthy. She eats a vegan diet."

"Which Gunner and Kimber don't like. Give the kids some meat, for Pete's sake."

"I'll talk to Anna."

I back off a little. "Thank you. By the way, who has legal custody of the twins?"

He gives me his sneery smile. "New Dawn, of course. All the children here are in the custody of New Dawn. It's part of the deal."

"When can I come again?"

"Remember, I'm calling the shots."

"Fine, but if I don't hear from you by next week, expect a visit from Children's Services."

He claps a hand on my shoulder. I shake it off.
He says, "I'm sure we can work something out."
I burn with anger all the way home.

Chapter Twenty-Nine

The next week passes slowly as I wait and worry. I take extra shifts at work and collapse, exhausted, into a deep, dreamless sleep each night. Ziggy isn't speaking to me. I can live with that. No calls from Mick. It's over. I can live with that too. Billy drops by the pub every night, looking hopeful. Kendra knows I'm in a funk and calls every day to cheer me up.

Six days after I threaten Hitchcock, he knocks on my door. I look through the peephole and see Anna standing next to him. Hitchcock's SUV is parked next to the curb. Hoping the kids are with them, I check it out. They're not. I ask, "Who's watching the kids?"

Two spots of red appear high on Anna's cheekbones.

Hitchcock says, "They're being looked after. Can we come in?"

I'm interested in getting a good look into Anna's soul and lead them into the living room. Anna watches as Hitchcock selects a straight back chair before she sits on the couch, as far away from him as she can get in my small space. I leave one cushion between us and join her on the couch.

Hitchcock says, "Anna has something to say to you."

She's perched, ramrod straight on the edge of the sofa. Robotically, she turns toward me, hands clasped together. Her gaze is fixed on a point lower than my chin. When she speaks, her voice is pitched low and totally without inflection. "Apparently, I haven't been feeding the twins properly."

She pauses and briefly looks into my eyes. I have very little time to evaluate what I see in her soul, but my gut tells me she's far from happy. It makes me wonder if Hitchcock has warned her not to make eye contact. Is there something in her soul he doesn't want me to see? Once again, I'd like to slap his smug face. It's obvious he's paid no attention to the twins since Jake died, and now he's found a scapegoat.

I nod, encouraging her to continue.

"I eat a plant-based diet and the kids aren't used to it. Jake rarely gave them vegetables and fruit, so I thought I was doing something good for them. I did notice they weren't eating much, but chalked it up to their loss."

She glances over at Hitchcock who has not taken his piercing gaze from her. I get the impression he's written the script for Anna and there's more to come.

She continues in the same flat tone. "Since your visit, I've added some lean meat and protein powder to their diet. I think they're eating more now."

I can't resist saying, "A little junk food wouldn't hurt."

She looks deeply into my eyes. "We pretty much eat what we grow and harvest at New Dawn, plus the meat provided by our hunters."

"No problem, I'll provide the junk food."

Her soul is a dull shade of blue, as if natural human emotions have been frozen or put on permanent hold in exchange for rigid self-control. I'd seen it before, usually when someone experiences a loss and tries to stuff it away instead of dealing with it. It makes me wonder what brought her to New Dawn. She turns away from me, her posture still stiff and forbidding. Apparently the recital is over and it's my turn to talk.

"Thanks for letting me know. Tell the kids I'll be there as soon as I can." I shoot a look at Hitchcock. "I'd be there every day if I could."

He stands and shrugs his shoulders like I'm a pesky fly annoying him. "I'll be in touch. Let's go, Anna."

There are so many things I want to say to him, a multitude of angry words stored up and bursting to get out. Not to mention, scurrilous insults to hurl. But, to do so would likely get me banned from New Dawn for life. Hitchcock bested me once again, cleverly deflecting my threat to report him to Children's' Services by forcing Anna to take the blame.

And then, there's Anna. Cold, emotionless Anna, the twins' primary caregiver. Does she tuck them in at night? Wipe away their tears? Give them hugs? I seriously doubt it.

Still fuming, I arrive at work and see Cowboy Jim seated at the bar.

His eyes light up when he sees me. "Hey there, sweet cheeks. Ready for another dance lesson?"

"Welcome back. We haven't seen you for a while."

Since our first lesson, Cowboy has been conspicuously absent from Nick's.

He removes his hat and holds it over his heart. "Grandma Edie wanted her ashes scattered in Texas, so I took a little road trip."

At that precise moment, all of my worries, anger and angst over the New Dawn situation coalesce into a great big fiery ball, and I hatch a beautiful, purely evil plan. Evil, but amusing.

"Is Ziggy here?" I ask Nick.

"Yeah, pouting in the kitchen."

I place a hand on Cowboy's arm. "As much as I enjoyed dancing with you, I have a lot going on now. Stay right where you are. I'm bringing you a new dance partner."

Cowboy says, "Okay with me."

Nick grins and gives me a thumbs-up. "I'll get the tunes ready."

I dash into the kitchen where Ziggy is folding dishcloths and wrap my fingers around her arm. "You have a new assignment. Come with me."

She tries to pull away.

I tighten my grip. "Don't mess with me today."

She wails, "Why are you always so *mean* to me?"

"It's your lucky day." I pull her through the swinging doors. "You're going to have fun, so quit your damn whining."

I march her over to Cowboy Jim who slides off his stool and gives her a courtly bow. "Afternoon, little lady. I hear you're my new dance partner. Let's get started."

Ziggy leans close and whispers, "I'll get you for this, Mel."

I beam at her. "You're welcome. Have fun."

I prep for the dinner crowd, wiping off tables and making sure they all have the proper set-up of condiments along with napkins, salt and pepper shakers and placemats. All the while, I keep a close eye on Ziggy, hoping she won't fake an injury and head for the door. Nick stays close by and watches her as well.

Cowboy isn't put off by her crappy attitude. He kids and cajoles her. When he insists on knowing her full name, he repeats, "Zelda. It's a beautiful name and that's what I'm going to call you."

After she loosens up, he shows her the proper dance position and guides her through the Texas Two Step. Although her face is bright red with embarrassment/self consciousness/anger at Mel (choose one) it soon becomes obvious she's getting with the program. She's a quick learner and masters the two-step faster than I did. Cowboy moves on to the waltz and soon they're spinning across the floor like old pros. Do I see a glimmer of a smile on Ziggy's face?

Billy comes through the door while "Waltz Across Texas" is playing. He walks to me, extends his right hand and says, "Miss, may I have this dance?"

I blink in surprise. "You know how to waltz?"

"Are you kidding? Prepare to be amazed." He pulls me into his arms, presses my body close to his and says, "Hang on, baby."

Billy is a gifted athlete and oozes self-confidence. I shouldn't be surprised he's a good dancer, but I am. Athletic ability does not always translate to a sense of rhythm, but Billy picks up the one-two-three tempo of the waltz immediately. I'll never know if he was blowing smoke or really knew how to waltz before this moment in time. At some point, I don't care because I'm having fun, floating across the floor like Cinderella at the ball.

When the song ends, I'm laughing and gasping for breath. The music stops, but he doesn't let me go.

"Guess you won't doubt me again."

I look up at him. "You and I never danced, you

know, before."

He whispers, "Unless you count the horizontal mambo."

My face warms up at the memory. "I mean, we never danced fully clothed."

"Maybe we should do it again. Dance fully clothed. Can we start with dinner? It's why I stopped by. I want to take you to dinner at a nice place."

I decide not to make it easy for him. "You mean other than here?"

He glances over at Nick. "The food's good here, but I want to take you to a place with white tablecloths, candles, snobby waiters and overpriced food. How about it? Has the red light turned to amber yet?"

"It's getting there. Can you give me another week? I've got stuff to take care of."

I look in his eyes and see disappointment float across his soul in a fleeting dark gray cloud.

He drops a chaste kiss on my forehead. "Sure, you're worth waiting for."

Chapter Thirty

On Sunday, Hitchcock calls to tell me he'll need my services twice in the following week. My feelings are complex. I resent being at his beck and call, but grateful for an opportunity to see the twins. To maintain a bit of self-respect, I push the boundaries and negotiate the day and time. After a slight hesitation, he agrees. I know he's large and in charge, but tough titties, if he wants to use my unique abilities, he'll have to learn the art of give and take.

"Tuesday morning works for me," I tell him. "We're breaking in a new waitress who will take over my lunch assignment, so I don't have to be at work until four. Friday is my day off. I'll be working late Thursday night and I'd like to catch up on my sleep. How about mid afternoon? The kids will be done with school and I'll be able to spend more time with them. Also, before the interview, you and I need to talk privately about what you expect from me. I'm not sure you're aware of my limitations." I hold the phone away from my ear as he heaves an exasperated sigh.

When he grunts an affirmative, I pump a fist in the air, celebrating my small victory.

Before my command performance on Tuesday, I think about what lies ahead. Maybe one of the appointments is with the ringer. If so, Hitchcock will already know the answers. It won't affect my ability since I see what I see. But, I might see something truly awful, something that might put the person in harm's way. Or, put other people in harm's way. Since I won't know who the ringer is, I'll have to decide how much to share. Just thinking about all the permutations makes my brain tired. Bottom line, soul reading is a complicated, risky business.

I'm still receiving sporadic texts and phone calls from Mick, but they've become fewer and farther between. Maybe he's found a new girlfriend. The thought stings a little, but then I remind myself, What did you expect, dummy?

When I arrive at New Dawn on Tuesday, Chad escorts me to the Hall of the Dead/Hitchcock's office.

He's behind the desk and looks up when I enter. "You said we needed to talk before the next interview. Go ahead, I'm listening."

He doesn't invite me to sit, so I grab a chair and pull it up nice and close next to his desk. He blinks rapidly like I've invaded his personal space, and it's offensive. Good, I want to catch him off guard. "Here's the deal, Ken," I say. "Is it okay if I call you Ken?"

He squints at me through bloodshot eyes. "Do you really care if it's okay?"

"Now who has the bad attitude?"

He rubs his bristly chin and mumbles, "Sorry, I've been trying to sort out some problems and haven't been sleeping well."

"Maybe you should consider delegating some of your authority."

I know it's a ridiculous suggestion. Men like Hitchcock trust no one but themselves.

"I'll muddle through. Now, please continue. You

mentioned you have limitations."

"The only way I can detect a lie is if I can look into the person's eyes, preferably longer than a second or two. There are a number of reasons it might not be possible. For instance, if you want me to take notes, I'll be looking at the paper, not the person. Also, some people are extremely uncomfortable making eye contact. It doesn't always indicate guilt. He or she may be shy or scared."

"Okay, I get it. No eye contact, no soul reading. No note taking. Anything else?"

His impatience tells me he's uncomfortable with our conversation. He won't be happy until I'm back under his thumb, where I belong.

"You also have to consider the physical appearance of the eyes. The shape. The size. Are they hooded with heavy lids? Does the person's gaze dart to and fro?"

"Is that it?"

"Pretty much. Rest assured, I'll do my best. If the person is reluctant to look at me, I try to engage him somehow, but it doesn't always work. Just so you know, I'm not a miracle worker."

He stands. "Are you ready?"

"That depends. It would help if you'd share background information, so I can ask semi- intelligent questions."

He starts for the door. "We'll be meeting with a married couple. The issue will become evident when I question them. Let's go."

As I follow him to the conference room, I wonder if he's heard a word I said.

Once again, a couple is seated at the table, a much older couple than Conrad and Shirley. They both look up when we enter the room. The man is dressed in typical New Dawn garb, camo all the way. The woman wears jeans and a baggy sweatshirt adorned with daisies. Her hair is iron gray. Her eyes are black, suspicious, heavy-lidded and familiar. I know this woman. She's Agnes the mail lady. Is this my test? If so, I have my work cut out for me, since the upper half of her eyes are covered by droopy lids. Great. Just great.

Ken and I sit across from the two and I am introduced as his *legal* assistant. Apparently I've jumped up a pay grade.

Agnes has no problem making eye contact. In fact, her black eyes spark with hostility. "I know who she is. I saw her with the Gunderson kids. Didn't know she was a *legal* assistant."

I give her a big, friendly smile. "I remember you too, Agnes. Is this your husband?"

The man yawns, stretches and then lumbers to his feet. He extends a hand. "Yep, she's my better half. I'm George. Pleased to meet you, ma'am."

We shake hands and I look into his bland, blue eyes. I'm surprised at what I see in his soul.

Hitchcock begins. "Agnes, you have an extremely important position at New Dawn, that of sorting and distributing the mail. I appointed you because you had my implicit trust. You have your instructions. Certain envelopes are to be opened by you and the contents put into my lockbox. Correct?'

Agnes narrows her eyes (damn), grips the edge of the table, leans forward and snarls, "Yes."

Hitchcock says, "I have reason to believe some items are missing."

He lets his statement hang in the air, probably for my benefit. Agnes squints angrily at George who ignores her and gives me a pleasant smile.

I'm pretty sure who the guilty party is.

I reach across the table and gently pat the white knuckles of Agnes's left hand. "How long have you and George been married? A long time, I bet."

Surprised by the question, her eyes widen. "Yes, a long time. Too long."

I pat her hand again and giggle in female solidarity. "I totally understand." I turn my gaze on George. "So, George, exactly how many years has it been since the two of you were wed?'

George ponders the question, his eyes rolling upward, sideways and back to center. Hitchcock gives me his, *what the hell are you doing* look. The man really needs to learn how to trust me.

George says, "Oh, maybe close to forty years now."

Agnes rolls her beady eyes. "More like thirty-five."

"Seems like forty," George says with a hearty chuckle.

Hitchcock has had enough. "I'm still waiting for an answer, Agnes."

Agnes' mouth opens and closes. She casts another look at her husband. As unlovable as Agnes is, I feel a wave of pity. I say, "I need to use the restroom. Will you excuse me for a minute?"

To emphasize my point, I kick Hitchcock beneath the table. He jerks a little but gets the message.

"Down the hall to your left," he says.

When I come back from the restroom, he's waiting in the hall.

Not one to waste words, he lifts his hands in question.

"Whatever she did, he made her do it," I say. "Somehow, he has the power. I don't know what he's holding over her, but she's scared and sad, afraid she's going to lose him. He may look like a big, lovable bubba, but don't let him fool you. He's one sharp cookie,'

"You're sure?"

"Absolutely."

He reaches out and grips my shoulder. "Good job. It's what I thought. I just needed to make sure."

I pull away. "Can I see the kids now?"

He glances at his watch. "It's a school day. Lunch is in fifteen minutes."

My time with the twins is short and uncomfortable. Anna stands on the front porch of the school and watches as I sit with the kids at the picnic table. Their lunch consists of mystery meat on coarse homemade bread and a bottle of water. To my credit, I don't pass out the potato chips and candy bars until they've eaten every bite. Both the kids are still underweight, but not as shockingly thin as they were last time. Gunner is quiet and apathetic. Kimber, still holding Blossom Bunny tightly, clings to me like I'm a lifeline in a tossing sea. Each time I'm with the twins, it becomes harder to leave them.

Anna rings the bell signaling the end of lunch. I watch the twins walk away and know I can't go on like this. I need a plan. Unfortunately, it involves Hitchcock.

Chapter Thirty-One

Hitchcock is still closeted with Agnes and George and, according to Chad, cannot be disturbed.

"I'm supposed to take you home," Chad adds.

Hands on hips, I narrow my eyes and snap, "Not going anywhere until I talk to him."

He flushes and backs away from me. "Whatever you say. So, are you going to wait here?"

"It's a nice day. I might take a walk. Or, is taking a walk against the rules at New Dawn?"

He squelches a grin. "Damn, girl, you got a mouth on you. Go ahead and walk. Just stay on the main paths. We spotted a cougar not far from here. I bet you'd make a tasty meal."

Even though the idea of a giant cat lurking in the woods gives me pause, I'm determined to show no fear. "I'll be careful."

Chad tells me he'll be at the range if I change my mind.

As I step outside, the weather takes a nasty turn. A black cloud floats across the sun, casting dark, misshapen shadows across the path I've chosen. An icy wind whistles through the pines like the shriek of a banshee. I shiver and raise the hood on my sweatshirt.

Curious about the industrial looking building, I meander down the path while constantly checking the trees and bushes for the aforementioned cougar. I hate to admit it, but Chad has me spooked. My frame of reference is Thunder Paws. He has wicked claws, sharp fangs and the ability to leap to ridiculous heights. I multiply his physical attributes by twenty. Yikes!

I'm also worried about the kids. If I would make a tasty meal, Kimber and Gunner would be snack food. I should cut Anna some slack. Maybe it wasn't me she was concerned about earlier, as she kept watch from the porch.

The path winds around the community building and then forks off in two different directions. One leads to the shooting range, the other to the building at the base of the hill. The sound of gunfire from the range reverberates through the forest. I meet nobody on the path. After a few more twisty turns, I'm looking at the building in question.

Several women stand outside the door, puffing on cigarettes. Somehow this shocks me. I associate New Dawn with a healthy lifestyle, hearty folk living off the land with venison steaks, organic veggies picked at their peak and preserved in a giant kettle of boiling water. Cigarettes? Not so much.

Since I'm encroaching on forbidden territory, I duck behind a copse of pine trees, ever mindful of the big cat. The women drop their cigarette butts into a container and head back to the building. One of them swipes a card into the reader and pulls the door open. The brisk wind catches the door and rips it from the woman's hand. It crashes back against the building. She grabs it and they all file in. The last woman in line places a something in the crack between the door and the threshold. She turns and calls out to a woman who is still puffing away.

I really, *really* want to see what's going on inside, so I wait until the lone woman looks away. I dart closer, pressing my body against the side of the building away from her view. I peek around the building and check her out. She looks younger than the others. After she finishes her cigarette, she goes to the door. When she opens it, the wind catches it again. It slips from her hand. I round the corner of the building, dash up behind her and grab the door before it bangs against the wall.

She turns, her eyes wide with surprise. "Oh my God, that wind is awful. I haven't seen you before. You must be new."

"Yep," I say with a winsome smile. "Brand-new."

I follow her through the door. We're in a foyer with vending machines and bathrooms. I spot the sign for ladies and say, "Be right with you. Don't work too hard."

She giggles. "No worries."

I wait inside the bathroom for a couple of minutes, and then slip back into the foyer to see if there's a hiding place should I need one. A plastic trash container with wheels rests against one wall next to a broom and dustpan. A quick peek in the trashcan reveals nothing of interest. Coats of every size and shape hang from of hooks in the wall next to the main door.

I peer into a large room lined with cubicles and hear the sound of female voices rising and falling. Kimber said this building is where females talk on the phone. For sure they're selling something, though I doubt it's window blinds. I need to get close enough to hear an actual conversation.

Feeling exposed, I duck back into the foyer and weigh my options. Nothing ventured, nothing gained,

Mel. I pull my hood forward until it covers my hair and stroll into the main room, carrying the broom and dustpan. I'm almost to the first cubicle when a woman's voice booms over the intercom. Startled, I leap in the air, legs churning, not unlike the roadrunner fleeing from Wile E. Coyote.

She exclaims, "Let's hear it for Carolyn. She just nailed down her tenth client today. She makes the rest of us look like slackers, so get busy, gals."

A smattering of applause follows her announcement.

I walk purposefully down the corridor dividing the cubicles as if I'm on a mission. At first the jumble of voices confuses me. Close to the end of the corridor, I luck out. One woman—maybe the infamous Carolyn—has a high-pitched distinctive voice and a deaf client.

She says, "Mr. Kincaid? Mr. Harold Kincaid? Yes, I can speak up. Can you hear me now?"

I slow down and listen to her pitch. "I'm calling from International Children's Fund. Yes, I know you are a current sponsor and we thank you so very much."

A long silence follows. I go to the end of the row, make a U-turn and walk slowly by the loud talker's cubicle.

She continues, "I'm more than happy to take care of this for you, Mr. Kincaid. And again, many thanks."

I continue walking back toward the foyer, picking up snatches of conversation along the way. In addition to the Children's Fund, I hear references to a Crippled Veterans Organization, Society for the Prevention of Lung Disease, Fund for Homeless Animals, Parents Against Drunk Drivers and others.

I know all these organizations are legit. Is it

possible the women have been hired as telemarketers? If so, why the locked doors and secrecy? Somehow, it doesn't make sense. Color me confused.

I've heard enough and skedaddle back to the foyer. I'm reaching for the door when I hear heavy footsteps and male voices just outside. I calculate the distance to the bathroom and realize I can't make it before they enter. Instead, I dive into the coat rack and slither behind a long raincoat. As I flatten myself against the wall, I hear the men come through the door. I look down. Damn, my toes are clearly visible beneath the coat. I don't dare move them. I can only hope it appears somebody parked a pair of shoes beneath the coat.

Just my luck, instead of going into the main room, they talk in the foyer. Hitchcock and Chad.

Frozen in fear, I hear Hitchcock say, "Go check with Donna. See if anybody's been in the building. I'll check the bathrooms."

I hold my breath as Hitchcock walks down the hall toward the bathrooms. Is it my imagination, or does he slow down a bit as he walks by my hiding place? In my terrified state, I'm afraid the sound of my heart banging like a kettledrum will reverberate through the coats. I let out a long, tremulous sigh when he walks on.

When I hear the bathroom door open. I slide toward the outside door on shaky legs. A peek into the main room tells me Chad is chatting up one of the women. I open the door, slip out and dash down the path like a pack of hungry wolves are after me. Maybe they are. I may not have learned much from my scouting trip, but of one thing I'm sure. Hitchcock doesn't want me in that building. Translation: he has something to hide. All I have to do is figure out what it is.

By the time Hitchcock and Chad return, I'm sitting on the bench in front of the community hall, hopefully the picture of innocence.

Chad says, "I'll go get the truck."

Hitchcock folds his arms across his chest and stares down at me. "Where were you?"

I know he's going for intimidation, so I cop an attitude. "What do you mean, where was I? I told Chad I was going for a walk."

"We checked all the paths."

"Apparently you didn't."

He pinches his lips together in disgust. "Too bad I can't look into *your* soul to see if you're lying."

I shrug. "Why would I lie?"

He studies my face. "You look pale."

"The cougar thing freaked me out a little."

With a snort of frustration, he changes the subject. "Chad said you wanted to talk to me."

He's towering over me and I don't like it. I stand and take a step closer, looking deep into his eyes. It works. He takes a step back and lowers his gaze.

"I'm concerned about Kimber and Gunner. They're living at the school with their teacher who isn't exactly the affectionate type. They deserve better."

"Define better," he says.

"I love those kids. I'd take good care of them."

He smirks. "Right. What are you, twenty-two, twenty-three years old? You're just a kid. You work in a bar. From the looks of your car, I doubt you have a big bank account. How could you possibly care for two kids?"

This isn't going well. I try to hang on to my dignity

and temper, even though he's pushing all my buttons. When I speak, I hear desperation in my voice. "I have resources, a wide circle of family and friends who support me."

"You're right. The children deserve better. I'm working on placing them with a family."

I have no words.

"Anything else?" he says.

"I'll be back Friday."

With a sinking heart, I wheel around and head for Chad's truck.

Chapter Thirty-Two

When I get home, I stretch out on the couch, close my eyes and attempt to fit pieces of the puzzle together. The call center. The so-called mini-blinds factory. The thieving mail lady. I try not to think about the twins, knowing what Hitchcock said is true. I'm young. I work at a bar. I don't have a lot of money. The truth hurts and I fight tears.

The furnace clicks on forcing air through the floor vents. Hope's red balloon, delivered days ago by Billy, bumps and bounces along the ceiling until it settles directly overhead. Bio dad Steve's words resonate in my fractured and despondent mind. The balloon is a reminder to let your sister into your life.

I gaze at the bobbing red balloon. "It's a good thing my name isn't Hope because, right now, I feel pretty damn hopeless."

On impulse, I stand on the couch and tug on the ribbon tied to the balloon. I wrap it around my hand, curl up on the couch and close my eyes. I will myself to relax and enter the fugue state halfway between sleep and wakefulness. The red balloon warms against my hand. Comforted, I ask Hope to come to me. She doesn't.

Frustrated and exhausted, I drift into a deep sleep fraught with terrifying dreams. I see the twins on a wooded path. Gunner, clad in camo, walks a few steps ahead of Kimber who is clutching Blossom Bunny. The two are unaware of the cougar perched high above them, its gaze tracking their movements.

Suddenly, I'm there too, trailing behind, a red balloon tied to my wrist. I try to call out, but I have no voice. I scream silently in my mind. Hurry, Mel, hurry! The kids are in danger. When I try to run, my feet are anchored to the ground. Unable to speak or run, I watch the cougar leap from the tree and creep up behind the twins who are oblivious to the danger. The wind howls through the pines, their frenzied branches whipping back and forth like living things.

I'm powerless. Helpless. A frustrated, soundless "No!" reverberates through my body. The ribbon, securing the red balloon to my wrist, wriggles and unwinds, releasing the balloon into the air. It floats upward, gently bouncing along the treetops before rising upward.

As it disappears, I feel strength and energy pour into my body. My feet fly down the path and I scream a warning. The big cat pauses and turns to face me. Its yellow eyes now fixed on me. The twins freeze. Then, Gunner pushes Kimber behind him. I look for a weapon and find nothing but a pile of pinecones. I begin hurling them at the cougar. As the makeshift missiles bounce off the animal, they turn into tiny red balloons and rise in the air.

Kimber screams in terror. Gunner picks up a stick and advances toward the cougar.

"No!" The scream rips me from the dream. I awake covered in sweat, my heart pounding, the inside of my mouth like cracked leather. My hands are shaking. While thrashing in my troubled sleep, the red balloon slipped from my hand. It now rests against the window, deflating slowly. I watch as it collapses, folds into itself and settles onto the sill.

I pace the floor. My feelings of fright and confusion will not subside. It's time to call the one person who truly understands the strangeness of my life.

Steve answers on the first ring. "Melanie, how are you?"

I hear voices in the background. "Sounds like you're busy. Are you working?"

"Hold on a sec."

I hear footsteps, a door opening and closing.

"Tell me what's on your mind."

The words pour out, my voice quivering with emotion. Steve listens attentively, interrupting from time to time to clarify a point.

By the time I finish describing the dream, I'm in tears. "You sent the balloon as a reminder to include Hope in my life. I called out for her but she didn't come. Now, I feel like she's slipped away from me. I don't understand."

When he speaks, his voice is comforting. "*Mi hija*, I'm so glad you called me. You're feeling abandoned, but it's actually very good news."

"How so?"

"It's simple, really. Hope knows you don't need her anymore. The red balloon deflating means her soul is at ease. She knows that you, Honor Melanie Sullivan, are capable of acting alone. She knows you are fearless and smart. The dream is a sign. It means this is the time to release Hope's spirit and let her rest in peace."

I stay quiet and let his words sink in. I so want to

believe him. Steve has always been straight with me, but my ego is still stinging from Hitchcock's spot-on analysis of my current life situation. Finally, I murmur my thanks.

"You're welcome, dear one. Call if you need me."

As I'm getting ready for work, Kendra calls. "Remember my mini blinds order?"

"Of course. It's the last time I saw Jake Gunderson."

"You know I really didn't need them. I just wanted to get a look at Gunderson and actually, I was a big help. Right?"

"Refresh my memory."

She clucks her tongue in annoyance. "I can't believe you've forgotten I was the one who found out Jake isn't the twins' real father. Geez, Mel. Anyway, I called today and cancelled the order."

When I don't respond, she says, "What's going on with you? You sound depressed."

"Sorry, I got some bad news about the kids today."

I fill her in on my trip to New Dawn.

"So, now what?"

I hear a familiar sound. "Hold on a sec. Thunder Paws is pounding on the door."

Her laughter follows me to the door. I open it and the cat darts through. He has something in his mouth. A large furry something with a tail. He looks up at me with a smug expression and drops the fattest mouse I've ever seen at my feet. It's virtually unharmed and scampers across the floor. Before it can duck beneath the couch, Thunder Paws follows it and re-captures it with a furry paw.

Startled, I yip in alarm and drop the phone. "Damn

it, Thunder Paws, bad kitty!"

I hear Kendra yelling, "What? What?"

The cat returns to me with his prize. I walk to the door and open it, hoping he'll take the hint. But, no, instead he makes a U-turn and stalks into the kitchen, the mouse still clamped between his jaws.

Breathless, I tell Kendra. "It's Thunder Paws. He has a live mouse. It might even be a rat. It's not dead. Damn, what shall I do?"

Kendra finds the whole scenario amusing. When she finally stops laughing, she says, "It's a sign of his love. He brought you a present."

"He's toying with it. He lets it go and then grabs it again."

"Yeah, it's a cat thing. No worries. Help is on the way. In the meantime, see if you can corner it and trap it somehow."

"Trap it?" I screech. "How am I—"

It's too late. She's clicked off. I leave the front door open, hoping the rodent will make a break for it. Trap it, Kendra said. My mouse-catching arsenal is pretty lame. It consists of a broom and plastic bucket. If I can get Thunder Paws to release it, I'll whack it with the broom and throw the bucket over it.

The cat is now under the kitchen table, playing with the mouse who still has plenty of life left in him. With one eye on Thunder Paws, I open the fridge and look for something he can't resist. Slim pickings. Yogurt? No way. Then, I spot a shriveled wiener hiding behind a package of buns. Knowing his love of garbage, it should work.

Armed with my broom, I wave the wiener in front of TP's nose. "Here you go, kitty. Yum!"

He's definitely interested and spits out the mouse, but pins it to the floor with his front paw. His nose twitches. I back away, holding the wiener. He squints at me, suspecting a trick. I crouch down and drag the wiener across the floor in a zigzag pattern. He stands and crouches, ready to spring. Yes! "It's all yours, buddy. Come and get it."

I drop the wiener and grab the broom with both hands. TP releases the mouse and pounces on the wiener. As the mouse scrambles away, I whack it with the broom. Thunder Paws emits a hideous yowl and leaps upon the kitchen table with the desiccated wiener. The mouse is stunned but alive. I trap it under the bucket, feeling proud of myself. Kendra told me to trap it and I did. Yay, me.

I whirl around at the sound of footsteps. Billy is standing behind me, his Glock clearly visible in a shoulder holster inside his sport coat. He's trying not to smile but amusement dances in his eyes.

"Kendra called to report a damsel in distress. Something about a mouse? I was in the neighborhood."

I point to the bucket. "It's there. I trapped it."

"That's terrific, Minnie. What do you plan to do next?"

Oh, yeah, the next step. I know he's toying with me like Thunder Paws was toying with the mouse. Not to be outdone, I say, "I'll scoot the bucket across the floor until I reach the back door and then, I'll...I'll..."

"Yes?"

"I'll set it free."

"What if it runs back into the house?"

I glare up at him. "Highly unlikely since there's a cat in the house."

"You sure about that?'

"Pretty sure."

He chuckles. "You know what I find funny about this situation?"

I shrug. "No idea."

"What's my nickname for you?"

I roll my eyes. "Minnie Mouse."

He points at the bucket. "He could be your first cousin."

"Oh, shut the hell up, Billy. Are you going to help me or not?"

He whips the gun out of his holster and says, "On the count of three, lift the bucket."

Horrified, I clap a hand over my mouth.

He laughs and slides the gun back into the holster. "Just kidding. Minnie, if you could see your face."

"Fine," I huff. "I'll take care of it myself."

"No worries." He clamps his hands on my shoulders, turns me around and points at the living room. "I'm on the job. Wait in there."

I want the damn thing out of my house so I take a seat on the couch. There's a scraping sound, a muttered, "Gotcha," and the back door opening and closing.

He comes into the living room. "No more mouse. By the way, there's a cat on your kitchen table."

I demand details. "Did you kill the mouse?"

"Nope. Threw it outside."

"With your bare hands?"

"Paper towel."

He walks over to me. "You can thank me now."

I dart in close, give him a brief hug and back away. "Thanks."

He grins down at me. "Don't trust yourself, huh?"

"Your ego is enormous."

"I hear Friday's your day off. I'll pick you up at six."

Before I can respond, he's out the door.

Chapter Thirty-Three

The next few days pass swiftly. Back in a prescribed work routine, I regain my equilibrium and good nature, even though worry about the twins nibbles at my mind. Resolutely, I refuse to think about my date with Billy. Not an easy feat since he stops by the pub every night after work with his cop friends.

When I deliver their food and drinks, one of his buddies asks, "Are you two back together?"

Billy gets a competitive gleam in his eyes. "It's a possibility."

"Better bring your 'A' game," I say, evoking a round of ribald laughter.

Thankfully, things have calmed down on the Ziggy front. She's had a couple more lessons from Cowboy Jim. Nick said he actually saw her smile once and declares he's cautiously optimistic. She even mucked out stalls at the Rockin' R without bitching and moaning. Still, I warn Nick to make sure he knows her whereabouts at all times.

"Really?" he says. "She's being responsible. I think she's earned a little more freedom."

I don't agree, but Ziggy is his kid, not mine.

When Friday rolls around, Chad pulls into my driveway at noon. I grab a shopping bag with treats for the twins. String cheese. Juice boxes. Several boxes of cute little crackers shaped like goldfish. It's my attempt at providing healthy junk food.

I deliberately bought an extra box of crackers, which I share with Chad on our trip to New Dawn. He digs in enthusiastically, leading me to believe he is also junk food-deprived. Perhaps this will lead to a new job description for me: Melanie Sullivan, New Dawn's Fake Food Specialist.

When we arrive, Hitchcock is still behind closed doors. Chad points to a chair in the hall. I don't want him to think he's the boss of me, so I tell him I'll wait outside. He's not happy, but joins me on the bench outside the hall. I'm sure he has explicit orders to keep a close eye on me after my disappearing act on Tuesday.

I pass the next thirty minutes tormenting Chad. "Do you like it here? Why? Do you have a wife? Girlfriend? Kids? What did you eat for dinner last night? When you're not driving me back and forth from 3 Peaks, what's your job? Do you get paid? How much?"

Finally, he turns red in the face and holds up a hand. "Gawd Almighty, woman, don't you ever run out of questions?"

"Are you kidding? Of course not."

He groans.

I'm feeling a little guilty, so I add, "If you ever come to 3 Peaks when I'm working, stop by Nick's pub and I'll buy you a beer."

He smiles. "You got it."

His phone vibrates. He looks at the read-out. "Mr. Hitchcock is ready for you."

The door to the meeting room is closed. Hitchcock stands in the hall.

He leans close and lowers his voice. "This might be a little confusing for you. I'm negotiating a deal with the gentlemen inside. It involves a considerable amount of money."

I can't resist saying, "They must want to buy a bunch of blinds."

A shadow floats across his soul and he grimaces like he's trying to control himself. Is it my imagination, or are his hands twitching because he'd like to wrap them around my neck?

He says, "I'm making a point here, Mel. You'll hear us talking about the product. I need to make sure they're good for the money. That's where you come in."

"So, is this the test? To make sure I'm telling you the truth?"

He blows a disgusted sigh. "If it were, do you think I'd tell you? Actually, you passed with flying colors. Like I told you before, I pretty much knew George was making Agnes steal for him."

"Well, goodie for me. So, what happened to Agnes and George?"

"Don't push it, Mel."

He takes me by the arm and ushers me into the inner sanctum, where I see two men sitting on one side of the table. Both wear red baseball caps emblazoned with the logo from a bait and tackle shop. One man is older with a scruffy gray facial hair and a ponytail tied back with a leather thong. The second man is a bit younger with olive skin and luminous dark eyes. When I'm introduced as Hitchcock's legal assistant, the older man frowns and rakes me with a look of suspicion.

Since Hitchcock hasn't bothered to tell me their

names, I look at frowny face and say, "And you are…?"

"Bill."

I beam at him like he's just passed the orals for his doctorate degree, and then look inquisitively at the other man.

He gets the hint. "I'm Oscar."

I plant my butt in a chair and pull it up nice and close. "Very pleased to meet you both."

Bill stares at Hitchcock. "Why do you need a legal assistant, especially one who looks like a teenage girl? Is this a joke?"

I return his frown and, while I'm at it, take a good long look into his soul. "I assure you, sir, this is not a joke and I am not a teenager. Would you like to see my identification?"

He squirms a little and harrumphs, "Aw, forget it. Still don't understand why you brought her in, Ken."

Hitchcock places a meaty hand on my shoulder. "Because I trust her judgment in business dealings. If you have nothing to hide, you have nothing to worry about."

Bill isn't happy but, thankfully, shuts the hell up.

Oscar leans across the table and looks into my eyes with a seductive smile. "Melanie, I think you must be very intelligent for a businessman like Mr. Hitchcock to have such trust in you. I am impressed."

If you only knew, Oscar. I give him a big, cheesy smile. "Thank you."

I think I detect a slight accent in Oscar's syntax, but need to hear more to make sure. I've already had the opportunity to map the landscape of both men's souls. If they lie, I'll know it.

Hitchcock says, "So, let's get started. I need to

make sure you have adequate funds to pay for the product. You told me some of money is in offshore accounts. How do I know you have access?"

Bill narrows his eyes. Damn, he's making me work way too hard.

He said, "If we didn't have the funds, we wouldn't be here."

Oscar adds in his silky tone, "Your insistence on cash added a layer of difficulty for us."

"The accounts are in both your names?" Hitchcock asks.

"We have accounts under a number of names," Oscar says. "But, no worries. The money is available."

Bill leans back and folds his arms across his chest. "Before we come to an agreement, we want to inventory the product."

"No problem," Hitchcock says. "I'll take you there shortly."

He glances over at me. "Mel, I believe you said you have another appointment."

I nod like a bobble-head doll.

He says, "I have a message I'd like you to deliver for me. Will you excuse us for a moment, gentlemen?"

In the hall, Hitchcock says, "Well?"

"They're both shady characters, but you already know that. To answer your question, they have the money."

His eyes gleam with avarice. "Thank you."

"Now," I say. "What's the message you want me to deliver?"

He chuckles, "Guess you weren't looking into my soul. It was a lie. Enjoy your time with the twins."

Chapter Thirty-Four

As Chad walks me down the trail to the school, I feel guilty for having been part of the transaction, like I've aided and abetted a pair of criminals, not to mention Hitchcock and his obvious greed. I only hope I'll have a chance to redeem myself.

School's out so I have more time with Kimber and Gunner. Recalling my dream, I ask if they know about the cougar.

Gunner straightens up to his full height and puffs out his chest. "Yes, I look everywhere when we go outside. I tell Kimber, no going off the path looking for wildflowers. It's my job to protect my sister."

It seems like Gunner is getting stronger, back to his old self. Maybe Hitchcock wants him to look good for his new family. I should be happy for them, but all I feel is a sense of loss. Kimber is still clingy. Blossom Bunny is clamped under one arm while she grips my hand with the other.

She says, "I wish you lived here, Mel. Then, me and Gunner could stay with you."

Her voice is wistful and tugs at my heart. "I'm afraid I can't, sweetie. I have a job and a home in 3 Peaks."

She brightens. "Maybe we can come live with you."

"I would love that."

We munch on crackers and drink our juice.

I point at the ceiling. "I've been meaning to ask you about the beautiful mural. Did your papa paint the moon and stars?"

Both twins nod solemnly.

"It's beautiful," I say.

A tear rolls down Kimber's cheek. "We miss Papa."

I put my arms around both kids and pull them close. "Remember when I told you I have a twin?"

Kimber nods.

"I miss her very much. She died when we were about your age."

I wrap my hand around the twin heart necklace. "When I touch this, it keeps her in my heart." I think for a moment. "I have an idea."

"What?" Gunner says.

"How about this? I'll take a picture of the beautiful ceiling your Papa painted. When I go home, I'll print out two pictures, one for each of you. That way, you'll always have your Papa with you."

Kimber drops Blossom Bunny on the floor and claps her hands.

Gunner pumps a fist in the air. "Yes!'

I grope around in my pocket for my cell phone before it dawns on me. As always, Chad took my phone when we came to New Dawn. Well, damn.

I walk to the window and peer out. Chad's sitting on the front porch steps.

I fling the door open. "Hey buddy, I need my phone to take pictures for the kids."

"No can do," he says, shaking his head. "I got chewed out big time when you went on your little stroll and couldn't find you."

I try my intimidating glare and he caves a little.

"I guess I could take the pictures," he says, "And send them to your phone after we leave."

I scamper onto the porch and give him a hug. "Chad, you're the best! Thanks."

His face turns bright red. "Whatta ya want me to shoot?"

He takes a bunch of photos, including one of the twins gazing up at the ceiling. After I thank him again, he steps outside and closes the door.

Kimber unzips one of Blossom Bunny's ears and pulls out a pen. "This was Papa's pen. I keep it here to remember him."

Gunner says, "And I wear camo stuff like Papa."

This time, I clap my hands. "Very good!"

It's time for me to go. I kiss the kids goodbye.

When my hand is on the doorknob, I hear Anna say, "Mel."

I turn as she emerges from her private quarters. She hurries across the room and presses a folded scrap of paper into my hand.

"Call me later." She turns and herds the twins from the room.

"Wait," I call, but the door closes behind her.

I slam a palm against my forehead in frustration. This place is giving me a major headache, as well as high anxiety. The last New Dawn person to give me his phone number died shortly after. The secretive manner in which Anna slipped me the note makes me wonder if Chad has been assigned to spy on her. I briefly consider tormenting him again to see if I can get at the truth, but abandon the idea. His fear and respect for Hitchcock far outweigh anything I'm capable of.

When I climb in the truck, Chad tells me, "The boss wants to see you before we go."

"Why?"

Chad shrugs. "He didn't tell me."

Irritated, I glance at the time. Billy plans to pick me up at six. It's now after four. After another conversation with Hitchcock and the one-hour plus drive to 3 Peaks, I'll be lucky if I have time to jump in the shower. And now, Anna's phone number is burning a hole in my pocket.

I assume we're heading for Hitchcock's office, but Chad drives to the range. It's busy today with at least ten people blasting away at paper targets. He stops next to a small building with dark-tinted windows.

"He's inside. I'll wait here for you. Got anymore of them crackers?"

I hand him the box. "They're all yours."

I walk to the building, grip the doorknob and pull. It flies open and my body slams into the man who's exiting. We both step back and mutter, "Sorry."

Then, we make eye contact. I'm looking into the dark, evil soul of the last person I expect to see at New Dawn. Paul Moen is blocking the doorway and he's carrying a gun.

"Why are you here?" he growls.

"Why are *you* here?" I retort.

We're at a stalemate. Neither of us budges, not even an inch. Instead, we engage in a game of *who will be the first to look away*. Not to be outdone, I refuse to blink.

Hitchcock's mirthless chuckle breaks the spell. "I see you two know each other."

Marilee Brothers

He claps a hand on Moen's shoulder and maneuvers him to one side. "Come in, Mel. This is a hostility free zone."

I know he's attempting to make a joke. It's not working. "Chad said you wanted to see me."

"In a minute. First tell me what's going on between you two. Relationship problems?"

"Trust me," I say. "I do not have a relationship with this man, but we do have a problem. I'd prefer he doesn't have contact with a teenage girl I'm fond of."

Moen sneers at me. "She sure the hell isn't fond of you."

"I don't want to be her best friend. I'm trying to keep her out of trouble."

"Where's your big beaner friend? Busy beating up innocent people?"

"I believe the big beaner you're referring to is my Uncle Paco, and he never beats up *innocent* people." I pull out my cell phone. "I've got him on speed dial. Any messages?"

Hatred spews from his soul. "I can think of a few."

He moves toward the exit, bumping his shoulder into mine a little harder than necessary. I stagger back a couple of steps to regain my balance.

When the door slams behind him, I turn to Hitchcock. "What's his story?"

"He bought a gun from us, passed the background check and has a concealed carry permit. He comes to the range to practice. Nothing more. I could ask you the same thing."

"Personal stuff I probably shouldn't share. Let's just say we're not close friends." I wait a beat, before asking, "What did you want to see me about?"

"Now that you've spent time with us, I hope I can convince you to change your mind."

"About what?"

He winks at me. It feels weird, almost flirtatious.

"You've been extremely helpful. I'd like to offer you a permanent position. Naturally, you'd have to move to New Dawn."

I so want to roll my eyes. It takes every ounce of self-control to stop myself. "Okay, lets spell it out. You're offering me a full time position, which means I move to New Dawn, give up all control over my life and work for no pay and the common good. Sounds a little like communism to me."

He shakes a finger at me. "There it is again, the bad attitude. Obviously, I would not expect you to work for nothing. And then, you should consider the twins."

I brace myself. "What about them?

"Under the right circumstances, they could live with you."

"I thought you had an adoptive family lined up."

He strokes his chin. "Naturally, I want the twins to live with a traditional family. We have a number of single men at New Dawn in need of a wife."

He pauses and checks my body like he's buying a prize heifer.

I take a deep breath to keep from blurting something obscene and therefore, inappropriate. "I appreciate the offer. I'll think it over." I won't, of course, but if it will buy me a bit more time with the kids, I'll fake it.

He pats my cheek and gives me a benevolent smile. "Very good. I'll call you soon."

Chapter Thirty-Five

When I get home, it's five-thirty. Before I jump in the shower, I text Billy and ask if he'll give me an extra half hour.

My hair is still wet when he raps on the door. When I open it, the first thing I see is the bouquet of crimson roses in his right hand. The second thing I see is his smile. The third thing is idling in the driveway, a long black stretch limo. After factoring in the visuals, I look into his soul. Stunned, I'm unable to speak.

Billy's brows draw together. "You okay, Minnie?"

"Beautiful, " I whisper.

He lifts the bouquet. "I'm glad you like them."

The roses are gorgeous, but the flowers are not what took my breath away. "Come in, I'll find a vase."

He trails me into the kitchen. "You look nice. I haven't seen you dressed up since Paco and Aida's wedding.

The memory of their bizarre wedding in the back of an eighteen-wheeler and my hideous bridesmaid dress makes me smile. "Thanks. You look nice too."

Actually I do feel pretty in my deep blue glittery top, snug-fitting black pants and strappy heels.

Billy fills the vase with water, inserts the roses and then, cups my face in his palms and presses his forehead against mine. "You saw something in my soul. What was it?"

His comment surprises me. At one time, my soul reading ability was a hot button issue between us. His soul churned with emotions caused by PTSD. Crippled by psychic pain, he didn't want me to think he was weak. It resulted in the incident that led to our break-up. Those negative emotions are no longer present in his soul, but I'm not ready to admit, even to myself, what I'm now seeing.

I place my hands over his. "I see something wonderful, Billy. I can't really put it into words. When I figure it out, I'll let you know."

He pulls away and cocks his head to one side, his typical posture when expressing doubt. "You're the boss. Let me know when you're ready to tell me."

Now, I'm the one who looks away. "Okay."

He takes my hand and leads me to the door. "I've got a surprise for you in the limo."

"You really jumped into this wooing thing with both feet."

"You'd better believe it, baby."

The surprise turns out to be Kendra and her hubby, Craig. Typical Kendra, she doesn't hide behind the dark-tinted windows, but bursts from the limo, clatters down the sidewalk in high heels and pulls me into a bear hug.

"Isn't this fun?" she exclaims, patting her hair back in place. "I get a few kid-free hours, dinner out and time with my bestie. Hard to beat." She drags me to the limo where I greet Craig who smooches me on the cheek.

Wedged between Kendra and Billy, I ask, "Where are we going?"

Kendra grabs my hand and squeezes. "Adele's. Do

you know how hard it is to get a table at Adele's?"

I admit I do not, since the majority of my days are spent in a sports bar.

Billy thumps his chest. "Chalk it up to my manly charm. Adele took one look at me, batted her fake eyelashes and said, 'Whatever you want, big boy.' "

"Oh, please," I say.

Craig chuckles and Kendra says, "Yeah, you're great at charming eighty-year-old women."

"Hey," Billy protests. "She's not a day over seventy-five."

The limo pulls up in front of a charming bungalow, painted sage green with white trim. A broad sidewalk lined with manicured shrubs leads to the double front doors. A white picket fence surrounds the property. Round flowerbeds filled with daffodils and tulips add a touch of color.

"Excellent example of Craftsman architecture," Craig announces.

Kendra and I exchange a quizzical look.

"Enlighten us," Billy says.

We exit the limo and Craig points out various features. "Craftsman homes are usually constructed of wood siding and brick, and feature low, gabled roofs and broad front porches. Check out the dormer windows. Wow, they're six over one."

I've never known Craig to be so eloquent and enthusiastic. Obediently, we look at the windows in the upper story of the bungalow.

"They're called six over one," he says, "because the upper sash has six panes and the lower, just one. It's the sign of a true Craftsman."

Kendra takes his arm. "Okay Mr. Architectural

Digest, it's time to eat."

The inside of the bungalow is just as charming. Dramatic dark red walls. A curved bar. Glowing lantern lights on each table. A menu priced way over my budget. More than likely, it's over Billy's budget too.

"I'm not that hungry," I say. "An appetizer will be fine."

In typical Billy fashion, he takes the comment as a challenge. "Fine. I'll order for the both of us."

Kendra and Craig are thoroughly enjoying our verbal sparring. Kendra doesn't say a word—highly unusual—and smiles at Craig, making me wonder if he's kicking her under the table.

The champagne arrives with a flourish. FYI, after working in a bar and seeing too many drunken fools, I usually stick to cranberry juice. Not tonight. It would be crass to refuse, since champagne is obviously an integral part of the wooing process. Naturally, the delightful bubbly goes right to my head. I begin to jabber like my tongue is tied in the middle and flapping at both ends, my mother's favorite saying about people who talk too much. Billy looks amused.

Over the entrees, blackened scallops with onion and pepper polenta as well as braised short ribs, I blurt, "I saw Paul Moen today. He hates my guts."

Kendra says, "Who's Paul Moen?"

Billy sets his fork down. "How could anybody hate your guts?"

"Apparently, he does."

"I heard you and Paco paid him a visit."

I frown at him. "And you know this…how?"

"A buddy of mine was in the same building where Moen has his office. He saw you and Paco go inside and heard a big commotion."

I sigh. "Is nothing secret in this town?"

Billy laughs. "I hope you scared the shit out of him."

"We did, but now he's got a gun. He goes to the shooting range at New Dawn. When he pulls the trigger, he's probably thinking about me."

Kendra gives me a goofy, drunken grin. "Maybe we need to go undercover again."

Craig and Billy say together. "No way."

My brain is still loopy. My tongue is still flapping. "Hitchcock wants me to move to New Dawn and hook up with some camo-clad guy so we can adopt the twins."

A long, stunned silence follows.

Finally, Billy says, "And your answer?"

"I didn't say yes and I didn't say no. Naturally, I have no intention of moving to New Dawn. But if I flat out refused, Hitchcock would make sure I never see the kids again." I take a shaky breath and feel hot tears sting my eyes. "And that's not okay with me."

Billy is not pleased. "So now, Paul Moen enters the picture."

Kendra says, "Maybe you should take a break from New Dawn."

Craig nods.

I swipe at my tears and grip the edge of the table. They don't understand. "I have to see the twins. They need me."

My weepy confession pretty much puts a damper on the evening.

Back in the limo, Billy puts his arm around me and pulls me close. He whispers, "I worry about you,

Minnie. You wear your heart on your sleeve."

I look up into his clear, hazel eyes and know the love he has for me is real. I've been in deep denial, trying to convince myself it's just a fleeting emotion. It's not. Several months ago, I asked Steve what romantic love looks like in the soul. He said, Like a deep crimson rose in full bloom. At first, it drifts across the soul, never touching down. In a committed relationship, it's in a fixed position and takes on a golden hue as if touched by a beautiful sunset. Tonight, when I looked into Billy's soul, I saw the deep red rose tinged with gold. It's uppermost in his soul and in a fixed position.

Feeling safe and in peace, I snuggle into his chest and doze off.

Chapter Thirty-Six

When the limo stops in front of my place, I jerk awake, rising up suddenly and striking Billy's chin with the top of my head. "Oops, so sorry."

He chuckles. "No problem. It brings back an excellent memory."

I know exactly what he's talking about. The first time we made love, we engaged in a mock sparring contest in which I bounced to my feet, struck his chin and practically knocked him out. I snicker at the memory. "Turned out okay though."

"Until I screwed it up."

I snuggle closer. "We don't have to live in the past."

The limo driver opens the door.

Kendra says, "Want us to leave you here, Billy?"

He shakes his head. "Not part of the wooing plan. I'll walk her to the door."

Yes, part of me is disappointed. But, God forbid, I should interfere with Billy's wooing protocol. Kendra and Craig find this hilarious. Their laughter trails behind us like musical footsteps, as Billy takes me to the door. He drops a chaste kiss on my forehead.

"Oh, come on," I say. "You can do better than that."

And he does, leaving me on shaky legs and weak with longing.

I have no pride. "Are you sure you don't want to come in?"

His expression is fierce and proud. "Yes, I want to come in and show you how much I love you, but I'll save it for another time."

Our gazes meet and I nod. "Okay, another time."

He spins around and jogs to the limo, like he's afraid if he looks back, he'll change his mind.

After I change into comfy clothes, I spot the scrap of paper with Anna's phone number. I check the time. Not quite ten. I dither a while. Is it too late to call? Maybe, like high security prisons, they have a lights out curfew at New Dawn. I decide to risk it and punch in her number.

She answers on the first ring with a tentative, "Hello?"

"Hi Anna, it's Mel."

Utter silence. It makes me wonder if she's alone.

"Anna? Are you there?"

"Yeah, hang on a sec."

Hmm, is Anna entertaining a rugged outdoorsman wearing camouflage jammies? My imagination begins to run wild. Settle down, Mel.

I hear a rustling sound and footsteps. A door opens and closes.

"There's something you need to know," she says. "Hitchcock has plans for the twins."

"Yes, he told me."

"What, exactly, did he say?"

"That he wanted them in a traditional family. Mother and father."

"Did he say where?"

I think about my last conversation with Hitchcock

and his attempt to entice me to move. "I assumed he was referring to New Dawn. Why?"

"He's got a deal going with people in Portland who are willing to pay big bucks for the twins."

Black spots dance before my eyes as the blood leaves my brain. My knees buckle and I sit on the edge of the bed. I whisper, "He's *selling* them?"

"Yeah, I thought you should know. I'm going to hang up now."

"Wait!" I desperately try to come up with something to keep her talking. I recall Hitchcock's words. *We have a number of single men at New Dawn who need a wife.* Anna is a single woman. "Anna, why aren't you married? Hitchcock says there's a bunch of eligible men. If you married, you could keep the kids."

"Long story," she says and clicks off.

I punch in her number, but she doesn't answer.

Sleep doesn't come easy. I toss and turn, punch my pillow and finally drift off into dreams jumbled with disturbing images of Kimber and Gunner being dragged into a car by a well-dressed middle-aged couple. Kimber is clutching Blossom Bunny and crying. Gunner, still dressed in camo, looks pale and defeated.

I fight my way to consciousness. It's still dark and I'm exhausted, but unwilling to slip back into dreamland. I opt for coffee instead. Seated at the table, I check the messages on my phone.

Nick. Last night. Eight-thirty p.m.

—Need some advice about Ziggy.—

Damn, when did I turn into The Designated Advisor of Teenage Girls?

****

"How long has she been gone?"

234

We're done prepping for the lunch crowd and taking a break before the doors open.

Nick says, "Since last night. She left me a note."

He slaps a sheet of paper on the bar. It says, "I'm spending a few days with a friend. No biggie. Don't panic. Just needed a little time off. I'll be in touch soon."

I study the note, obviously written on a computer with a word processing program. The only hand-written item is the large Z scrawled at the bottom in black ink. I splay my hand across the paper. "Do you think she wrote this?"

Nick nods.

"Does she have access to a computer and printer?"

"Yeah," he says. "In my office."

"And, you have no idea who the friend is?"

He shakes his head. "Is it time to panic? Call the cops?"

"I don't know. Maybe." I think about the note, how easy it would be for anyone to type it up, print it out and sign it with a Z. "Does she usually sign her name with a Z?"

Nick shrugs. "Hell if I know. She never left me a note before."

"Do you want to report her missing? I can call Billy, ask him how it works."

He says, "It hasn't been twenty-four hours yet, so they probably won't consider her a runaway, especially with the note she left. I'm thinking, give it another day and see what happens."

"Okay, fingers crossed."

Billy comes in for lunch. I want to tell him about Ziggy, but he has another agenda.

"You planning on going up to New Dawn again?"

"It depends." I fill him in on the soul reading I'm doing for Hitchcock. "It's the only way I can see the kids. And, I have to see the kids."

His forehead furrows in suspicion. "Have you seen anything shady at New Dawn?"

I think about what I observed in the call center, and my last meeting with the two guys paying big bucks for *product*. I'd like to dump all this information on Billy, but I can't. I don't want to jeopardize our tentative, new relationship. If I share my sketchy knowledge, he'll jump in with both feet. Then, I'll have to sneak around in order to see the kids. I pick my words carefully. "I have no definite proof of any wrong doing, but I'll keep my eyes open."

"Do you feel safe there?"

"So far, I do."

"What do you mean, so far?"

I put a hand on my hip and cop an attitude. "Hey, you're talking to a girl who can field strip a Glock and recite the Twelve Golden Rules of Safe Gun Handling."

He chuckles. "But, can you shoot one?"

"Sort of."

"Is it on your person? Can I pat you down?"

I fake-punch his shoulder. "Not on my person, but you can still pat me down."

His eyes light up with enthusiasm. "Hold that thought."

He leaves a twenty-dollar tip on the table. I catch him at the door and try to give it back. "It's too much."

He waves me off. "My choice. Live with it."

As I clear off the table, Nick saunters over. "You two back together?'

"We're working on it. It's a little awkward right now." I describe the wooing process Billy is so fixated upon.

When he stops laughing, Nick says, "I have an idea."

He leans close and whispers his suggestion.

At first, I gasp in surprise. Then, I think it over. "Brilliant," I say.

Chapter Thirty-Seven

During my break, I attempt to contact Hitchcock. After talking to Anna, I'm hearing *tick, tick, tick*. How much time remains before he decides to make money selling a couple of cute little kids? In our conversation yesterday, I told him I'd think about moving to New Dawn, even though I have no intention of doing so. Still, I have a skill set he wants. I need to take advantage of it as long as possible. He's using the twins as a pawn. In spite of Anna's fears, I don't think he'll act if there's a possibility of luring me to the compound.

His phone goes to voice mail. I leave the following message. "Ken, I'm arranging my work schedule for next week and need to know if you'll require my services. Please let me know."

I check every fifteen minutes for a reply, to no avail. Therefore, I'm free to carry out the plan suggested by Nick. I send a text to Billy.

—I'm off at midnight. If so inclined, meet me in Number Ten.—

His response is lightning fast.

—I'm SO inclined.—

I give Nick a thumbs up and at eleven thirty, he hands me the key to unit number ten. "Take off. You need to get ready."

I look down at my Nick's Pub pink T-shirt, jeans

and apron. "Yeah, I look real sexy."

Nick guffaws. "Somehow, I don't think it will matter."

I smooch his bristly cheek. "I'll check with you tomorrow and see if Ziggy is back. If not, we need to contact the authorities."

One of his eyebrows shoots up. "Unless I'm mistaken, one of the *authorities* will be available in Number Ten."

My face heats up and I mutter, "Oh, yeah, you're right."

His laughter follows me as I exit through the kitchen.

When I unlock the door to Number Ten, I'm swamped with a tsunami of emotions. This was my first home away from home. I'd arrived in 3 Peaks with little but the clothes on my back. Even with my lack of waitressing experience, Nick hired me and gave me a place to call home. Yes, I've paid my dues. Under the iron thumb of Connie, Queen of the Motel Maids, I earned my keep, cleaning up more than one disgusting room. Fortunately, I've become more valuable as a server and no longer under the thumb of Queen Connie.

Number Ten has history. If the walls could talk, I'd be blushing. Billy and I first got together in Number Ten and I remember every teensy detail. The heat had been building between us and it was inevitable we would act upon it. Billy was experienced. I was the novice. Not that I was virginal, but most of my encounters had been in haste, fumbling in the cramped back seat of various and sundry automobiles. In other words, Billy initiated me into the joys of sexual union. His goal was to make me happy. And, he did, at least, until he cheated on me. No, I haven't forgotten. I wish I could, but I can't. But, I will do my best to put it out of my mind tonight.

In all fairness, as I step into the shower, I wonder if Billy is thinking about Mick, like I'm thinking about his fling with Haley, last name unknown. It's hard to forget and forgive when the love of your life cheats on you. I know he was screwed up with PTSD at the time, but a little nagging voice in my brain says, "What if he does it again?"

Note to self: ask Billy what he thinks about my relationship with Mick. Do you really want to know, Mel? Yes, I do.

Squeaky clean and sprawled on the bed, I check my messages, hoping to hear from Ken Hitchcock. Nothing. I'm tempted to call Anna and check on the twins, but come on, it's almost midnight. Not much I can do until tomorrow. Let it go, Mel. You can cut loose once in a while.

Billy arrives at five minutes after midnight, another bouquet of red roses clutched in his hand. I answer the door with a towel wrapped around the essential parts. His eyes widen in appreciation.

"You didn't have to bring roses," I say. "I still have the ones from yesterday."

He says, "I'd like to bring you roses every day."

I take the roses to the bathroom, put some water in the basin and make sure the stems are covered.

When I return, Billy holds out his arms. "Get in here, Minnie. We've got some catching up to do."

I step into his embrace. The towel falls to the floor. He sweeps me up and sits on the edge of the bed with me on his lap.

"Talk first," he says.

Safe in his embrace, I look into his eyes and smile.

He meets my gaze without hesitation. "Isn't it about time to tell me what you see?"

I think about my options. I can tell him what I see, or I can fudge a little as I did before. L-O-V-E. Such a little word. So easily uttered insincerely by people with an agenda. I believe I'm seeing the real thing in Billy's soul, but what if I'm wrong? Maybe Billy is thinking about all the beautiful roses he wants to bring to me. I decide to go for it. "I've seen the same thing in your soul for the last few months. I didn't know what it meant and asked Steve." I pause and take a deep breath.

He says, "What did you see?"

I describe the crimson rose, how it floated across his soul, and is now in a fixed position with golden highlights.

"Is that a good thing?"

I nod. "Yes. It's a very good thing. I don't want to tell you what you feel and, if I'm wrong, no hard feelings."

He sets me down on the bed and cups my face in his hands. "You don't have to say another word. The rose is a symbol and what you're seeing is my love for you."

My chest feels tight. Tears well in my eyes and spill down my cheeks. "Yes."

He leans closer until his lips are against my ear. "You don't need to read my soul to know that."

I know the response he's looking for. I love Billy. I do. But, it will take time for me to regain trust and utter the words. Thankfully, he understands. He stretches out next to me. I feel him shaking with need. When I look into his soul, I see desire burning hot and barely under control.

I lever myself up on one elbow and stare down at him. "You're still fully clothed. Why?"

He needs no more encouragement and strips off his clothes. He is lean, muscular and magnificently aroused.

I hold out my arms, inviting him in. "Wow, I think you're glad to see me."

"You have no idea."

His lips are warm as he trails kisses down the length of my body. "You first," he murmurs. "You first. Always."

His warm, moist lips linger on my belly a little longer than necessary. I twitch and moan. He looks up and we make eye contact. I see the old competitive gleam is back. For a brief moment, I wonder if he's thinking, *I need to be better at this than Mick,* and I almost smile. But then, his lips move lower and I'm in a fever of need. His warm, wet tongue flicks over the heated, sensitive bit of flesh so eager for his touch. I stiffen as my climax sweeps over me in waves of ecstasy, stealing the breath from my body.

True to form, he holds off on his own desire until he's sure I'm fully satisfied. He covers my body with his, taking care not to crush me with his weight. I welcome him into my body in the familiar way of experienced lovers.

Later, much later, I murmur, "Now what?"

He props himself up and gazes down at me. "Have you heard from Mick after he moved?"

"He texted me a few times. Nothing lately."

He shakes his head as if he can't believe it. "I

would never leave you behind, Minnie. Never. If I needed to move for a job and you decided not to go with me, I'd stay. That's a promise."

I gaze into his soul and know the words he uttered are sincere. "I believe you. I just need a little time to sort things out."

"Take all the time you want." He presses his forehead against mine. "Somehow, I don't think I'm competing with another guy for your attention. I think it's a pair of five-year-old twins. Tell me about them."

My heart is full and the words spill out like water bursting from a high-pressure hose. "Oh, Billy, they're so sweet and I love them so much." I tell him about their past, how Jake Gunderson raised them as his own and now, about their precarious situation living with Anna in the school house. Finally, I finish with "Anna says Hitchcock has plans to sell them."

Billy frowns down at me. "You can't sell kids. It's against the law."

"I'm sure he's figured out a way to make it legal."

Billy turns me over until we're in a spooning position. He's quiet for so long, I think he's fallen asleep. Finally, he says, "So, do you have a plan?"

Good question. "I'm working on it."

He sighs. "That's what I thought. I'll help if I can." His breathing evens out as he drifts off to sleep.

Not me. My mind is still racing and I realize Kimber and Gunner are not the only worry keeping me awake. I blurt, "Ziggy took off."

Billy awakes with a jerk. "Huh?'

After I fill him in on the latest Ziggy crisis, he says, "Aw, give it a rest, Minnie. It'll wait until tomorrow. After twenty-four hours, Nick can report her missing."

My mind doesn't work that way. Once I start fretting about something, sleep is not an option.

After Billy is sleeping soundly, I slip from his embrace and go to the window. I part the drapes and peer through the crack. It's well after midnight. Most of the hard-core drinkers have split and the motel is flashing a *no vacancy* sign. I smile as I spot Thunder Paws sitting on the back steps of the pub, waiting for a handout. Is it possible I miss living in a motel?

Finally feeling drowsy, I'm ready for bed. As I release the drapes, I glimpse a car pulling into the parking lot. I pull the drapes apart again and spot an old junker car with primer on the sides and a tan, flaking vinyl roof. I know this car. It belongs to green-haired Benny. Is he the friend Ziggy is spending time with? I watch as it stops, make a U turn and drives slowly out of the lot. Benny is clearly alone.

Where the hell is Ziggy?

Chapter Thirty-Eight

Billy has an early shift and leaves before I'm awake. When I pry my eyes open, I find a note pinned on his pillow.

"Hey, Minnie Mouse,

Sorry to bail out so early. I made coffee. I'll check with you later. Let me know if you need help with Ziggy."

The note is signed with a giant, somewhat egotistical, B to which he's added a pair of legs astride a Harley Davidson. The note ends with a string of hearts pierced with arrows, followed by multiple X's and O's. I can't help but snicker. Who knew Billy was so creative?

Over coffee, I check my messages. Nothing from Hitchcock. I try calling him again. He doesn't answer. I leave another message, even though I'm afraid it sounds a bit desperate. "Still waiting to hear from you. Let me know if you need me next week."

I follow up with a call to Nick. "Ziggy back yet?"

"Nope. I called the school. She didn't show up."

A half-baked plan is forming in my tired brain. I need to follow up with Benny, see what he knows. Ethically, I need to keep Nick in the loop. "Last night, I saw one of Ziggy's friends pull into the parking lot. She wasn't with him, but he might know something. I know where he lives. If it's okay with you, I'll pay him a visit."

"Damn, girl, would you do that for me?" The relief is palpable in his voice.

I know I'm enabling him. Nick's the dad. He's the one who should be out searching for his daughter. I can't help myself, because I remember how screwed up I was when I was sixteen. But then, I had Sandra, who would move heaven and earth to save me. Besides, I've got nothing to lose. Ziggy already hates me. Maybe I can salvage her relationship with Nick.

As I gather my belongings and head for the door, my ears are assaulted by a familiar *squeak, squeak, squeak.* It's a sound I know well. Connie, Queen of the Motel Maids is pushing her squeaky-wheeled cleaning cart, making her rounds. I sit on the edge of the bed, waiting for her to pass by, after which I'll zip out the door and dash to the car. At least, that's my plan.

The sound stops directly outside the door of Number Ten, blocking my escape route. Then, the jangle of keys and the door flies open.

Connie, now sporting bright red hair streaked with pink highlights, screeches, "*Ay, caramba*, it *is* you! Why you back? Want a job? Number twelve needs cleaning."

I shake my head. "Just visiting."

She cocks her head to one side and studies the bed. "*Si*, I think Billy the Keed is still in your life. Billy the Keed is macho man. Is Connie right?"

Unable to speak, I nod.

She takes a step closer and lowers her voice to a seductive purr. "What about your Uncle Paco? Tell him Connie still has *mucho caliente* dreams about him."

All I want is to get the hell out of here, so I choose

not to inform Connie of Paco's marital status and impending fatherhood. "I'll be sure to give him your regards, Connie. Gotta run. Bye."

Before she can press me into service, I slip by her and head for Buttercup. I fire up the engine and pull out into the traffic streaming by the pub. I'd like to go home and freshen up before launching into my plan, but somehow, I think earlier is better for what I'm about to do.

When I arrive at Benny's apartment complex, I'm relieved to see his disgusting-looking car in the lot. In the back of my mind, I'd considered driving to the school where he and Ziggy are enrolled. Silly me. Of course, he decided to cut classes after his late night doing who knows what?

I'd also thought about calling Paco. He'd be willing and eager to scare the crap out of Benny again. Same story with Billy. But, I decide to opt for a woman's touch. Even though Benny isn't much younger than me, he's still a kid. Smoking a butt load of marijuana tends to stunt your emotional growth. If I'm right, Benny is probably working things out with the mental capabilities of a fourteen-year-old boy. I could be wrong, but it's worth a try.

As I walk his door, I remember the elderly gentleman who is not fond of Benny. I rap on his door. Footsteps approach.

The door opens a crack and a bristly face appears. "Do I know you?"

I give him my dimpled smile. "Hello there, sir. We met a while back when I came to retrieve my sister from your neighbor, Benny. Do you know if he's home?"

247

"Yeah," he growls. "The little shit's home. Came in late last night. Blasted his damn music 'til three in the morning. Had to call the manager again. They need to throw his ass out of here."

"Okey dokey, then. Thanks. Have a good day."

He opens the door wider. "You a friend of his?"

"Not really," I admit. "I'm trying to track down my sister again and thought maybe she was here."

"No," he says. "I saw him come in last night. By himself. The walls here are thin. If he had a girl in his apartment, I'd have heard her. I'm not deaf, ya know."

"Many thanks," I say and edge away.

He watches as I move to Benny's apartment and rap on the door.

"Waste of time," he growls. "Not an early riser." With that, he retreats, but keeps the door open.

When Benny doesn't respond, I hammer the door with my fist and yell, "Open up, Benny. It's Mel. Don't be scared, I'm by myself."

The drapes part narrowly. A heavy-lidded bloodshot eye topped by a lock of greasy green hair peers out at me. The eye darts back and forth, checking for danger. When he sees none, he opens the window a crack. "Where's the gang banger?"

"I told you, I'm alone. Can I come in?"

He slams the window shut, shuffles to the door and opens it. I'm treated to a full-length view of his scrawny bod, clad only in grubby beige pajama bottoms barely clinging to his bony hips. His bare chest sports a tattoo of a full-sized marijuana plant, the words Mary Jane, and the image of a nubile young woman clad in short shorts and a halter-top. I'm momentarily speechless.

His head swivels left and right, his nostrils flaring, sniffing the air for danger. "You sure you're alone?"

"Yes, Benny. I'm alone."

Aware of his lifestyle, I'm betting he has the munchies. "How about you get dressed, my friend, and I'll take you to breakfast. You look like you could use a good meal."

His expression brightens and he steps out onto the landing. "Far out, man."

I take him by the shoulders, turn him around and give him a little push. "I *said*, go get dressed. Pants. Shirt. Shoes. Got it?"

He shuffles inside. "Yeah, yeah, I got it. No shirt, no shoes, no service."

Once inside the diner, I make sure were seated well away from the crowd. Benny orders the Big Boy special, the three-egg omelet with diced ham along with biscuits and gravy. My tummy is growling after a night with Billy, so I settle for a veggie omelet with hash browns. I feel super righteous about the vegetables.

We wait for our order, slurping coffee and gazing suspiciously at each other across the table. I let the silence settle, hoping Benny will be uncomfortable. He leans back against the bench seat and closes his eyes, awakening only when our food arrives. We dig in, still not talking. I thought I was good at waiting, but Benny is better. I know when I'm beat.

I say, "Saw you last night. You drove into the parking lot at Nick's, then turned around and drove away. I thought maybe Ziggy was with you, but she wasn't."

He scrapes the last bit of food from his plate and stuffs it in his mouth. I admit I'm surprised when he uses his napkin to wipe his mouth. It makes me wonder if Benny has a caring mother somewhere who taught him table manners.

Finally, he says, "Yeah, about that. I wanted to check and see if she made it home, but I chickened out when I saw her dad come out the back door."

I don't want to spook him so I try, very hard, not to sound threatening. "Back from where?"

He shrugs. "Well, you know. From there."

I want to reach across the table, wrap my hands around his scrawny neck and scream, "There? Where the hell is there?" But, I don't. Instead, I take a deep breath and try to think like a fourteen-year-old. "I guess you're worried about her too. Her dad is waiting for her to come home. Do you know where she is?"

He blinks rapidly. "You don't know?"

"No, Benny. I don't know. That's why I'm feeding you breakfast and asking you."

"Aw, man," he says. "Maybe she's with Darcy."

Calling on the last shred of my patience, I say, "Who's Darcy?"

He gives me his full, frontal sleepy-eyed stare. "She's a chick from school. I think she and Ziggy are tight."

"Ziggy told her dad she was staying with a friend. Do you know where Darcy lives?"

"Yeah, I gave her a ride once."

Maybe Ziggy was telling the truth in her note to Nick. Maybe she's hanging out with a girlfriend. But, something doesn't ring true. I need to pry more information from Benny. "Obviously you care about Ziggy. Otherwise, you wouldn't have been checking on her last night. Talk to me."

His furtive glance darts around the room. Then, he gazes at the tabletop and lowers his voice to a whisper. "I could be wrong, but the last time I saw her, she was hanging with some bad dudes. That's why I'm worried about her, man. She's a sweet kid. She doesn't know what's she's getting into."

"Like what?"

"Aw, shit! I guess you don't know."

"So, tell me."

He peers into my eyes. "I heard they hook girls on drugs and then, you know, make them do bad things."

I lean across the table and whisper, "Like prostitution."

He nods. "Exactly."

"Will you show me where Darcy lives?"

"Sure."

The good news? He's not lying. The bad news? Benny's memory has been heavily influenced by the love affair with his favorite girlfriend, Mary Jane.

Chapter Thirty-Nine

Benny directs me to a shabby trailer park at the edge of town. He points out Darcy's home, a vintage thirty-five foot trailer with a flaking paint job and aluminum foil covering the windows. A series of warped boards are propped against the bottom of the trailer in a feeble attempt at skirting. My empathy for Darcy is growing by the second. No kid should have to grow up in a place like this.

Benny stays in the car while I climb onto the cement blocks serving as steps and rap on the door. I hear a television program playing in the background and the sound of shuffling footsteps.

The door opens, revealing an elderly woman with bright blue eyes. Her head is crowned with fluffy, white hair like a dandelion gone to seed. She's clad in red polyester pants, a baggy white sweater and slippers. Another thought circles my brain. No old lady should have to live in a place like this.

She looks me over. "What can I do for you? Are you from the school? Did Darcy skip out again?"

I explain that I'm looking for Ziggy and ask about Darcy's whereabouts.

She frowns and a cloud of suspicion shoots through her soul, dimming the brightness of her gaze. "My granddaughter isn't here. Haven't seen her for two days. When I got home from bingo that day, she was gone. Left a note, said she was staying with Ziggy."

"I was hoping I'd find Ziggy here."

"More than likely, they've run off together. Darcy does it on a regular basis." She heaves a dispirited sigh. "I'm too damn old for this."

She fetches the note. It's similar in content to Ziggy's, obviously written on a computer and signed with her name scrawled at the bottom.

"Maybe you should report her missing."

She waves a dismissive hand. "Why? She'll turn up in a few days. Probably Ziggy too."

I give her my contact information and ask her to call if she hears from Darcy.

I join Benny in the car. His chin rests on his bony chest. It's morning naptime. When I slam the door, he snaps to attention, rubbing his eyes.

"No Darcy?"

"No Darcy or Ziggy," I say.

"Bummer. Now what?"

"You said Ziggy was hanging around with some bad dudes. Do you know where I can find them?"

He pulls out his cell phone and steps out of the car. "Give me a sec." He strides away from the car and turns his back.

I can't make out his words, but there's a whole lot of gesticulating going on with his free hand.

When he returns to the car, his sleepy eyes sparkle with excitement and he offers a fist to bump. "Damn, this is cool. You and I make an awesome crime-fighting duo. Like Batman and Robin."

I return the fist bump and bite back a sarcastic response. Batman and Robin, also known as, Nosey Mel and her stoner sidekick, green-haired Benny. I say,

"So, I guess we're on our way to a new location. Right?"

"Wrong. I don't know the location yet. The guy I talked to has to talk to another guy who might know. It's how stuff like this works."

"Enlighten me."

"These dudes have a bunch of drug houses. If things gets hot in one place, they move to another."

It's time to cut to the chase. "Bottom line, Benny. Does your friend know where the girls are?"

His brow furrows in concentration as he tries to formulate an answer. "Maybe." His cell phone buzzes and, once again in spy mode, he steps out of the car to take the call. He nods and, using his pointer finger, he writes on Buttercup's dusty hood. He opens the car door. "This isn't a sure thing, but I got the address of one of the drug houses. Good thing you don't wash your car and it ain't raining, cause I don't got paper and pencil."

He does his best to guide me. We make frequent stops to check his notes on the hood. Just when I think we're hopelessly lost and going in circles, he points at a street sign labeled Ponderosa.

"Turn there."

Buttercup screeches in alarm as I crank her into an abrupt left turn. The asphalt peters out and we're on a rutted dirt road.

"You sure about this?" I ask Benny.

"Yep. Keep going.

We bump along for at least a mile. The houses are spaced farther and farther apart.

Benny leans forward and points at a one-story cement block rambler set back from the road. It looks like a typical family home with an attached garage and kids' bicycles parked under the overhanging roof next to the front door. "There." After his one word declaration, he slithers down in the seat until he's out of view from oncoming cars or anyone else remotely interested. He whispers, "These guys are dangerous. They might think I'm a narc."

It's then I realize half my intrepid crime-fighting duo has an extreme case of the jitters. I pat his knee. "No problem. I'll handle it now." I drive past the house. "I have a plan. Since I'm going solo I'll need a wardrobe change. Take off your shirt."

"Huh?

Actually my plan isn't entirely fleshed out, so let's call it a glimmer of a plan.

A quarter mile down the road, I make a U turn and stop. I strip off my denim jacket and pull the Nick's Pub T-shirt over my head. I hand it to Benny who is seemingly in a state of suspended animation. Not surprisingly, his gaze is locked on my boobage, which I would describe as not voluptuous, but adequate in size and perkiness. I snap my fingers in front of his face. "Shirt. Now."

Still staring at my chest, he smiles dreamily and whips off the black T-shirt emblazoned with a death's head. I dig a tissue out of my purse, wipe off my lipstick and run my fingers through my hair until it's standing on end. I look over at Benny. "Do I pass?"

"As what?"

"As a teenage girl you might see at a rave, who's looking for drugs."

Benny's eyes widen in appreciation. "You definitely pass. So, you're playing the drug angle?"

"Got a better idea?"

"No, but you need to be careful."

I drive slowly to the house, pull into the driveway and park. I reach for the door handle. "You keep watch, okay?"

"Well, duh, of course I will. We need a secret sign, though. In case something goes wrong. Partners always have a secret sign."

"How about this, Benny, if I turn around and scream, 'Call 911,' that will be our sign."

"Okey dokey. Good luck."

I pick my way across a sparse lawn dotted with patchy weeds. As I step to the front door, I hear shrieks of laughter and applause from a TV game show playing in the background. Drapes covering the front window part briefly. A face appears. Before I lift my hand to knock, the door flies open. A large, muscular man steps through, closes the door behind him and joins me on the porch.

He grins and laugh lines appear around his startling blue eyes. His gaze roves over my body. "What can I do for you, sweet thing?"

I'm momentarily struck dumb. Not sure what I expected, but this guy is hot. Clad in jeans and a white, strapped T-shirt, commonly known as a wife beater, he's oozes sex appeal. His well-defined biceps are emphasized with elaborate tattoos. Add to the picture, a casual brush cut, a dark five o'clock shadow, those mesmerizing eyes and what do you get? The perfect honey trap for teenage girls. Judging from my visceral reaction, I should add, and women of all ages. I give myself a stern warning. He's one of the bad guys, Mel.

I'm still trying to string a few words together when

he says, "What's your name, honey? I'm Pete."

"I'm, uh, Jamie."

He points at Buttercup. "Is that your car? Kind of a beater, huh?"

"Yeah, it was my Grandma's car. I got it when she died."

He folds his arms and gazes down at me. "What brings you here?"

I shiver a little and use the back of my hand to wipe my nose. "My friend, Ziggy said I might be able to get some stuff from you guys. You know what I'm talking about. Right?"

Something flickers across his ice-cold soul when I mention Ziggy. Is he one of her captors? Is she inside the house? I'm so tempted to scream out her name, but that would be incredibly stupid.

"So, you're a friend of Ziggy's?"

"Yeah, is she here?"

As the words come out of my mouth, his gaze flicks away from mine. I'm not able to see in his soul, but his body language indicates he's uncomfortable with the question.

"No, why would she be here?"

When I don't answer, he looks me over again. "Such a pretty little girl. Sounds like you need something to make you feel as pretty as you look."

A blush warms my cheeks. "I guess so."

"Got any money?"

"Ten bucks."

"Can't get much for ten bucks, honey. Hmm, let me think." He steps closer to me and traces a finger down my cheek.

I have to stiffen my resolve to keep from backing

away.

Once again, he flashes his engaging smile. "Lucky for you, I do take other forms of payment. I'm sure we can work something out."

Quick as a cat, his right hand grips the back of my neck and he pulls me up against his rock-hard body. His left hand fondles my butt. My face is smushed against his neck. I'm longing to use every ounce of strength in my body to smash a knee into his manly parts. In fact, I'm trembling with the desire to do so. Fortunately, he mistakes my attempt at self-control as awe and fear.

He releases me. "So, do we have a deal?"

"You mean, right now?"

He chuckles. "I'm kinda busy right now, babe. Hit me up a little later in the week and we'll talk business."

I feign disappointment. "You're not going to help me out?"

"Here's your lesson of the day, babe. The payment always comes first. Then, you get the goods. Got it?"

"Got it."

Head hanging, I slouch back to the car, feeling like I need a shower to wash away his touch. On the way back to 3 Peaks, I fill Benny in.

He's aghast. "OMG, he was totally groping you? Do you think Ziggy and Darcy are in the house?"

"Yes, I believe they are."

I know I'm in over my head. Time to call in the troops.

Chapter Forty

Billy, Nick and I are huddled in Nick's office, trying to decide the best course of action. Nick chomps at the bit, ready to break a window or beat down the door. I can tell by Billy's expression, he'd love to do the same. But, his situation is different. He's not a private citizen. As a member of the 3 Peaks police department, he has to do everything by the book. To act otherwise would put his job in jeopardy.

"Can't you or another officer knock on the door and ask about Ziggy?" I say.

"Sure, we could do that, but without a search warrant, we can't go in."

"What about probable cause?"

"Based on what? Did you ask if Ziggy was inside?"

"I did, but he looked away when I asked him. I couldn't see into his soul, but I'm pretty sure he was lying."

Billy's expression is grim. "The girls haven't been reported missing and it sounds like Ziggy's friend Darcy is a chronic runaway. Not to mention, most of the information is from a kid whose life is dedicated to smoking weed. I doubt there's a judge in 3 Peaks who would issue a search warrant."

Nick pushes away from his desk. "Screw it! I'm going out there."

Billy warns, "Don't go alone. There are probably

guns in the house. Call Paco. He knows how to deal with bad guys. I'll follow you out there and we'll be in touch by cell phone. If you need help, I'll call for reinforcements."

I whip out my phone and punch in Paco's number.

He listens carefully. "So these are the dudes who kidnap girls, hook them on drugs and force them to turn tricks to support their habit?"

"Yes."

"And Billy says I can beat the shit out of them?" His tone is gleeful at the prospect.

"No, Unc, I didn't say that. Sometimes your mere presence is extremely persuasive. You're coming along as a bodyguard for yours truly and Nick. Okay?"

To say Paco is enthusiastic is an understatement. The prospect of meting out justice to bad guys who kidnap teenage girls brings joy to his heart. "I'll be there as fast as I can. Right now, I'm grocery shopping with Aida at some friggin' organic food store."

Uncle Paco? Grocery shopping? For organic food? I try, unsuccessfully, to stifle a giggle.

"I heard that," he mutters. He lowers his voice, "The bigger her tummy gets, the happier she is. I don't want to mess it up, so cut me some slack."

An hour later, he shows up on his Harley.

Before we take off, Billy pulls me to one side, his hands cupping my face, his forehead touching mine. "I want you to be careful. We're dealing with nasty guys here. From what you said, this Pete dude probably can't wait to get his hands on you."

Although I didn't mention the groping incident, Billy zeroed right in on the risk.

"I'll be careful."

He tips my head back until I meet his gaze. "Promise?"

"I promise."

Paco and I pile into Nick's truck. The intrepid crime-fighting team has expanded to a trio. Paco, Nick and me. Four, if you count Billy who will be parked nearby, ready to help if need be.

Twenty minutes later, we're standing on the front porch of the drug house. I press the doorbell. Paco doubles up a fist and pounds on the door. Utter silence. The house has an empty feel to it. I try the doorbell again. Nothing. Nick twists the doorknob. Locked.

We step off the porch and scan the front of the house. The drapes are tightly closed. Definitely a no peek zone. Nick heads for the back of the house. Paco and I follow, checking out the dusty basement windows concealed with pull-down blinds.

The backyard has an ancient picnic table and a rusty swing set. Leaving no stone unturned, we rap on the back door and try twisting the knob. The place is sealed up like Fort Knox.

"Screw this," Paco says and pulls a slim device from his pocket.

Despite his ham-sized hands, he has a delicate touch with a lock pick. In less than a minute, the back door is open.

I'm on the phone to Billy. "We're going in."

He says, "Paco?"

"Yeah."

"Leave your phone on. Check for an alarm. If you see one, get the hell out."

We close the door behind us. No alarm. It takes a moment for our eyes to adjust to the gloom. The air inside is cold and musty and reeks of spoiled milk, greasy food and garbage. I swallow hard to keep from gagging.

Paco pulls a small but powerful LED penlight from his pocket. He flashes it around the greasy kitchen and the adjoining living room, illuminating a ratty couch, two hardback chairs and a small TV on a stand.

"We need to check the basement," Nick says, charging ahead of us.

The door leading to the basement is tightly locked. Paco picks it open and fumbles for the light switch on the wall. He flips it up and down a few times and mutters, "Power's off."

He aims the light downward, illuminating a rickety, wooden staircase. It creaks ominously under his weight.

"Be careful, little girl," he warns and grips my hand as we descend the steep stairs with no handrail. I reach back and take Nick's hand.

My feeling of dread grows as the light flashes around the small, dingy basement, completely devoid of human life. The air is permeated with the stench of raw sewage. Two cots with rumpled sleeping bags are pushed against one wall.

Paco shines his light on a plastic bucket covered with a board. "Makeshift toilet."

Nick sputters, "God damn it! The girls were here. I know it. Where the hell are they?"

I get on the phone and tell Billy what's going on.

He says, "Check the garbage. If you see anything that looks like evidence, don't touch it."

Though none of us are eager to hang around longer than necessary, we track the beam of light as it bounces around the room.

"There," I say. "A garbage can under the laundry tub. I doubt it's been emptied lately.

As Paco reaches for it, I caution, "Don't touch it."

He pulls the sleeve of his shirt down to cover his hand and extracts the stained, plastic wastebasket from beneath the grubby laundry tub. It's jammed with fast food cartons empty water bottles and greasy paper towels. Paco tips the wastebasket to one side and dumps the contents onto the concrete floor. He uses his foot to separate congealed French fries and bits of moldy lunchmeat. One final nudge of his foot loosens a nasty mash-up of wadded toilet paper.

Four dirty syringes tumble out. I clap a hand over my mouth to keep from crying out.

Paco swears.

Nick's eyes glitter with fury.

Where the hell are the girls?

Chapter Forty-One

The next few hours are filled with a flurry of activity. We visit Darcy's grandmother and convince her to come with us to fill out a missing person report, along with Nick. While Billy guides them through the process, I collect Buttercup, pay another visit to Benny and tell him what we found.

"Here's the deal, Benny," I say. "You called somebody who knows about the drug house. You need to talk to the cops, give them the name of your contact. Or, you could tell me and I'll tell them."

His eyes roll with panic. "No way. Those guys are bad news. If I get labeled as a snitch, it's all over."

"I know you care about the girls. You told me you were worried about them."

I keep talking, trying to wear him down, but his fear of reprisal is stronger than my powers of persuasion. I strike out and leave feeling despondent.

Billy promises he'll light a fire under the higher-ups in the department, try to convince them it's a matter of urgency, not simply a case of two teens on the run. Nick and I go back to the pub and get to work, although our hearts aren't in it.

By the time I get home, it's well after midnight. I'm physically and emotionally drained. I check my phone one last time, hoping to hear from Ken Hitchcock or Anna. Despite the drama with Ziggy, the twins are always there in my thoughts.

I climb into bed, but sleep eludes me. My body is tired, but my mind is revved up and treating me to images of Ziggy, helpless and in a drug-induced stupor. When I finally drift off, I wake frequently to pound my pillow into submission and straighten the bed covers I've kicked off.

At three a.m., I'm awakened by the shrill summons of my cell phone. Blindly, I reach out and knock the phone off the bedside table. I switch on the light, retrieve the phone and glance at the screen. Riley Rathjen. A jolt of alarm zips through my body. I'm now fully awake. Why would Riley be calling me in the middle of the night? "Riley? What's wrong?"

"It's Ziggy, Mel. She's here and she's not in good shape. You need to come out. Now."

My brain is still a bit foggy. "Ziggy?" I repeat. "She's at your place? Darcy too? But…?"

"Not Darcy," he says. "Get out here as fast as you can."

I pull myself together. "I'll bring Nick. What about Billy? Should I call him?"

He doesn't hesitate. "Yes, bring Billy. Ziggy thinks Darcy is in big trouble."

After a quick call to Nick and Billy, I throw on some clothes and fire up Buttercup. On the drive to the Rockin' R ranch, Nick and Billy question me.

Finally, I lose my patience. "Look, guys. I've told you everything I know. Ziggy is at the ranch. Darcy isn't. We'll have answers soon."

The Rathjen house is ablaze with lights. Buttercup screeches to a stop and we run for the house. Being fleet of foot, I'm the first one to dash through the door.

The entire Rathjen family is in the living room with Ziggy who's shaking and wrapped in a blanket. When she sees Nick and me, she begins to sob.

"Daddy, Mel, I'm so sorry. I'm so, so sorry."

The Rathjens part so Nick and I can join Ziggy on the couch. We both murmur comforting words. She clings to Nick as he wraps his arms around her.

He says, "You're okay now, kiddo. Daddy's got you."

Leaving Ziggy in Nick's care, I join Billy and the Rathjen family.

Rick says, "It was the weirdest thing. It's my poker night with the guys, so I was out late. I'm heading home in the Rockin' R truck when something catches my eye. A flash of white in the ditch and it's moving. I stop the truck and roll down the window. That's when I see the girl. Guess she recognized the logo on the truck. She sort of staggers toward me, screaming, "Help me!" Didn't realize it was Ziggy at first. She looked like shit." He pauses and re-thinks his words. "Sorry. Guess you can see for yourself how she looks. Strung out. Dirty. Panicky. She said some guys were after her. Anyway, I brought her home and told Riley to call you. We didn't ask her a bunch of questions. Just tried to get her to calm down."

Billy offers his hand to Rick. "Thanks, man. A lot of people wouldn't have stopped. We'll take her to the hospital, get her checked out."

Before we leave, Ziggy goes to Rick and hugs him. Her voice is muffled against his chest. "Thank you. Thank you. You saved my life."

Rick looks embarrassed, but pats her back. Riley tells Ziggy she can have her job back whenever she wants.

We load Ziggy into the car. Nick sits in the back seat with her. Billy and I keep our mouths shut as she pieces out the story. Her tears continue to flow and she murmurs in disjointed sentence fragments

"Should have listened to you, Mel...we were stupid...should have known better...they shot us up."

The last bit makes my blood run cold, but I don't need an apology. "It's okay, sweetie. Everything will be okay."

"Darcy," she mutters. "We gotta find Darcy. Oh, God, I think she's dead."

Between sobs, the story comes out. She and Darcy were invited to a party at an abandoned warehouse, a place well known for illicit drugs. Aware they would never get permission to attend, they concocted the 'staying with a friend' story. The girls were scared and nervous about attending and made a pact that they would stick together. Drugs were being used openly and booze was flowing. The girls were handed a drink and the rest of the evening was wiped from their memories. They woke up, sick and disoriented, locked in a grubby basement.

"We had to use a bucket to go to the bathroom. Two guys were in the house. When they came into the basement with food, they wore clown masks and then..." she pauses and takes a hiccupping breath. "They injected stuff into our veins." The deeper she gets into the story, the more agitated she becomes. "Darcy freaked out. She's diabetic. She needed her insulin."

"Did she have it with her?" Billy asks.

"It was in her backpack when we went to the party.

When we woke up in the basement, it was gone. She begged the guys to find it for her. They just ignored her. One guy held her down, the other guy injected her and told her she'd be feeling better soon."

From listening to her story, I'm sure the girls were being held in the house we broke into. "Did you hear a doorbell ring or knocking on the door yesterday?"

"Yes, I heard it. Darcy was passed out and I was trying to get her to wake up. A little later, I heard a bunch of yelling. One of the guys came downstairs. He was talking on his cell phone. I couldn't hear much, but it sounded like he was getting chewed out. He said stuff like, 'Yeah, it might have been her. Black hair. Blue eyes. Short. Hey, chill. How the hell would I know who she is?' " Ziggy takes a shaky breath. "That's when I knew it was you, Mel, who rang the doorbell and knocked on the door. I had to pull myself together. I had to get help for Darcy."

We all listen without interrupting as she relates the rest of the story.

Ziggy overheard snatches of the phone conversation and knew they would be moved to another location after dark. She says, "I figured it was my only chance to get away, but first, I needed them to think I was totally out of it."

Fearful she's about to be injected again, she feigns unconsciousness. Darcy doesn't have to pretend. She's slipped into a diabetic coma.

Sometime later, the men return to the basement. One of them picks up Darcy and hauls her up the stairs. Ziggy forces herself to remain limp as she's lifted and carried from the house. Darcy is thrown onto the back seat of a four-door sedan. Ziggy is tossed, feet-first onto the floorboards. When they slam the door, it bangs against her head. It hurts like hell but she doesn't dare cry out. Ziggy is banking on men's carelessness. Obviously, they believe the girls are not an escape risk.

"It seems like we drove around for hours. Probably wasn't that long since I wasn't exactly myself at the time. My stomach was upset, big time. I kept praying I wouldn't puke. I tried to stay really still, but I was able to reach under the front seat. That's when I touched something. I ran my hand over it and realized it was one of those little umbrellas that fold up. I wrapped my fingers around it." She continues, "The car finally stopped. The driver got out, told the other guy to keep watch. I'm praying they'll take Darcy first. Please, take Darcy first. I lucked out. The driver opened the door and offloaded Darcy. He closed the door and I heard him walk away. A few minutes later, the other guy opened the door. He grabbed my shoulders and started to drag me out of the car. I, I…" She gulps back tears.

Nick pats her back. "Take your time."

"I waited until the upper half of my body was out of the car. Then, I managed to get my feet under me. I remembered Mel telling me to go for the throat, nose or eyes if I ever got attacked. I gripped the umbrella like a baseball bat and swung it at him as hard as I could. It slammed across his throat. When he staggered backward, I jammed the point of the umbrella into his crotch. He doubled over, hit the ground and started yelling for the other guy."

I reach back and pat her leg. "I'm proud of you, Ziggy."

She hoped to jump in the car and drive away but the keys weren't in it, so she took off running, knowing the men would give chase. Her only hope was to find a house, knock on the door and ask for help.

"I kept running and hiding every time I heard a car coming. In the ditch, behind trees, anywhere I could find something to duck behind. It was really dark. I tripped and fell down a bunch of times. I kept looking for a house, but there weren't any. Not sure how much time went by. Seemed like forever. I was so tired I could barely move. When I heard Rick's truck, I just dove into the ditch. Then, I saw Rockin' R Ranch on the door and who it was."

I glance into the back seat and see Ziggy is cradled in Nick's arms, her head against his chest. She whispers, "Darcy. We have to find Darcy before it's too late."

I glance up at the starry sky and direct a fervent prayer to my sister, Hope and to all the angels in heaven on behalf of Darcy. I pray they're listening.

Chapter Forty-Two

Back in 3 Peaks, I park in front of the hospital emergency room entrance.

Billy says, "Wait here. I'll go in and explain the situation."

Nick follows him in. Five minutes later, an orderly approaches the car, pushing a wheelchair.

Ziggy huffs, "Geez, I don't need a wheel chair. I'm not *old*."

Her feistiness makes me smile.

The orderly says, "Sorry, kiddo. I'm the boss."

A young ER doctor takes charge and makes the decision to keep Ziggy overnight. He gently questions her about her treatment. She tells him they had both been injected with needles several times during the two days of their captivity.

"Do I need to order a rape kit?" he asks.

She stares at the floor. "No, we were scared they would, but they didn't."

An hour later, the paperwork is done. Nick decides to stay with the Ziggy.

The doc kicks Billy and me out. "Go home," he says. "Get some sleep. We'll clean her up and check her out. There's nothing more you can do here."

Since we arrived at the hospital, Billy's been on his cell phone, trying to get the search for Darcy under way. His irritation grows as he keeps getting bumped up the chain of command. He finally gets results when he says, "Listen to me! This girl will die if she doesn't get her insulin. Picture the headline: TEEN GIRL DIES WHILE POLICE DELAY SEARCH." He listens for a moment and then flashes the thumbs up sign. He gives them directions to the house, clicks off and mumbles, "Bureaucracy sucks."

On the drive home, I question him. "What happens next?"

"A detective will be assigned to the case, probably not me. Ziggy and Nick will be brought in for questioning. They'll want to talk to you too. In Oregon, kidnapping with the intent to terrorize a person is a class A felony. When you factor in the age of the girls, it will definitely be taken seriously.

"If Ziggy hadn't escaped, where would she be right now? And, Darcy…" My voice breaks. "If she dies, she won't be of any use to them and they'll dump her somewhere. She might never be found. Somebody needs to talk to her grandmother."

"I'll do it tomorrow."

Dawn is breaking in cold, gray light when I park in Billy's driveway. I pull out my cell phone. "She's probably asleep, but I'm calling her now. She needs to know what's going on."

I punch in the number, hoping the elderly woman will answer in the wee hours of the morning.

After five rings, I hear her creaky voice. "Hello? Is that you, Darcy?"

"No, it's Mel."

"Why are you calling now? Did you find the girls? Did you find my Darcy?"

When I tell her we found Ziggy, but Darcy is still

missing, she begins to weep.

"I'm so sorry," I tell her. "But, I wanted to tell you the police are searching for her right now."

She pulls herself together and thanks me. "At least she took her insulin with her. I saw it was gone. She's a diabetic, you see."

I haven't the heart to tell her the insulin is missing. When we end the call, I'm feeling even more depressed.

Billy wraps an arm around me and pulls me close. "Stay with me, Minnie. You'll feel better after you sleep. We'll have answers soon."

We stumble into his house and collapse onto the bed, fully clothed. I pull a quilt over us and snuggle into Billy's warm embrace, my head against his chest. The steady beat of his heart comforts me and slows my racing thoughts. Before I'm borne away on waves of blissful slumber, I wrap my fingers around the twin pendant and murmur to Hope, "Ziggy is safe."

A gust of wind rattles the window and I hear her soft reply. "And, so are you."

****

It's noon and I'm in Nick's office. He brought Ziggy home from the hospital, tucked her into bed and held her hand until she fell asleep. His eyes are bloodshot with deep shadows beneath. A few gray whiskers are visible on his bristly chin. He's aged ten years overnight.

"So, the girls were shot up with the hard stuff," I say, feeling sick to my stomach.

"Yes. I saw the tox screen they did on Ziggy. The doc said it was lucky she got away when she did. Another couple of days and she'd be craving it."

273

"Not to mention, carted off somewhere and forced to turn tricks to get the drugs." I pound a fist on Nick's desk. "Damn, this sucks. We need to find Darcy. Does Ziggy have any clue where they might have taken her?"

"I asked her and she started to cry. She said it's like she has holes in her memory." Nick yawns and rubs his eyes. "She's been through a severe trauma. The doc said not to push her."

"Here's an idea," I say. "Go get some sleep. Spend time with your daughter. I can handle things here today. Helen will be in soon and I'll give the new girl a call. She said she wanted more hours." I grab his hand, pull him out of the chair and push him through the door.

"Bossy little thing," he grumbles, but doesn't resist. "Booze delivery this afternoon."

"I can handle it."

He heads toward the kitchen exit and stops. "Almost forgot. Yesterday, a guy came in looking for you. Said he went to your place, but you weren't home."

"Did you get his name?"

"Hitch something."

"Ken Hitchcock. I've been trying to get in touch with him. Did he say what he wanted?"

"He said he has a job for you." Nick grins, points at his head and twirls his pointer finger. "Somehow I got the impression it has something to do with your, um, unique ability."

I smile at him. "Your impression is correct. I'll call him."

"I hope he's paying you for all that heavy-duty mind-melding."

"He's paying me, but not with money. It's a long

story. I'll tell you about it soon. Now, go get some sleep."

After I sort things out in the restaurant, I find an empty booth and call Hitchcock. "I hear you were looking for me yesterday."

"I've got a job for you. When can you come up?"

"I've got something to take care of tomorrow and I work late the next day. How about Friday?"

"Chad will pick you up at five. The guy I need you to see can't get here until after six."

"I've been calling you."

"Sorry, I had business out of town. With the two guys you met last time."

He doesn't sound sorry at all, but we're not exactly best buds, so I let it slide, even though I wonder what his out of town business with two shady guys might entail. "All right, see you Friday. I'll plan on spending some time with the kids."

A long silence ensues.

Finally, I say, "I *will* be able to see Kimber and Gunner. Right? If not, I'm afraid I won't be able to help you."

"Yes, you'll be able to see the kids. I have someone I want you to meet as well."

I stifle a groan. It's highly possible Ken Hitchcock has lined up a camo-clad potential suitor for my perusal.

"And this person is…?"

His raspy chuckle assaults my ear. "Someone you'll like. Trust me."

When pigs grow fins and swim with the fishies.

"See you Friday."

Chapter Forty-Three

Though the wheels of justice usually turn slowly, Billy manages to apply a little grease to speed them up. My old friend and (sort of) colleague, Candy Talbot, is the lead detective investigating the kidnapping. Ziggy, Nick and I will be interviewed. Ziggy, though quieter than usual, seems to be coping. Nick is setting up counseling sessions for the two of them. As strange as it sounds, the horrific ordeal strengthened their father/daughter bond.

When I look at Ziggy, I see fear in her soul. She tries to cover it up with bluster. I know how paralyzing fear and panic can be and offer to teach her Brazilian Jui Jitsu. Since I'm petite, it's served me well in a couple of scary situations.

Without hesitation, she says, "Yes, when can we start?"

The day after my conversation with Hitchcock, Candy summons me. In her usual no nonsense fashion, she begins, "So, once again, you're in the middle of a screwed-up mess."

I smile sweetly and wait for her to continue. She activates a small recorder. "Start at the beginning."

"I knew Ziggy hadn't come home for a few days and ran into a friend of hers who was looking for her."

She narrows her eyes at me. "Name?"

"Benny something. He said he was worried about

her."

"Why?"

"Because he'd seen her hanging out with some guys he called bad dudes."

I'm purposely vague about Benny. Because of his fear of reprisal, I doubt if he'll be willing to cooperate. I go on to explain how Benny was able to find directions to the house. I described my interaction with Pete.

"Did you go into the house?"

"No, he stepped out on the porch and closed the door."

"What did you do next?"

I'm aware she and Billy have discussed the case and she already knows the answer. I see no reason to lie. If she wants to charge me with breaking and entering, so be it. "I told Billy and Nick what I'd seen. Nick and I went back to the house and managed to find a way in."

"How?"

I reach over and turn the recorder off. "For God's sake, Candy, you've talked to Billy. You know exactly what happened. There's no way I'm going to involve my uncle in this, so you better figure out a way to get around it."

We lock gazes. I see confusion in her soul and give myself an imaginary pat on the back.

She sighs. "Look, I'm just trying to cover my butt. I've got a bunch of people looking for the other girl and I need an official record."

We discuss possible ways to answer the *how* question and finally come to agreement. She turns the recorder on.

"We knocked on the door. No response. There was

no way could we walk away if the girls were inside, so I used a hairpin to pick the lock."

"What did you find?"

"No one was inside. We found rotten food, garbage, a makeshift toilet and used syringes."

She skips ahead to the phone call I received.

"Rick Rathjen called me." I go on to describe my relationship with the Rathjens and their connection to Ziggy.

When we get to Ziggy's story, she listens without interruption and scribbles notes. Once again, I'm certain Billy has already filled her in. Maybe she's checking to see of our stories match. When I finish, she stops the tape and glances at me, her eyes sparking with anger.

"Damn, I want to nail these guys." She leans back in her chair and folds her arms.

I notice she's now giving me guarded glances, like she suddenly remembered I could plumb the depths of her soul.

"We're off the record now. Tell me about Paul Moen. Billy said you had a run-in with him."

"I suspected he was giving Ziggy fentanyl. He laughed at me when I asked him to stop, so I recruited an assistant."

Candy's mouth twitches like she's trying not to smile. "Yes, I heard about the incident."

I continue, "I have absolutely no proof, but I believe Moen is basically a bully who thinks I'm the weakest link. There's no way he would challenge my, um, assistant."

"Yeah, I get it."

She rises, signaling our interview is over. "I'll be

talking to Ziggy this afternoon. I'll check out the Paul Moen angle. It sounds like you think Moen planned the kidnapping to get back at you, to show you who's boss. Sounds extremely unlikely to me. Would he really go to all that trouble because you pissed him off?"

I ignore the question, scoot my chair back and stand. "Are we done? Keep me posted."

She gives my body an appraising onceover. "If I don't, I'm sure you have another source of information."

I leave before I can say what I'm thinking. Screw you, Candy, and your confused little mind.

My annoyance grows as I walk to the parking lot. I climb into Buttercup, but don't start the engine. Candy Talbot's derisive and superior attitude ticks me off. If Paul Moen is the guy who orchestrated the kidnapping, I don't want him overlooked because Talbot thinks I'm an attention-seeking, self-centered, wannabe soap star.

After I ponder the dilemma a while longer, I arrive at a solution and an evil chuckle slips out. I'm sleeping with one of her colleagues. Why not use it to my advantage?

I punch in Billy's number.

He picks up after the first ring. "Minnie. How did the interview go?"

"It was okay, but I'm pretty sure she's blowing off the Paul Moen connection. She says it sounds extremely unlikely. Billy, I know I don't have proof, but I know, I just *know* he's involved in this. We can't let him walk away."

After a long moment, Billy says, "I'll talk to Candy. This is a big case for her. She might be feeling a little overwhelmed. If I offer to look into the Paul Moen angle, I think she'll jump on it. Sound okay?"

"Thanks, I owe you."

His voice lowers to a sexy growl. "Trust me, I'll collect. See you tonight."

My body responds to the heat in his voice. I grip the phone tighter. "Tonight? What about right now?"

Though his hand is over the phone, I hear him say, "Anybody have a problem with me taking an early lunch?"

I hear laughter and a couple of comments. "Enjoy your lunch, Billy." "Give her my regards."

"See you in five minutes," he says.

"Make it twenty. I'm not home."

We arrive at the same time. Once inside, I rip off my clothes and jump into his arms, my legs wrapped around his waist.

His breathing accelerates and he grins. "Wow, Minnie, have I been neglecting you?"

I nibble at his neck. "Yes, but we've been busy. Now, get your clothes off."

"Yes, ma'am." He walks us into the bedroom.

We come together in a heated rush of desire, no foreplay required. I let go of all my worries, relax and revel in sensation. I feel the warmth of his breath on my cheek. His muscular body pressed against mine. His feathery touch to the most sensitive, intimate parts of my body. I breathe in his unique scent. Motorcycle leathers. Minty toothpaste. Pine-scented air.

My Billy. My love. For this moment, I am at peace.

Chapter Forty-Four

It's Friday and I'm waiting for Chad to pick me up. I'm toting a shopping bag full of stuff for the twins, including framed pictures of Jake's stunning artwork on the schoolhouse ceiling. I also have two boxes of the little goldfish crackers Chad is so fond of. One for him. One for the twins.

At four forty-five, I get a call from Chad. "My damn truck broke down. I'm getting it towed into 3 Peaks right now. I doubt your car can make it up the mountain. Want me to call Ken?"

I think for a moment. "You're right, Buttercup can't handle it, but I'll see if I can borrow my uncle's car. Call you back."

Twenty minutes later, I'm behind the wheel of a sleek, black 1964 Pontiac GTO, which, according to Uncle Paco, is *the* classic muscle car. I'm paying close attention to Paco's directions and dire warnings.

"Listen up, little girl. This here is a powerful machine. It's like having a motorcycle gang under your hood. They're all revving their engines, itchin' to get on the road. You got it?"

Actually, I'm having a hard time imagining an entire motorcycle gang under the Pontiac's hood, but dutifully nod my head. "Got it."

"In other words, feather the accelerator, don't stomp it. Take it easy on the curves. You're going up a mountain road. Right?"

I nod again.

"Want me to drive?"

"I'll be fine."

The next step is driving Paco home. I know it's a test, so I barely touch the accelerator when I back out of the driveway. The Pontiac leaps backward. I hit the brakes and screech to a stop.

Paco shakes his shaggy head. "See what I'm talking about?"

By the time we reach his house, I'm getting the hang of it.

Paco still has his doubts. "Call if you need me. I'll hop on the Harley and be there in a flash."

"I'll be back late, so don't worry."

He kisses the top of my head, pats the hood of the car and heads for the house.

I pick up Chad at the repair shop. When he sees the Pontiac, his eyes light up. He opens the door on the driver side. "You better let me drive. This thing is way too powerful for you."

"No."

"Aw, come on, Mel. Please?"

"Maybe later."

He sulks for a bit, but cheers up when I give him the goldfish crackers.

The route to New Dawn is familiar, but with all of Paco's warnings swirling through my brain, I'm taking it slow.

Chad can hardly bear it. "Damn it, woman, we won't get there until morning if you don't speed up."

I increase the speed to thirty-five mph. "Who's the guy Ken wants me to see?"

He mumbles. "Not supposed to talk about it."

"If you tell me, I'll let you drive."

He can't wait to spill his guts. "Actually, there are two guys. Ken wants you to sit in on the interview with one of them. Apparently, he has a particular skill Ken needs."

"Which is?"

He shrugs.

"What about the second guy?"

He shoots me a sly grin. "Don't shoot the messenger, but let's just say Ken's hoping you'll find your forever soul mate and move to New Dawn."

I don't respond, although I'm thinking, fat chance.

True to my word, I pull over and let Chad take the wheel. First, I give him a stern warning. "No funny stuff. This car belongs to a three-hundred-pound Mexican gangbanger who will kick your ass six ways from Sunday if he sees a single ding or scratch."

Chad turns pale, but nods.

I have to admit, he handles the car well. His expression is joyful as he speeds up on the straightaways and slows for the curves. We reach New Dawn in record time and, when the guards see Chad, we're waved through the gate without a hitch. We pull up in front of the community hall. I hold out a hand for the car keys.

Chad says, "I should probably keep 'em since I'll be driving you home."

"Give me the damn keys, Chad."

"Okay, okay, don't get testy."

He takes my cell phone and follows me into the hall. "Ken said for you to go to his office first."

"Oh, yay, the hallowed hall of dead animals," I

mutter. "Their glassy eyes freak me out."

Chad emits a strangled laugh disguised as a cough.

Hitchcock is waiting for me and wastes no time on pleasantries. "You're late."

I bare my teeth in a fake smile. "Hello to you too, Ken. How are you this evening?"

He rubs his bloodshot eyes. "Sorry. I know it wasn't your fault. Damn kid should take better care of his truck."

"Cut him some slack. Some things can't be helped. We're here. Isn't that what matters?"

He nods absently. His mind is clearly somewhere else. "The guy I'm about to interview has a somewhat shady past."

"What's new? Doesn't everybody here have a shady past?"

He ignores the question. "He was referred by a friend of a friend. I'm not sure he's the right fit for New Dawn."

"Then, why bother with him?"

Clearly uncomfortable, he pinches his lips together before he answers. "He has a skill we need at New Dawn."

"Which is?"

"You don't need to know."

"Oh, please," I say. "How can I help you if I don't know what you're looking for?"

He pushes away from his desk and stands. "I'll ask the questions. Your job is to figure out if he's lying."

I don't budge out of my chair. "What's his crime? Why is he running?"

"Can't tell you that."

I follow him out of his office, bitching all the way.

"I hope you realize you're putting me in an impossible situation. It's like I have two hands tied behind my back and I'm trying to scramble eggs, or type a letter, or…"

He waves a dismissive hand in my direction. "Yeah, yeah, I know. Just do the best you can."

I tap him on the shoulder. "Before we start, tell me about the other guy you want me to meet. I have a boyfriend, you know."

"Later," he says, and opens the door to the conference room.

Clad in a short-sleeved white shirt and dark trousers, the man seated at the table startles at our approach. Painfully thin, his prominent Adam's apple is clearly visible in his long, narrow neck. Oversized glasses rest upon his beak of a nose. His hairline has retreated to the middle of his scalp where tufts of dark hair rise up as if seeking the light.

Hitchcock says, "Howard, this is my trusted assistant, Melanie."

Trusted assistant? Guess we'll see how long that lasts. I reach across the table and offer him my hand. "Nice to meet you Howard."

He springs to his feet, knocking his chair over in the process. His sallow cheeks redden with embarrassment as he retrieves the chair and grips my hand with ink-stained fingers.

"Pleased to meet you, miss." His voice is high-pitched and squeaky with nerves.

He's not an eye contact guy, so I need to get him talking and put him at ease. I go with my forte, mindless blather. "Wow, Howard, what do you think about driving these mountain roads? Kinda twisty and dangerous, huh? You know that one turn where you look straight down? It's terrifying. Did you drive here or did someone bring you?"

Hitchcock rakes me with a skeptical look.

Tough shit, Ken.

Howard swallows loudly, his Adam's apple bobbing up and down. He glances into my eyes. "Oh, I drove myself. You're right. It's scary. I'm from Kansas and it's pretty flat."

"What brings you to Oregon?'

He glances over at Hitchcock. "I needed a fresh start."

Hitchcock says, "If you qualify, you'll get one here. Of course, we…"

I interrupt before he can finish his sentence. "Is it true, what they said you did?"

Startled, Howard looks directly into my eyes. "She told me she was eighteen. How was I supposed to know she was only fourteen?"

"I bet she was glad to take your money."

"Oh, there was no money involved. She just wanted a friend."

I lean back in my chair, feeling slightly ill.

Hitchcock asserts himself. "As you know, Howard, your protection will be guaranteed, providing you're able to offer the services we spoke of."

Apparently, Howard has been warned not to describe his particular skill while the *trusted assistant* is present.

He says, "I gave you samples of my work."

Hitchcock says, "If I give you the supplies you need, can you produce a foolproof product?"

Howard lifts his gaze to Hitchcock. I lean close to get a good look. "Yes, bring me the stuff and I'll do it right now."

Hitchcock stands. "I'll be right back."

We huddle in the hall.

His eyes burn with anger. "What the hell was that?"

I don't back down. "It was me getting at the truth. Isn't that what you want?"

"Which is?"

"He's not lying. But now, you'll have a pedophile living at New Dawn. Is it worth it?"

He avoids my gaze. "It's complicated. We'll keep an eye on him."

I shake my head in disgust. "Are we done?"

"For now. Enjoy your time with the kids. You'll probably never see them again."

I spin around and walk away, his words drilling a gigantic hole in my heart.

Chapter Forty-Five

I sit in the car for a few minutes, waiting for my anger to simmer down. Shall I walk to the schoolhouse or drive? I opt for driving down the rutted road instead of taking the forest path. Just as I insert the keys into the ignition, Billy calls.

"Hey Minnie, I have good news and bad news."

My heart kicks up a beat. "Lay it on me."

"Good news, Darcy has been found. Bad news, she's in a diabetic coma, critical condition. The docs aren't making any promises, but they did say youth is on her side. I picked up Grandma. She'll stay with her."

"Where was Darcy found?"

"It's like you said earlier. They panicked and dumped her alongside a deserted road. No houses nearby. It's a miracle she was found at all. A young kid driving an ATV spotted her and called 911."

"Did you tell Ziggy?"

"Yeah, she and Nick are on their way to the hospital."

"Thanks for letting me know. Looks like I'll be late getting back. No worries, okay?"

"I hear you're driving the Pontiac. Be careful on the curves."

I blow an exasperated sigh. "Do you and Paco have a Melanie hotline?"

He chuckles. "Pretty much. Oh, one more thing. I

stopped by Paul Moen's office. Nobody home. Closed sign is up. I tried his phone. Goes straight to voicemail."

"Interesting. Maybe things are getting too hot for him in 3 Peaks."

"I'll keep digging."

It's dark by the time I navigate the dirt road to the schoolhouse. The car lurches in fits and starts as I attempt to control the snarling beast lurking beneath the Pontiac's hood. As I pull to a stop, the door bursts open and the twins spill out, tripping over each other in their eagerness. I spy Anna standing in the doorway, her watchful eye on the kids.

Gunner stops, places his hands on his hips and cocks his head to one side. "You never said you had a car." His voice has an accusatory tone.

Kimber sets Blossom Bunny on the front fender. "Your car is pretty. Can we go for a ride?"

I glance at Anna. Her expression is stoic, neither indicating yes or no to Kimber's question.

I grab my backpack. "It's my uncle's car. My car's is called Buttercup and she's too old and tired to make it here. How about we go inside? I've got pictures for you."

"You do?" Kimber grabs Blossom Bunny and dances up and down with excitement.

Gunner glances over at Anna and whispers, "Did you bring any good food?"

"Maybe," I say, to prolong the suspense.

Anna steps aside so we can enter. Her face is pale and drawn, her body tight with tension. The dullness in her eyes tells me she's not sleeping.

I place a hand on her arm. "Are you okay, Anna?"

She pulls free and turns away. "I'll give you some time with the kids."

She walks toward her private quarters, places a hand on the doorknob and stops. Her voice is so low, I can barely make out the words. "Blossom Bunny's ears are pretty interesting. Maybe Kimber would like to share some of her treasures with you."

Before I can answer, she slips through the door.

The kids and I settle around a kid-sized table. Their gaze is riveted on my backpack. I unzip it and pull out two framed photographs. One of the schoolhouse ceiling, the other of the twins gazing up at Jake's artwork.

"Oh." Kimber sighs. She plants a kiss on each of the pictures.

Gunner glares at her. "You slobbered on the pictures."

"No harm done," I say, wiping the glass with the sleeve of my sweatshirt.

Gunner's angst is forgotten when I offload the rest of the goodies. Once again, chips and bean dip for Gunner. Chips and cheese dip for Kimber, along with juice and crackers for them both. I also slip them each a packet of chocolate-coated candies.

Before the kids dive into the food, Kimber thrusts Blossom Bunny into my hands. "Forgot to tell you last time. Papa said I needed to share her with you."

The strangeness of Jake's comment piques my interest, not to mention Anna's statement about bunny ears. While the twins are absorbed in their goodies, I pick up the stuffed toy and sit at Anna's desk. Blossom Bunny's ears droop for a very good reason. They are loaded with Kimber's treasures. Fortunately, the pictures I brought today are too big to fit. In one ear, I find two pencils, purple and pink crayons, a handful of goldfish crackers, a folded piece of paper inscribed with the twelve golden rules of gun safety and a tiny ceramic kangaroo.

I strike gold in the other ear. Along with a little rubber ball, a set of jacks and a Beanie Baby, I discover an envelope with my name on it. It's been sealed shut but slit open at the top. By Anna?

I extract a slip of paper inscribed with tiny, perfectly printed words. So perfect, it looks like it was created on a word processor. A tiny smudge of ink near the bottom of the page tells me it wasn't.

The note is dated the day of Jake's death.

"Mel,

I'm scared. I've stumbled onto something so dangerous, I fear my life may be in danger. First, a little background. As you've probably figured out, most all of us at New Dawn have a secret. Not only a secret, but a criminal background. You once admired my sketches. Yes, I have talent, but I went down the wrong path. Document fraud. Forgery. I'm very good with pen and ink and creating documents needed by people seeking a new identity. I was making money hand over fist until I got caught.

Out on bail, I ran and found a home at New Dawn. Nobody at New Dawn is free. We all have talents needed by Hitchcock. At first, it seemed like the perfect fit. Then, I realized I was in over my head, especially after the twins came into my life. The window blinds industry isn't totally bogus, but it's a good cover for delivering long guns to people willing to pay big bucks for them, people who can't buy guns legally. Some are foreign nationals, but that doesn't matter to Hitchcock. He's all about the money.

When I found out about the illegal gun sales, I told him I wanted to leave and take the twins. He laughed at me, said, 'What will happen to the twins when you're locked up for fraud?' Bottom line, I may be stuck, but I need to get the kids out of here. They deserve better. I hope you can help.

J."

An icy chill grips my body as Jake's words take up residence in my heart. *I need to get the kids out of here.* It all makes sense now. The day of his death, he was on his way to see me, probably to ask me to take the kids. Since he put the letter in Blossom Bunny's ear, he must have had a hunch he was in Hitchcock's crosshairs. I'm pretty sure Jake's unfortunate accident was no accident, but it's too late to prove it now.

I know exactly what I have to do and the hell with the consequences. Even though I'm bummed about leaving my cell phone behind, I call to the kids, "Hey, you two. Let's go for a ride."

Gunner pumps a fist in the air. "Yes!"

Kimber jumps up and hollers, "Let's go!"

I knock on Anna's door. She opens it a crack.

"The kids are excited about the car. I'm going to take them for a little ride."

She nods. "Good idea since it's their last night here."

I recall Hitchcock's words. *You'll probably never see them again.* Guess again, Ken.

"Their last night? Where are they going?"

"Not sure. I guess somebody's adopting them." She shrugs like she doesn't give a rip and closes the door.

"Grab your coats, kids."

"Not cold," Gunner says."

"Me either," Kimber adds.

Hands on hips, I give them my best I'm-the-boss look. "Then, I guess we'll stay here."

They grumble but fetch their coats. Gunner brings GI Joe and Kimber tucks Blossom Bunny under one arm. I swallow hard, realizing what few possessions they have will now be left behind.

"I've got an idea," I say. "Let's take the pictures for a ride."

This appeals to Kimber's sense of whimsy and she giggles. Gunner looks dubious but collects the pictures. My heart is racing when I load the kids into the back seat of the Pontiac. My plan is half-baked, but time is running out and a half-baked plan is better than none at all. I pop the trunk, hoping to find a blanket or a tarp, anything to cover up a pair of five-year-olds. Nada. Time for plan B.

First, I start the car. Then, I climb out and open the back door. The twins have been taught to use seatbelts and both are fastened in. There's no good way to do this. I know I'll be putting them in danger, but once I clear the gates, I'll rectify the problem. I unlatch the seatbelts and whisper, "Can you keep a secret?"

Both nod solemnly.

"I want to take you to my house for a visit. Is that okay with you?"

Kimber squeals, "Oh, Mel, I've wanted to go to your house forever."

Gunner frowns. "Will we get in trouble?"

"Not if I can help it."

"Don't be a baby, Gunner. This is an adventure.

Right, Mel?"

"Right. Now, here's what you need to do until we're through the gate. First of all, you have to make yourselves as tiny and quiet as possible."

Fortunately, the Pontiac is a big car. When I back around and head for the gate, the kids are curled up on the floorboards, pressed against the base of the front seats, virtually out of sight unless the guard decides to search the car. In the past, we've always been waved through. New Dawn is all about keeping strangers from coming into their hallowed ground. They don't seem to care if you're leaving. An irritating little voice natters inside my head. You've always been with Chad. Now, you're not. Will that look suspicious? "Oh, shut up," I mutter.

Kimber pipes up, "But we were being quiet like you said."

"And doing a good job of it. I was talking to the voice in my head."

Gunner says, "Shhh, quit talking."

I slow the powerful car to a rumbling crawl as we approach the gate. On the plus side, there's only one guard on duty tonight. On the downside, he appears smitten with the car.

I lower my window and wait for his approach.

He looks the car over and lowers his body so his face is level with mine. "Sweet car. You're the female who's helping Mr. Hitchcock. Right?"

I lean toward him with a winning smile, hoping he's up for flirtation. "You're right and we're done for the day."

A little smirk blooms on his face. "Okey dokey, I'll open the gate."

Warning bells clang in my head. Surely this is way too easy.

He presses a button and the gate swings open. I wave my thanks and punch the accelerator. The car leaps forward and I peel out leaving a trail of dust. I'm barely a hundred yards down the road when, in deference to the children in the back seat, the poo-poo hits the fan.

Chapter Forty-Six

The blackness of night vanishes as a pair of high-beam headlights appears in my rearview window. As I round a curve, I see a line of vehicles following behind the first. Looking ahead proves to be more troublesome. Two large four—by-fours are angled across the road, making it impossible for me to squeeze through.

"Oh, shit," I mutter, aiming the Pontiac toward the narrow shoulder. Enough room to bypass the roadblock? No way. Not unless I want to risk the front tires hanging over the edge of a cliff. I'm screwed.

"You said a bad word." Kimber's voice.

Gunner's head pops up. "Guess we're in trouble."

I guess we are. My mouth goes cotton dry as panic threatens to overcome my ability to think. I take a couple of deep breaths and try to slow my racing heart. I need to stay calm for the kids. I finally find my voice, though it sounds a little shaky. "You two stay in the car. I'll be right back." I hope.

I slip out of the Pontiac and into a solid phalanx of large male bodies.

A massively built man wearing a Top Gun ball cap speaks into a hand-held walkie-talkie. "We've stopped the female."

He listens for a minute. "Hang on. We'll check the car."

He makes a move toward the car. I jump in front of

him. "The kids are in the back. Please don't scare them."

With a sneer, he shoves me out of the way. "I give the orders. You follow them."

He yanks the car door open. I peer around him. The twins are still curled up on the floorboards. Kimber is whimpering in fear. Gunner is silent, but trembling.

Top Gun slams the door and speaks into walkie-talkie. "The kids are here. Uh huh, uh huh. Yes, right away, sir." He takes my arm in an iron grip and calls, "Mike, get your ass over here."

A young man separates himself from the others and joins us.

My captor points at the car. "Drive this hunk of metal back inside. I'll take the female."

Mike opens the driver's side door as Top Gun drags me to his truck. Now, I hear both kids' pitiful cries.

Kimber screams, "Mel! Mel! I want you. Please come back."

Gunner's response breaks my heart. "Don't cry, sissy. It will be all right."

My own tears are flowing as I'm tossed into the truck. The door slams and Top Gun walks around to the driver's side. I try the door. It's unlocked. Yes, I could run, but I got the kids into this mess. There's no way I can leave them now.

Top Gun taunts me on the way back. "Stupid, stupid, stupid idea, trying to kidnap our kids. Did you actually think you could get away with it? That we weren't tracking your every move?"

I don't bother to answer. In my heart, I know he's right. It was stupid, stupid, stupid.

He doesn't let up. "Ken will deal with you now. If you're not officially scared, the time has arrived. As you may have gathered, he's not overly fond of females."

Unwisely, I can't resist saying, "Does that mean he's overly fond of males? No worries. It's acceptable in today's world."

Whack! Top Gun has a wicked backhand. I don't have time to duck. The powerful blow slams across my face with such force, my body flies against the passenger door.

"Or maybe not," I mutter when the world stops spinning and my power of speech returns. The pain in my head throbs in rhythm with the pounding of my heart.

He continues to taunt me. "Why is it females never know when to shut the hell up?"

Wisely, I don't respond.

Our little convoy passes through the gates. As they close behind us, I'm swamped with a sense of dread. I'm the mouse in the trap. Hitchcock is the cruel cat who wants to toy with me before he puts me out of my misery. Even worse, I'm carrying a heavy load of guilt. I so wanted to give the twins a better life. In doing so, I put them in peril.

I look out the back window and see the Pontiac turn left off the main road. Is he taking the kids back to Anna?

The truck comes to a stop in front of the community hall. Top Gun grabs my left arm, drags me across the bench seat and sets me onto the ground. I hear car doors slamming and the mutter of male voices.

Ken Hitchcock is standing on the wide front porch,

arms folded across his chest, gazing at the assembled masses like a king inspecting his fiefdom. Our gazes meet. I'm too far away to read his soul, but I already know what makes Hitchcock tick, and it doesn't bring me comfort. Without uttering a word, he spins around and enters the building. Escorted by two large men gripping my arms, I'm marched to Hitchcock's office where he awaits me.

He's leaning against his desk, arms still crossed, eyes burning with fury. He dismisses his underlings. "Thanks, men. I can handle it now. Go home."

They leave, closing the door behind them. Hitchcock pushes away from his desk and closes the gap between us. I steel myself for what's coming next, using every ounce of will power to keep from showing fear. He moves into my personal space, expecting me to back away. When I stand my ground, he reaches out and brushes his finger across the swelling on my face. His touch is surprisingly gentle. Sort of like a cat's paw with the claws retracted.

"What happened?"

I hold back a shudder. "No biggie. Your guys don't like females who have a mind of their own. But, you already know that."

He sighs. "Melanie, we've already established you have a smart mouth."

"Guess I'll never learn."

He stares down at me. "Now, what am I supposed to do with you? You're a valuable asset to our community, yet you try to steal our children."

"Maybe you should call the authorities. Turn me in for kidnapping."

"You'd like that, wouldn't you?" He folds his arms

again and looks me over, from top to bottom. "We were so hoping you would choose to stay with us, pick a mate, settle down. Be a mother to the twins. Frankly, we would welcome your genetic material. I have somebody in mind."

When I don't respond, he says, "Now would be the time to speak up."

"So, if I don't want to die, I have to marry one of your Neanderthals, produce a batch of soul-reading babies, and be an obedient little female who knows how to keep her mouth shut. Right?"

"Crudely put, but accurate."

"Thank you, but I have to decline your generous offer."

He shakes his head sadly, as if I've somehow disappointed him. I know it's an act because I can see into his soul. It shimmers with red streaks of pent-up violence and cruelty, waiting for release. Barring a miracle, I know my time on earth is short.

He says, "I thought you'd say that."

Quick as a striking rattlesnake, he grabs my arm, opens the door and drags me into the conference room where another man waits. I can't hold back a gasp of surprise.

Hitchcock smiles down at me. "I believe you remember Paul Moen. He's looking forward to a session with you. I'll be here too, of course, in case he gets carried away. After all, we have all night."

Mel, you are so screwed.

Chapter Forty-Seven

Moen stands next to the table, gun in hand. I know what a Glock looks like and this is definitely not a Glock. It's bigger and heavier. The large bore is aimed directly at my head.

As sometimes happens when I'm in an impossible situation, a sense of calm settles over me. Am I ready to leave my earthly bonds to be re-united with my sister? No, I think it's a defense mechanism that kicks in when I know my chances of survival are slim to none. On the plus side, Hitchcock and Moen think I'm a helpless female, totally at their mercy. Guess what? I know Brazilian Jujitsu and I can probably kick at least one ass before I go down. The gun is a bit troublesome, however.

I place a hand on my hip and taunt Moen. "Pretty tough when you're holding a gun. What a man!"

He rises to the bait and sets the gun on the table. His eyes narrow and he spits his words out as if they taste bad. "Actually, shooting is too good for you. And, it would spoil the merchandise. After you're softened up a bit, you can take the place of the little teenyboppers I had to get rid of. When I get done with you, you'll be begging for the needle."

I take a step toward him. "I figured you were behind the kidnapping. Ziggy proved to be too much for your boys, and then you got scared and dumped poor

Darcy 'cause you thought she was going to die. Well, guess what? She didn't."

Hitchcock grips the back of my neck and squeezes a little harder than necessary. "I'm trying to help you, Mel, but you won't listen. You could have found a home here. Now, I can't save you."

When I speak, I add a little tremor of fear to my voice. "You don't want to save me. I'm the female who refused to go along with the plan. Okay, you win."

Speaking of plans, I really want to take out Moen first. He's got the gun. But Hitchcock's proximity is too hard to resist. I relax in his grip and drop my head like I'm giving up.

His grip loosens a bit. As my instructor taught me, I visualize a tightly coiled spring running through the core of my body. I jerk free, whirl and do a move that is *so* not sanctioned by the Brazilian Jujitsu association. Instead, I heed my mother's voice. *Go for the 'nads, Mel.* I gather all the strength in my body and lash out with a vicious kick, slamming my right foot into Hitchcock's crotch. He bellows in pain and slowly crumbles onto his hands and knees.

Moen's gun is still an issue. Actually, it's an enormous issue. I dive behind Hitchcock, hoping his body will conceal me. Stupid. All Moen has to do is walk over and plant one right between my eyes. I peek over Hitchcock's crumpled body, pleased to see Moen is having second thoughts. Perhaps the little female isn't as helpless as he thought. Think, Mel, think. The door isn't that far away. Can I get through it before he shoots me in the back? It's worth a try.

I slither across the floor toward the door. Moen walks toward me. His right arm is extended. He's peering down the barrel, ready for the kill shot.

It's now or never, Mel.

Just as I get my feet beneath me, the door flies open and Anna bursts through, holding a shotgun.

"Watch out," I cry. "Moen's got a gun."

Moen lifts the gun and points it at Anna. She doesn't hesitate. She aims and pulls the trigger. The blast hits Moen squarely in the chest. The gun flies from his hand. Deafened by the shot in such close quarters, I pull myself together and run over to retrieve it. Moen is alive and bleeding profusely, but I'm unable to work up a shred of sympathy.

Hitchcock is still incapacitated and groaning, thank to *moi.* I give myself an imaginary pat on the back.

He manages to get to his feet, though he's clutching his injured private parts. "Anna," he croaks. "Stop her. She's crazy. She tried to kidnap the twins."

She aims the shotgun at his head and snaps, "Twins you planned to sell."

"But I…"

Her grip tightens on the shotgun. "Don't say a word, asshole. You're the one I really want to kill."

I'm speechless with surprise. My gaze flickers back and forth between the two. Hitchcock moans and buries his face in his hands. I know there's a backstory. I pinch my lips together and wait.

Anna marches over and places the muzzle of the shotgun against Hitchcock's head. He's shaking with fear.

"You did it. You killed my baby."

"Anna," he pleads. "I took you and your boyfriend in when nobody else would. If I hadn't, you'd both be locked up. Nobody was more surprised than me when

Bobby took off. But, like I told you from the start, New Dawn isn't for everyone. When the baby got sick, we did everything we could to help her."

Angry red splotches appear on Anna's pale cheeks. Her finger tightens on the trigger. "Everything?" she repeats. "That quack of a doctor had no idea what was wrong with Frannie. I begged you to let me take her to a real doctor in 3 Peaks. I got on my knees and *begged*. But you refused and my baby died. I've been waiting a long time for this, Ken. A very long time. Remember your motto? A life for a life. It's time you paid for your sins."

Visualizing the horror of what she is about to do, I find my voice. "Anna," I say. "Please don't do this. We'll call the police, the sheriff, and the feds. They'll handle it the right way. Hitchcock will pay for his crimes. You shot Moen in self-defense. If you kill Hitchcock, it's cold-blooded murder and you'll be locked up. I promise I'll help you."

The shotgun remains firmly planted against Hitchcock's head, but her trigger finger relaxes as she glances over at me. The pain in her soul is almost more than I can bear. Her eyes brim with tears. "But he killed my baby."

"I know and I'm so sorry."

It takes both my hands to lift the heavy handgun. I take the correct shooting stance and point it at Hitchcock. I speak softly to Anna, praying my words will penetrate her emotionally unstable thoughts. "Here's what we need to do. I'll stay here and make sure Hitchcock doesn't get away. If he tries to run, I'll shoot him. Find a phone and call 911. Can you do that?"

Her soul is a kaleidoscope of conflicting emotions. Rage. Bitterness. Loss. Sorrow. As she gazes into my eyes, I see a glimmer of green. The presence of hope in the human soul appears as a pale green beacon, the color of the sea on a sunny day. The flash of green tells me Anna hasn't completely lapsed into a state of hopelessness and despair.

When she backs away and lowers the shotgun, I smile and nod. "I knew you could do it. I'll be right here."

Hitchcock lifts his head as she opens the door. I see his muscles tense like he's preparing to make a run for it. I steady my grip on the handgun. Can I pull the trigger if I have to? Oh, yeah, I can. "Don't even think about it, Hitchcock."

Before he can form an answer, there's a commotion in the hall, stomping feet and loud male voices. One loud voice, in particular, brings joy to my heart.

"Where are you, little girl? Uncle Paco is here!"

I slip out of the room and close the door behind me. Moen is bleeding out. I kind of hope Hitchcock will try to escape. If so, he'll have to fight his way through Paco and the ten Los Habañeros gang members in the hall, fully armed and spoiling for a fight.

I take Anna's arm and drag her over to Paco. "Hi, Unc. This is Anna. She's kind of pissed off at a guy in the conference room. Maybe you can convince her to give you the shotgun."

He looks me over and holds out a hand. "What about the cannon you're packing?"

I give him the gun. "I'll fill you in later. I have to do something first."

As I scurry away, I hear him talking to Anna in gentle tones. "Hey, sweet lady. I'm here to help. You don't have to do a thing. Give me the shotgun and I promise you, the bad guy won't get away."

When I exit the community hall, I see Paco and his boys haven't arrived alone. Billy and a SWAT team pile out of armored vehicles, apparently late to the party.

"Mel," Billy calls. "You okay?"

"I'm good. Talk to you later." I scurry away before he can respond.

Must find Kimber and Gunner.

Chapter Forty-Eight

I peer through the inky darkness, beyond the cluster of cabins. With a feeling of hopelessness, I realize the kids could be hidden anywhere. In an outbuilding, the blinds factory, the call center or even a musty basement like the one Ziggy and Darcy were in. The thought makes me shiver. I know I should wait until the cops fan out and do a thorough search. But, I simply can't bear the idea of the kids, alone and scared, thinking I've abandoned them.

After a brief hesitation, I turn and trot back into the building. Paco and his men are mingling with various and sundry law enforcement folk. A handcuffed Hitchcock is in the custody of two large men. His hateful glance follows me as I approach Paco, who's cradling Anna in his arms and murmuring softly to her in Spanish. Paco has a special talent for comforting hysterical women. One of his men is holding Anna's shotgun.

I tug on Paco's sleeve. "I need to speak to Anna."

Gently, he turns her around to face me. I look into her soul. Warring emotions still bubble beneath the surface, but a modicum of calm and reason has returned.

I lean close and whisper. "I need to find the twins before a bunch of armed men bust in and scare the crap out of them. Are they at the schoolhouse?"

She shakes her head. "The last time I saw them is when they left with you."

"Any idea where I should look?"

I jump in surprise when one of the SWAT guys clamps a meaty hand on my shoulder. "Billy wants you to wait in his car. We're organizing a search. Apparently there are a lot of heavily armed people here. He wants you out of danger."

I thank him despite the fact I have no intention of waiting in Billy's car.

When he stomps away, Anna pulls a small flashlight from her pocket and slips it into my hand. She whispers, "Go through the kitchen and out the back door. Wherever they are, the kids will be locked in and alone. That's how Hitchcock does things if somebody steps out of line. Check Jake's cabin first, then try the call center. It will be deserted this time of the night. Good luck and, Mel…thank you."

I give her hand a squeeze and check on Billy's proximity. He's deep in conversation with his cohorts, but spots me immediately. First, he points at me and then toward the parking lot. The meaning is obvious. *Get your butt into the car.* I smile agreeably and duck behind Paco whose huge bulk obliterates Billy's view. Thankfully, Paco, who's just as protective as Billy, is still absorbed in comforting Anna.

I make myself as small as possible and slip between the men gathered in the hall. Hitchcock's office has been cordoned off and, as I pass by the conference room, I see two men tending to Moen. Sirens in the distance tell me an aid car is on the way. Nobody challenges me as I walk through the kitchen and out the back door.

In a matter of minutes, a team of armed men will cover every inch of the compound. The SWAT guy has it right. The residents of New Dawn are not only heavily armed, but practice regularly at the range. As I slip into the shadows, I wonder if they're capable of functioning without their leader. The alternative is frightening. Guns blasting. Innocent children caught in the crossfire.

Must find the twins.

Reluctant to turn on the flashlight until I'm out of sight, I stumble down the rough, winding path leading to Jake's cabin After I do a face plant on the pine-needle-covered trail, I whisper, "Damn it!" and flip the switch, taking care to aim it directly in front of my feet. Most of the cabins are illuminated and I see people huddled together, hear snatches of worried conversation.

As I pass by one cabin, a woman calls out to me. "What's happening?"

"Not sure," I say and hurry away.

Unlike the others, Jake's cabin is pitch dark and silent. I approach it with caution. The hair on the back of my neck prickles with alarm. If the kids are inside, there may be someone guarding them. A heavily armed someone. I step onto the porch, aim the flashlight at the door and see a hasp fastened with a sturdy padlock. I switch off the flashlight, take a couple of steps to the left and crouch.

Hopefully out of range if a shooter lurks behind the door, I call, "Kimber? Gunner? It's Mel."

I press my ear against the outside wall. An owl hoots its disapproval. The wind carries a cacophony of voices in the distance. Then, I hear a sound that makes my heart leaps with joy. A faint whimper.

Tightly closed blinds conceal the windows in the front of the cabin. I switch on the light and hurriedly check the rest of the windows. The last one I check is on the left side and has a narrow gap from slightly askew, bent slats. Thank God for cheap blinds. I focus the beam at the opening and peer through. My breath hitches in my chest when I see the twins curled up together in an overstuffed chair. Gunner appears to be sleeping, his head propped against the arm of the chair. Kimber is wide-awake and clinging to Blossom Bunny. She stiffens and gazes at the window, her eyes wide with fear.

Shaking with both relief and fury, I wonder what kind of animal locks a pair of five-year-olds in a dark cabin so he can sell them for top dollar. I want to race back to the community hall and give Hitchcock forty whacks.

I pound on the window. "Kimber, it's Mel. Hang on, I'm going to break the window."

Kimber runs to the window, tears streaming down her face. "Mel," she sobs. "I knew you would come. I tried to unlock the door and so did Gunner, but we couldn't."

I look around for a big rock and tell Kimber to back away. The window is no match for my pent-up anger. I shatter it easily and pick at the broken glass. "Kimber, see if you can find a blanket and bring it to me."

Gunner, now fully awake, beats her to the bedroom and returns, carrying a heavy comforter. His face is ashen, but he manages a weak smile. "I'm so glad to see you, Mel. Mr. Ken said we were bad and had to be locked up."

I spread the comforter across the bottom sill and wriggle my way into the cabin without serious self-harm. After I hug both kids, I tell Gunner, "Mr. Ken is no longer in your lives, but I am and I promise to keep you safe."

The kids cling to me like we're duct-taped together

Kimber says, "Can we leave now?"

"Yeah," Gunner says. "It's dark and creepy in here."

I go to the window. Brilliant lights illuminate the path. Then, Billy's amplified voice. "This is Detective William McCarty from the 3 Peaks Police Department. I'm here with Sheriff John Dunbar and Special Agent Sanderson. Please remain in your homes. Place your weapons outside the door and wait for further instructions. You are not under arrest. I repeat, you are not under arrest. We will do our best to return you to your homes after the search."

I lead the kids to the big chair and settle them on my lap. "Guess what?" I say, hugging them close.

Together, they say, "What?"

"The voice you heard belongs to my friend, Billy. I've told him all about you and he'll be here real soon. We're going to wait right here until he comes. It won't be long. Is that okay?"

Kimber slips her arms around my neck and whispers. "Promise you won't leave us here."

"I promise."

We snuggle in the chair and, to pass the time, I tell them about another set of twins called Hope and Honor, how they celebrated their birthdays with red and blue balloons.

Gunner says, "Can we have a birthday party with red and blue balloons?"

"But we don't know when our birthday is, brother," Kimber says.

I squeeze them tight. "Even better, because now we can do it anytime we want."

The sound of the approaching search party grows louder. Lights flicker across the front of the cabin.

I extricate myself from the twins. "You two stay here." I cross to the window and call, "Billy, it's Mel. I'm here with the kids. We're padlocked in. You need a bolt cutter."

Billy, in full riot gear, splits off from the others and trots to the window. He sets his weapon down, cups my face in his palms and presses his forehead against mine. "Big surprise. You're not waiting in the car."

"I had to find them, Billy. They were all alone in the dark."

He nods. "Yeah, I get it. We'll have you out of there shortly."

True to his word, Billy is the first one through the door. He tells the others to wait and walks over to the chair where I'm seated with the kids. He squats until he's eye level with Gunner and Kimber. Flashing his heart-melting grin, he says, "I'm Billy. Let's get out of here. Who wants a piggy-back ride?"

Gunner wiggles out of my embrace. "Me! Me!! Can I shoot your gun?"

"Nope."

Kimber's thumb is in her mouth and she's clinging to me. Billy tickles her tummy. "What about you, sweetie? I've got room for two."

She gives me a questioning gaze. I nod. She tucks

Blossom Bunny under one arm and slides out of the chair. Both climb aboard Billy's back. He takes my hand. The four of us step through the door, leaving the darkness behind.

Chapter Forty-Nine

The rest of the night is hectic and noisy, yet satisfying. When Billy takes us to his car, I make a request. He thinks it over and nods his approval. The twins and I climb into the back seat. Billy starts the car and drives it through the gate to the world beyond the boundaries of New Dawn. He finds a blanket in the trunk and tucks it around the three of us.

Before he returns to the fray, I say, "There's a kid inside named Chad. He's a good kid who's been brainwashed by his dad and others. Make sure he's okay."

"Got it."

"Oh, and tell Paco to look for his car. I sort of lost it a while ago."

He puts his hands on his hips and grins down at me. "Anything else, Madam?"

"Yes, we need to look out for Anna. If not for her, I wouldn't have kidnapped the twins."

He frowns at me. "I don't want to visit my girlfriend in jail. You weren't *kidnapping* the twins. You were *rescuing* them. Got it?"

"Got it."

I take his hand and kiss it. "Thanks for showing up."

He leans over and brushes his lips across mine. "No thanks necessary."

After he leaves, Kimber says, "I like Billy. Is he your boyfriend?"

"Yes."

"Do you love him?"

"Yes," I answer without hesitation.

The words, spoken so freely, burrow into my heart and take root in my soul, their tendrils smoothing the jagged edges of grief, anger and guilt inflicted by the past. If I had the ability to look into my own soul, I know I would see a cluster of incredibly beautiful crimson roses. I breathe deeply and swear I can smell their fragrance. At that moment, my world, so often tilted sideways or even upside down, shifts and rights itself. A sense of peace steals over me as I wrap my arms around Kimber and Gunner and close my eyes.

The next few days pass in a whirlwind of confusion. The kids and I stay with Kendra while Billy deals with the legal aspects. My old archenemy and occasional working partner, Candy Talbot, proves to be a big help. Her current boyfriend, an attorney specializing in family practice, uses his influence with the Department of Children and Family Services. They cut through red tape quickly and allow the twins to be temporarily fostered at Kendra and Craig's house. Nick gives me time off so I can be with the kids.

Since I'm feeling cut off from the world, Billy retrieves my cell phone from the pile of confiscated items and fills me in on New Dawn. "It's a real mess. Fortunately, a lot of folks are ready to spill the beans in exchange for immunity. Among other things, New Dawn trafficked in illegal gun sales and operated a call center specializing in identity theft. Dozens of people were receiving benefit checks that didn't belong to them. Hitchcock made sure he got his hands on the checks. They also created and sold fake documents. That was Jake Gunderson's job. From what we've heard, he got wind of the gun trafficking thing and couldn't handle it. Nobody's admitting it, but the circumstances around his death are pretty suspicious. 3 Peaks P.D. will be out of the loop soon, since the feds are swarming in. They're taking over the investigation."

Three days after the New Dawn raid, my cell phone rings. The area code is 617, Boston, MA.

When I answer, I hear. "*Maylsh?*"

"Mick?"

A long silence follows as both of us struggle to find the right words.

Finally, he says, "Congratulations. I heard you were a big help in the New Dawn bust." He pauses and chuckles. "I should have known better than to tell you not to go there. You never fail to surprise me. I talked to some guys at DHS and you're getting a reward." He names a figure.

The amount makes my knees buckle. "No way!"

"It's true. The Department of Homeland Security would like to show their gratitude. Plus, they will have work for you in the future."

I stammer a bit but manage to thank him.

"I talked to Billy," he says. "He's right for you, *maylsh.* I know it now and I wish you happiness."

My eyes fill with tears. The lump in my throat won't let me speak. I take a few hiccuping breaths and fight for control.

"Don't cry," he says. "Just tell me goodbye."

I manage to say, "No goodbyes right now. We're still friends."

When the call ends, I feel a sense of closure, like the last piece of the puzzle has been found and slipped into place, completing the picture.

Five days after the bust, Kendra decides the twins need a birthday party, though we have no idea when they were born. Kimber and Gunner are wildly excited and demand red and blue balloons. It's a beautiful spring day and, because we have a gaggle of messy little kids, we opt to hold the event in the backyard.

Billy shows up before the party begins. "Who wants to go for a ride in a police car?"

Gunner and Aaron race for the door. Kimber, who's been my shadow, looks up at me with a worried expression. "If I go, will you be here when I get back?"

I pick her up and whirl her around until she giggles. "Where else would I be, silly?"

Billy holds out his hand. Kimber peels away from me and places her hand in his. When they reach the door, she turns and shakes Blossom Bunny at me. "See ya later, silly."

The party is a hit, complete with red and blue balloon bouquets, little faces smeared with fruit punch and chocolate frosting, as well as adult beverages for the grown-ups.

Nick is there with Ziggy and Cowboy Jim. Because of her hair-raising, potentially fatal encounter with Moen, Ziggy is toeing the line and seems to be a much happier kid. She tells me Darcy is on the mend and out of the hospital.

Cowboy Jim puts on some tunes and soon has the whole group line dancing, including Paco and Aida. Until you've seen a three hundred pound gangbanger line dancing with his pregnant wife, you haven't lived life to the fullest.

When the party winds down, Billy and the twins disappear inside the house. Kendra and Craig usher me to a lawn chair.

"What's going on?" I ask.

The door flies open. Kimber runs to me and places Blossom Bunny in my lap. Billy and Gunner follow.

Kimber says, "Blossom Bunny has something special for you in one of her ears. See if you can find it."

I look up at Billy, expecting to see a mischievous grin. Instead, his expression is solemn. I peek into his soul. Along with the sun-kissed crimson rose, I see a streak of anxiety. What the heck is going on?

Gunner and Kimber lean close. I run my fingers down the length of Blossom Bunny's left ear and feel the outline of crayons and a pencil.

Kimber whispers loudly, "The other ear, silly."

Her comment breaks the silence. Amid a chorus of laughter, I unzip the other ear and thrust my fingers inside. I'm beginning to think this is a practical joke until I explore the pointy tip of poor, worn-out Blossom Bunny's right ear. I hook my finger around the object, pull it out and place the sparkling diamond ring in the palm of my hand. I gasp in surprise.

Billy loops his arms around Kimber and Gunner and drops to one knee. "Honor Melanie Sullivan, my Minnie Mouse, will you marry us?"

I'm speechless for a moment. The silence grows. The kids look scared. Billy waits, his gaze never leaving mine.

Tears streaming down my face, I stammer, "Of course I will, silly."

Epilogue

Six months later

Gunner kneels on the couch, looking out the window. His little body tenses with anticipation and then he leaps off the couch and flies through the front door. Gunner is my early warning system. Billy has just pulled into the driveway.

I'm sprawled in a recliner with my feet elevated. Can you guess why?

Kimber is on the floor next to me, totally engrossed in cat beautification. Strangely, Thunder Paws is smitten with Kimber. Maybe it's the fish-flavored cat treats in Blossom Bunny's ears. He follows her around and growls at anyone who invades her space. Today, he's decked out in a red bandana and miniature cowboy hat. She's painted his toenails a matching color. Yes, Kimber has tamed the monster.

Billy comes through the door with Gunner on his back. He gives Thunder Paws a wide berth and holds out his arms to Kimber who runs to him. With the kids hanging on him, he crosses to the recliner, cups my face in his palms and kisses my forehead, my lips and both cheeks. He caresses my growing belly and whispers, "How's everyone doing today?"

I set my hand on top of his. "I think they're swimming laps. What do you think?"

His hand remains on my tummy until the babies begins to stir. Yes, that's right. Babies. Plural. We will soon be a family of six when our twin boys are born in January. Billy failed to tell me his father was a twin. With my history, we couldn't miss. No names yet, so we call them Thing One and Thing Two.

Every morning, without fail, Kimber runs to me, places her mouth two inches from my belly and yells, "Hi little thingies. It's your big sister, Kimber. I can't wait to see you. Mama Mel says you have to stay inside her tummy a while longer. Have fun, sillies!"

If all goes according to plan, by Christmas, Kimber and Gunner's adoption will be final. Their true names will be Kimberly Honor McCarty and Gunner William McCarty. My mother is already planning the party and will stick around until the babies are born.

I am so blessed. When I reflect how my life has changed since I arrived in 3 Peaks, I'm overwhelmed with gratitude. I found a man who loves me and accepts the weirdness of my soul-seeking nature, the gift I formerly considered an affliction. I have a loving extended family. Along with the unconditional love I receive from my mother and stepfather, my biological father shares my gift and gently guides me along my chosen path. And then, there's Kendra, whose best friend, Dani, was *my* best friend and the reason I came to 3 Peaks. May you rest in peace, sweet Dani. Your baby girl, Destiny, has a wonderful home with Kendra and Craig.

I'm saving my last chunk of gratitude for Uncle Paco. His devotion and ability to deliver rough justice saved my life more than once. He and Aida welcomed little Paco Junior two weeks ago. Billy and I gave the baby a tiny leather jacket with the words Lil Biker printed on the back. Aida was horrified and declared, "No motorcycle for my baby, Paco, and I mean it!"

I know my journey will not always be smooth. Every road has hairpin curves, potholes and unexpected detours. But with the loving support of family and friends, I will persevere.

My heart is full.

A word about the author...

Marilee Brothers is a former teacher, coach, counselor, and the author of ten books. Marilee and her husband are the parents of three grown sons and live in central Washington State. After writing six young adult books, Marilee is once again writing romantic suspense for the adult market, including the first two books in the Soul Seekers' trilogy: *Affliction* and *Allegiance*.

She loves hearing from people who have read her books. Feel free to contact her on social media at:

www.facebook.com/marilee

Twitter: @MarileeB

Marilee's blog is Book Blather, where she features aspiring and published authors as well as some tidbits of her own.

http://bookblatherblog.blogspot.com

http://www.marileebrothers.com

Thank you for purchasing
this publication of The Wild Rose Press, Inc.

If you enjoyed the story, we would appreciate your
letting others know by leaving a review.

For other wonderful stories,
please visit our on-line bookstore at
www.thewildrosepress.com.

For questions or more information
contact us at
info@thewildrosepress.com.

The Wild Rose Press, Inc.
www.thewildrosepress.com

Stay current with The Wild Rose Press, Inc.

Like us on Facebook

https://www.facebook.com/TheWildRosePress

And Follow us on Twitter
https://twitter.com/WildRosePress